I closed my eye: the crack between true sleep and wakeful presence. My muscles relaxed, and my thoughts began to float.

"I think they see us. They're coming this way." The IV drip of excitement drained from Josh's voice. "Mel, what's it look like to you?"

I fought my heavy eyelids as I peered over the tombstones. I swayed for a moment, then staggered toward Gabe. He tensed as if preparing to catch me.

"Gabe, Camera Two." Josh pointed at the camera cases by the crates. Gabe, being the gentleman he was, hesitated a moment before leaving my side. I'd seen the pained look on Gabe's face when I'd fallen a few times. Occupational hazard.

"Go," I whispered and waved him on. Despite his heavy muscles and large frame, he took off like a shot. My mind rolled on the shore of dreams. Each wave of REM stage that washed toward me threatened to sweep me away. I fought the tide as spirits spiraled past us. Where were they going? I reached into an icy current and caught another hand rough with the burdens of his former life. He closed the memory of his callused fingers over mine.

"What's wrong?" I asked the ghost. He fixed me with the deep-sea eyes of a faded mariner. His uniform came into view, and I heard the wet clang of a ship bell ringing.

"She's here." His voice trembled. "My apologies, miss. There is no time. You must run!"

Praise for Hunter J. Skye

A GLIMMER OF GHOSTS
is the winner of four RWA awards.

~*~

"Riveting, dark, sexy read."
~Alexandra Christle, award-winning author

A Glimmer of Ghosts

by

Hunter J. Skye

The Hell Gate Series

A Glimmer of Ghosts

Cover Art by *Kristian Norris*

The Wild Rose Press, Inc.
PO Box 708
Adams Basin, NY 14410-0708
Visit us at www.thewildrosepress.com

Publishing History
First Fantasy Rose Edition, 2020
Print ISBN 978-1-5092-3004-4
Digital ISBN 978-1-5092-3005-1
The Hell Gate Series
Published in the United States of America
Lyrics from "Beautiful Dreamer" by Stephen Foster (July 4, 1826-January 13, 1864) are in public domain.

Dedication

To my amazing parents
Dean and Peggy
for fostering what they thought was a healthy
imagination.
Clearly, the fault lies with them.
&
In memory of
Ricky Price
The colonel of our hearts

Acknowledgments

For their steadfast support and endless encouragement, I thank my husband, Keir, my children, Cameron, Leah, and Ben, and my brother, Dean.

I also thank my Chesapeake Romance Writers family who always keep me moving forward. Many thanks to author Alexandra Christle, for believing in this story and forcing me to do something about it.

Heartfelt thanks, as well, to The Wild Rose Press, particularly Dianne Rich and Amanda Barnett for taking a chance on me.

For inspiring various elements of this story and allowing me to share specific information, I would like to thank the Gaffos family, Anne Mcgowan, the Albertson family, Dr. Nikki Graves, RavenCon, Trinity Episcopal Church, the Portsmouth Public Library, the Oak Grove Cemetery, the Cedar Grove Cemetery, and the City of Portsmouth, VA.

The following sources were of great use to me in writing and researching this story: *History of Portsmouth, Virginia* by Dean Burgess, The Book of Common Prayer, and The Holy Bible.

I also acknowledge that narcolepsy is not the joke Hollywood has made it out to be. Though I've altered facts and descriptions for the purposes of this story, narcolepsy is a serious disorder. I know firsthand the debilitating effect it has on one's life. I have the utmost respect for persons suffering from this or any disabling medical condition.

Chapter One

Beautiful Dreamer, wake unto me.

Everyone with narcolepsy can feel the Shadow, and the Shadow can feel each and every one of us. So I kept my head on a nervous pivot, watching every angle and blind corner of the cemetery. I'd slipped into the hypnogogic state—the stage between waking and sleeping—three minutes ago, and the clock was ticking.

"Something's touching me!" My voice rang hollow against the headstones. The hot, spongy breath of the graveyard hung above our heads like a sodden blanket. Its misty tendrils reached for our necks like ethereal nooses.

"Mel, you have a six-foot perimeter. Nothing is touching you," Josh assured me, but I pointed to my foot, and his sharp, gray eyes dropped to the cable slithering across my sandal.

"Son of a bitch! Matt!" Josh's voice grated across my nerve endings. Ordinarily, I liked the low rocky tumble of testosterone in his voice. It matched his muscle-corded arms and his wide-shouldered frame, but tonight it pulled at my peace of mind. We were all on edge. Something was wrong with the cemetery.

Matt dropped the cable he had been dragging across my foot, and I kicked it away without looking at it. I could already hear it hissing to life. The cool rubber had warmed to soft serpent skin. I knew it hadn't transformed into a real snake, but the hallucination triggered the same razor slice of adrenaline through my body. All four members of the Ghost Towne Investigations team knew not to come in contact with my skin or hair when I was in the hypnogogic state. The transition from wakefulness to full sleep was tricky. I'd learned how to prolong it and even walk, talk, and think while in it, but the smallest stimuli confused my senses. Even contact with my clothes set off hallucinations.

"It's okay. I'm okay," I offered gently, but Matt avoided my eyes. Part of me wanted to strangle him with the pit viper he had just caused my mind to conjure, but who could stay mad at that handsome face and runaway curls? His angular features were the fleshed-in, finished painting to Josh's roughly sketched lines. Both brothers were handsome in a sun-freckled Viking sort of way with the same strong jaw and perfect lips, but Josh was just…unfinished.

"Go help Gabe and Seth with the crates," Josh barked. Matt was the oldest by a year and a half, but Josh called the shots. I watched through my peripheral vision as Matt struggled with his usual demons. He was shorter than Josh but packed the same muscle as his brother. A confrontation was boiling to life between the two, but Josh's wide stance said it wasn't going to be tonight. Matt abandoned the pile of cable at his feet and stomped off through the darkened tombstones. Voiceless heat-lightning laced across the sky, warping his shadow into something skittering and sinister.

"He didn't mean to touch me," I whispered. I was the only one who talked back to Josh when he was angry. He didn't scare me. Somewhere down the line, when we'd first started Ghost Towne Investigations, we'd taken the measure of each other and come up equal. Equally driven, equally stubborn, equally lonely. That type of synchronicity can change lives, and since neither of us likes change, we were very happy to file it under *things that Mel and Josh don't talk about.* I don't know about him, but I kept it in the folder next to *the kiss we've never spoken of or tried again.* I guess some things aren't meant to be.

"Don't defend him." Josh simmered.

"He was just trying to get the cables out of the way so I wouldn't trip." The tension in that strangling mist pressed against us. The crickets buzzed with it. The trees trembled with it. An argument was brewing.

"Fine, but a little caution is all I'm asking for. What if you freeze again?" Josh gripped the slender, high-altitude rescue inhaler he carried along whenever we ghost-hunted. Portsmouth, Virginia, was as sea level as you could get before you were actually standing in the Chesapeake Bay. The O_2 wasn't for altitude sickness. He kept it for me in case sleep paralysis shut down my autonomic systems again. It had only happened a few times, but a few times of not being able to breathe was enough. Just another life-threatening party favor from the neurological fiesta that is type one narcolepsy.

"Don't get me wrong—our viewers love it when your lips turn blue and you pass out." Josh shoved the oxygen into his back pocket and hefted Camera One.

Of course I didn't want to pass out. I didn't want to be in the hypnogogic state at all. No narcoleptic does. The longer you're in, the more time the Shadow has to find you.

Tick. Tock.

I stood and waited while my cerebellum tried to convince me up was down and down was up. We came to an agreement, and I began to walk.

Our base of operations for Oak Grove Cemetery was the Weeping Angel. Not because of the funerary sculpture's high levels of paranormal activity—quite the opposite. As long as we stayed within twenty yards of the front gate, our batteries wouldn't drain. The giant angel was less than twenty yards in and near enough to the main path to use hand trucks. It was also a fan favorite because of the otherworldly tear stains leaking from the angel's eyes. I was pretty sure it was just lucky lichen growth, but who am I to reject paranormal claims?

I walked ahead, listening to Josh's rockslide voice as he time-stamped the video and began narrating. I stood by myself at the edge of the camera's red, night-vision light. It was time for my "parlor trick."

I pushed at the strands of hair escaping my bun. I'd gone with an anime-slash-goth, *little girl lost in the big, dark graveyard* look tonight. It worked with my pale skin and dark hair—well, mostly dark hair. I had one streak of white trailing from my left temple. I'd woken up with it one night after a particularly nasty encounter with the Shadow—another oddity added to my strange collection of half Irish, half Latina features. There was still a little green paint mixed into the streak from my messy painting class, so I'd added green eyeshadow to finish the color scheme. My lips were always a little blue, so all I did for my mouth was add gloss on the plump spots to form a glistening heart. I didn't wear that much makeup in my daily life, but the viewers seemed to like it, and it showed up well on camera.

"Ready?" Josh's voice scattered my thoughts. They fluttered around me like moths. We'd promised our online audience we'd explore Potter's Field in the very back of the graveyard, but by the feel of it, the entire cemetery was awake and restless. I still couldn't put my finger on what was wrong with the thickening air, but something was just off. I turned to see Josh six feet behind and to the right of me.

"I don't think we're going to make it," I slurred. My brain slipped a little further into the hypnogogic state. Cataplexy began to set in, weakening my knees until I resembled a zombie shambling along in search of brains. If hemophilia was the inspiration for the vampire myth, then the sudden narcoleptic weakening of certain muscle groups, known as cataplexy, might very well have been the cause of zombie reports. I hadn't craved brains yet, but it might be a better option than the open can of fuzzy tuna waiting for me in my fridge.

"Movement," I called out. Josh followed as I stumbled forward. We'd only made it about ten feet down the main path when the first peripheral movements flickered into focus. Folds of fluttering cloth shivered through the air as weightless torsos rushed by. "There's a lot."

"Can you tell how many?"

"No. There's too much confusion."

"What's wrong with them?" Concern sneaked into Josh's voice. We were already taking a chance with the rainclouds sweeping in. Add a graveyard full of agitated ghosts, and our electrical equipment would be in serious jeopardy. He was right to be worried.

"Can you feel it?" I turned to face the camera. Josh put his fingers to his mouth and whistled for the rest of the team. I winced as the sound triggered an auditory hallucination of a screaming woman.

"Voices," I logged as sounds stirred around us. Josh's whistle had cut through the night's held breath, and secrets were spilling out.

"Can you tell what they're saying?" His words dripped with excitement. He tugged one headphone over his ear and left the other ear uncovered. I shook my head and tried to focus.

Matt reached us first with the electromagnetic field detector. Then Seth, our charming and always camera-ready gadget guy, trotted up and found a flat spot on a mausoleum step to set up the other infrared camera. I narrowed in on one of the movements and reached into its spirit stream. It was a casual gesture like dipping my hand into a touch pool at an aquarium in hopes of feeling a sting ray gliding by.

I caught one as it swirled past. My fingers tingled with a deadening chill, but I lost it. I reached again as a flash of silk sleeve and lace bodice drifted by. This time I made a connection. Antique perfume powdered the sticky air. My arm went cold, leaving the rest of my body to sweat in the hot July night. I touched her hand, and she turned anxious eyes to me. She may have seen me, but I lost the connection almost as soon as I'd established it. All I could catch from her was panic.

"I'm getting multiple cold spots," Seth announced. Josh swung the camera toward his view screen a few feet away. The alarm on the EMF detector in Matt's hands whined urgently, then fell silent.

"What's going on, Mel?" Josh angled the camera

back to me but kept walking toward Seth.

"I'm not sure. They're moving so quickly. It's almost like they're…fleeing."

"Are there any Haunted Tours tonight?" Gabe asked to no one in particular. We all turned to look at the big, mahogany-skinned man. Gabe rarely spoke when we were filming. Seth and Matt didn't mind being in front of the camera. Josh and I were in most of the shots. Gabe usually hung back.

"Not that I'm aware of." Matt pried the battery cover off the EMF detector and jiggled the batteries. "There are a few walking tours of the Olde Towne District, and in the summer the civic league hosts an evening Lantern Tour."

"The Haunted Tours are only in October. Why?" Josh asked, but Gabe just pointed. We all turned and looked off in the direction he indicated. On the far side of the cemetery, orbs of oily light flickered between the gravestones.

"Lanterns," Matt whispered.

"It can't be ghost hunters if they're using lanterns." Seth studied the infrared screen. "How many are there?"

We squinted at the bobbing lights.

"Five, maybe six," Josh counted.

"Uh, that's not right." Seth spoke more to himself than anyone else. He swung the infrared camera away then pointed it back at the group again. "Besides the lanterns, I'm only picking up two heat signatures." We looked again. There were clearly more than two people moving through the graves.

Josh moved carefully past me and balanced his camera on a smooth headstone. He adjusted the lens and pointed the directional microphone at the wandering group.

"I see them. They must be reenactors. Two women. Four men." He shook his head. "They're laughing."

"I'm telling you, there are only two people." Seth's words crept across my brain on spider's legs. "Look." He held the infrared monitor out so that Matt and Gabe both had a view of the glowing screen.

I took a deep, steadying breath and blew it out. I closed my eyes and wedged myself deeper into the crack between true sleep and wakeful presence. My muscles relaxed, and my thoughts began to float.

"I think they see us. They're coming this way." The IV drip of excitement drained from Josh's voice. "Mel, what's it look like to you?"

I fought my heavy eyelids as I peered over the tombstones. I swayed for a moment, then staggered toward Gabe. He tensed as if preparing to catch me.

"Gabe, Camera Two." Josh pointed at the camera cases by the crates. Gabe, being the gentleman he was, hesitated a moment before leaving my side. I'd seen the pained look on Gabe's face when I'd fallen a few times. Occupational hazard.

"Go," I whispered and waved him on. Despite his heavy muscles and large frame, he took off like a shot. My mind rolled on the shore of dreams. Each wave of REM stage that washed toward me threatened to sweep me away. I fought the tide as spirits spiraled past us. Where were they going? I reached into an icy current and caught another hand rough with the burdens of his former life. He closed the memory of his callused fingers over mine.

"What's wrong?" I asked the ghost. He fixed me

with the deep-sea eyes of a faded mariner. His uniform came into view, and I heard the wet clang of a ship bell ringing.

"She's here." His voice trembled. "My apologies, miss. There is no time. You must run!" He slipped from my grasp and twisted through the air. Gabe slid to a stop on the gravel path just as the spirit whipped past us. The midshipman's shoulder passed through Gabe's arm. The big man shuddered so violently he almost dropped the camera.

"Something touched me!" Gabe's eyes went round and white as he backed away. The tour group was close. I heard the crush of velvet and the sway of silk. Six people moved down the main path toward us.

The guide wore a full-length, forest green dress that bounced and swayed with what might have been upper-class Victorian flair. As she drew near, I saw the attention to detail in her costume. A trail of black velvet buttons ran from a small, matching black collar to her cinched waist. Full-length sleeves ended in delicate bells of black lace circling her long, black velvet gloves. She'd finished the ensemble with a sweeping up-do adorned with green and black ribbon spraying out from a single peacock feather. It was hard to make out the exact color of her hair in the flickering lamplight. It had the cold glint of steel, as did her eyes.

Orbs of light danced around lanterns held by the guide's two companions. The man to the left removed a gray hat from his dark hair and tucked it under the arm carrying the lantern. His black suit coat was tailored perfectly to his slim form. It hung open over a crimson four-buttoned vest. The lantern light and our red night-vision camera beams gave the silky material the tint of oozing blood. His wide black tie, shiny black shoes, and expertly tailored gray-striped pants gave him the elegant air of a Victorian gentleman.

The costumer who'd outfitted the first two had definitely not dressed the other man. The blond coming to an abrupt stop on the other side of the guide wore period clothing as well. His dull, black coat bagged around an equally dull, black vest which puckered between too many buttons. The only color on him was a hastily tied royal-blue tie that somehow lacked any royalty. He was handsome in a pencil-sharp way. Pale, wavy hair and a thin mustache carried well on his gaunt face. His sharp chin and jaw saved his masculinity from the rest of his otherwise delicate features.

Just entering the pool of lantern light behind the guide was a stunning woman in what looked like full evening attire. And, like the guide, she was also covered head to toe despite the heavy July night. The wavering light danced along her silky, flared, frost-blue skirt. A graceful matching collar and slanted pocket strips shimmered against her fitted black bodice. A tiny black hat with a frill of floating black feathers topped her auburn hair. A young, haughty look rode her porcelain features as her mouth carved out a slow predatory smile. Everything about her clashed with the man who stepped into the lamp light beside her.

The third man wore the shadows as if they were cut and stitched just for him. His costume seemed made to imitate an earlier time when lean waistlines were the result of a lack of food, not a fashion statement. And sleeves were cut wide to accommodate swollen muscles from hard work, not a whimsical trend.

I tried to make out the shape of his heavy brow or

the tint of the icy circles glinting in the unknowable depths of his face. He seemed familiar in the way some people do when I'm on the verge of sleep.

The last of the small group had clearly missed the memo regarding costumes. He wore a regular suit shirt, the kind that came folded and pinned to a cardboard square. His slacks were an indeterminate brown, and he wore scuffed shoes and a striped tie of inconsequential colors. He turned anxious eyes to me, visibly sweating in the dense night air.

The group floated to a stop about a dozen paces in front of us. The misty ceiling swirled above their heads. Even in my drifting state, I sensed the awkwardness of that distance.

"Out for a stroll among the headstones?" The tour guide obviously had voice training. Her soft tones practically slid along the skin. The city of Portsmouth employed several actors who worked year-round mingling with the tourists, handing out maps, and offering dining suggestions in old-fashioned accents. This gal was better than most. Their group felt more like a training session than an actual tour.

"Ghost Towne Investigations," Josh offered, slipping the headphones off. "We have permission to record tonight."

The woman in green broke the boundary between our two groups and drifted a few feet closer. None of her party followed. A dank scent of wet clay and freshly turned soil filled the space between us. The fragrance closed over me like a coffin lid.

"Investigators." She emitted a cultured giggle. "Of the…paranormal."

I was fascinated by how her red lips held their

femininity no matter what shape her words took. In fact, her entire face seemed unable to strike anything less than a flattering pose. It must have been her theatrical training. Though she stood squarely in front of me, she seemed less a real woman than the idea of one. Whose idea, I didn't know, but she was definitely a lovely invention.

"Mel!" I was suddenly aware of someone calling my name. I turned from the woman to look at Josh. His face had changed into a mask of worry. What had I missed? Had he said my name more than once? I turned back to the woman. She smiled at me in a private way as though I were the only one in front of her.

"Time to wake up," Josh said, but I couldn't bear to look away from the woman in green. I was in Stage One sleep when I could choose which dreams to stay with and which to discard.

I must have stumbled forward a few steps because suddenly the gunmetal of the woman's eyes loomed in front of me. I was mistaken. It wasn't metal. Her eyes were moonstones, deep and secretive. Were her lips really that close? A warm flush rose to the surface of my skin.

"*Beautiful dreamer, wake unto me.*" She began to sing, and a soft melody spun to life in my mind. "*Starlight and dewdrops are waiting for thee.*" I knew that song. I'd heard it before…somewhere. "*Sounds of the rude world heard in the day.*" Music whirled in my head. "*Lulled by the moonlight have all passed away.*"

Someone must have touched me and triggered a hallucination. The red night-vision light bled from the air, taking the rest of the world with it. All that remained was the echo of her voice and darkness. I hovered for a beautiful moment in that soft, velvet embrace of nothingness until a scream tore the whispering fabric in two.

I opened my eyes to the woman in green above me. I hung from her bony arms with my face pressed against the moldering material of her gown. I freed my mouth and coughed grave dust from my lungs. A woman shrieked again. I took a panicked look around. The woman in frost blue hovered like a nightmare a few feet off the ground. She turned to the woman in green, and half her face rotted away before my eyes, revealing a blackened row of cracked teeth.

"A Shade," she keened, pointing a bare-boned finger toward the back of the cemetery. The thick night air sucked into her rattling chest.

"Let her go." A man's voice shook next to me. I turned to see Josh. His hand clamped onto my wrist like a vise. He stretched upward, muscles straining.

I tried to move my sluggish legs and arms, but they barely responded.

I was freezing up.

I tried to inhale again, but my diaphragm sat like a stone beneath my ribs. Fear wrapped me in its bonds. I couldn't stay like this any longer or the Shadow would find me.

My head rolled against the woman's arm as she pulled me close. Her moonstone eyes had dried to dust. She blinked parchment lids over the crumbling orbs of her eyes, and an ichor-black smile slid across her withered face. "Beautiful Dreamer," she whispered again. The soft scrape of boney fingers crossed my cheek. My scalp tingled with horror. Then I was falling.

I hit the ground, and a hallucinatory earthquake

trembled around me. Tombstones swayed, and tree roots groaned. Something tall and dark moved among them.

"Wake up, Mel!" Josh shouted next to my ear. He hoisted me into his lap, but I could barely move.

The mist-shrouded night swallowed the lady in green and ate the man in the bloody vest too. The woman with the frost-blue skirt vanished as well. I looked around at the remaining people. Matt was wide-eyed and pale, still clutching the EVP recorder. Gabe was down on one knee slapping at Seth's clothing. Seth was rolling on the ground with little trails of smoke wafting up from his shirt.

The man with the icy stare seemed to hesitate for a moment. Something hovered on his lips. His eyes searched me from their shadowed caverns. He turned to scan the darkness behind him, and with a last lingering look in my direction, he folded into the devouring night and was gone.

The messy man in the royal blue tie seethed at us for one fiery moment, then turned and wove his way back through the headstones. That left the man in regular street clothes shaking before us. He opened his mouth to say something and thought better of it. He turned to leave but spun around again.

"I'm sorry." His strained voice barely whispered. With that, he grabbed the remaining lantern and left us in true darkness. Something moved through the thick, black night. It peeled away the mist, searching for me.

"Mel." Josh's voice drifted in and out. He shook me. I was in those final moments of sleep paralysis, when my brain tried to kick-start my neuroreceptors, but it lacked the necessary chemicals. It was like trying to get a car engine to turn over without gasoline. Luckily, Josh and I had a back-up plan.

He smacked me.

Hard.

The world flowed into place as something tall and blacker than the space between stars surged over the last gravestone. Its icy fingers grasped for me as I slipped from the sleeping world.

A feathery lick of loathing traced across my skin as the smothering July heat rolled over me. Cicadas electrified the trees. My mouth tasted of dirt. I was awake.

Josh handed me the oxygen canister. I inhaled deeply and asked just one question.

"Did we get the footage?"

Chapter Two

There are some things even a milkshake can't fix.

We huddled in the fluorescent light flooding the fast food restaurant. Not the chicken place right next to the cemetery. We agreed that was too close. Instead, we chose the burger joint across the Parkway.

Seth's burns weren't bad enough to see a doctor, but we'd had a brief parting ceremony for his vintage superhero T-shirt in the parking lot. He looked like a kid devouring a double cheeseburger in Gabe's gigantic Hawaiian shirt. Bright blue flowers bloomed across his chest over an eye-searing sunset.

He was okay, I reminded myself for the millionth time. I wished I could say the same for myself. I could still feel that tingling, almost sensual, compulsion to drink in the woman in green. A violent shiver shook my body as I thought of her moonstone eyes. It wasn't a cold shiver. It was warm like the press of a palm against secret places.

"You okay?" Josh frowned.

I nodded.

"Your eyes are still dilated." He suddenly felt too close. His face seemed only inches from mine.

I scooted my chair back and stood too abruptly. "I'm sorry. I think I need some air."

We all looked toward the front door, through its

plate glass, and out into the night. The parking lot was orange with floodlights, but beyond that was darkness. No one wanted to be in that darkness just now, not even me.

"Why don't you wait for the rest of us?" He reached for my wrist. His fingers stopped just above my skin.

I jerked my arm away. I could still feel the pain of his grip pressing my wrist bones together. I was pretty sure I'd have a bracelet of bruises the next day. I must have unconsciously started to rub it.

Josh's eyes suddenly filled with guilt. *Guilt!* From the guy who saved me from being carried away by a ghost to God knows where for God knows what reason.

I put my hand over his. "I'm okay...thank you." The tension around his eyes relaxed a little.

"I'm pretty sure I got a shot of the infrared's display on Camera One before it went up in flames." Josh turned to the rest of the table. "I need time to go through the footage."

"I'm telling you, someone's fucking with us." Everyone stopped chewing at once and looked at Gabe. I'd never heard him curse before, and from the looks of it, neither had any of the others. Seth started chewing again.

"Why? Why would someone do that?" Matt looked incredulous. "Why would someone go to such lengths to punk us? That was too elaborate, man. Why can't you accept what you saw? That was real."

"No...no way." Gabe shook his head again.

"So what do you think we've been hunting for the last few years?" Josh said it with a little too much sarcasm. "We hunt ghosts! Did you think Mel was just making it up?"

"I don't know. Okay? I don't know what I thought!" Everyone in the restaurant stopped chewing and looked at us. No one had ever heard Gabe yell before either. "I wasn't expecting that."

"None of us were, dude." I knew Josh was struggling as much as the rest of us, but he had at least managed to put a calm face on. He started to look my way but stopped. Clearly, he wanted to say something but was afraid he'd worry me.

"I'm going to get a milkshake. Anybody want one?" No one answered me. They shook their heads. "Fine." I got up and walked to the counter to order.

Josh waited until I was a few feet away. "I'm worried about Mel. That thing was solid...and strong! I was pulling with all my strength. We can't mess with stuff that's stronger than us. She can't be near stuff like that."

"None of us should be." Gabe regulated his tone to a whispery shout.

I let the guys talk it out while I waited for my shake. We were in shock. None of them had ever dealt with a full-body apparition. Certainly not one who could talk and walk and seem perfectly alive. Multiply that by four. It was different for them. I'd seen, heard, and felt ghosts my whole life. All they'd ever experienced were cold spots and a few whispered Electronic Voice Phenomena. I watched them talk for a couple of minutes.

Seth was on his third double cheeseburger. He was five feet four inches without his boots and had little to no body fat. I wasn't really sure where the protein went once he inhaled it. I'd met him first. It was hard to believe I'd only been with these guys for two years. Seth and I had been on the same panel at PoeCon, a convention aptly named in tribute to Edgar Allen Poe, celebrating all things supernatural. He'd saved my butt a few times, by answering questions directed at me that were way out of my depth. I'd known little to nothing about the mechanics of ghost hunting back then. I was there for the psychic perspective.

Seth had been, by far, the cutest guy at the convention. What he lacked in height, he made up for in swagger. I remembered trying to have a conversation after the panel, but random women kept coming up and touching his hair. It was the perfect icebreaker, apparently.

His locks were a silky shade of strawberry gold that swung down the full length of his back. He wore it down a lot then, but recently he'd started twisting it into a man bun. I can't believe now that I'd been that attracted to him. He was such a hyperactive mess. Without his electronics to occupy his attention, he could be downright annoying.

I'd met Gabe at the end of the Con. He'd shown up to help Seth load his equipment into the van. Like Seth, Gabe had not gone unnoticed by the ladies. If you liked the tall, dark, heavily muscled, gladiator look, Gabe was your guy. I'd been shocked when I'd learned he and I were the same age. He looked thirty-something, not twenty-something. All the construction work in the beating sun had given him a rugged, "works with his hands," African-American cover-model look.

Gabe and Seth had been friends since elementary school. Gabe saw how attentive Seth was with me. He'd backed off and, dutifully, never flirted with me even once. I liked Gabe. He was a good guy.

After PoeCon, I'd agreed to drive to Colonial Williamsburg to help them with a ghost hunt at a small cemetery the following week.

That was when I'd met the Brothers Grimm, aka Josh and Matt. Their last name was Grimes not Grimm, but whatever. To this day, I wasn't sure if Seth's invitation had been intended as a date or if the four-guy band needed a little feminine eye candy for their web videos. Either way, they'd tested me on an active graveyard. I got the job. Still, it hurt to know Gabe wasn't sure about me.

"...and what about that guy? The one in the shadows?" Matt was saying when I rejoined them.

"He looked familiar," Josh added.

"That's what I thought," I chimed in, rejoining them.

Gabe was finally eating, which was a relief. Matt's color had returned, and Josh was putting on a good front. They looked at me as though I'd just climbed up to a podium. It was definitely an uncomfortable silence. I didn't have a speech to give. I couldn't undo what had happened and put the world right for them again. I wished I could.

I looked at their faces under the fluorescent light. Matt's short curls had gone frizzy with too much nervous wiping. His full mouth looked wrong without a smile. Josh had the same shapely lips hidden under a dark blond, closely trimmed beard and mustache. I was used to him not smiling, and not for any particularly bad reason. Merriment wasn't Josh's default setting. He was contemplative and sometimes taciturn, but when he did smile, it was intoxicating and worth the wait. None of them smiled now. My friends, all strong men whose lives had just been changed forever. What could I say to them?

"Look," I started, then paused to take a sip of my milkshake. I gathered my thoughts and tried again. "When I was a little girl, my parents would take me to church every Sunday. I was so squirmy that at some point during the sermon, my mom would take me out into the churchyard to run it off. Maybe she was just bored or maybe I really was being disruptive, but as a result, what I learned about God and the afterlife didn't come from the priest. It came from the gardener." A trace of a smile pulled at Josh's mouth.

"Mom would sit on one of the benches and let me run around while the gardener tended to the flower beds and the markers on the historic graves. Some headstones were simple, and some were ornate, but he took care of them all the same.

"His name was Billy. Even though he was old, he was happy to see me." I smiled, remembering Billy's dark face and powdered donut hair like someone had shaken flour over his head and he'd left it in his hair for fun. "He told me people are made up of tiny pieces and the space that holds them together. He said when we die, the pieces stay here, but the space goes to God. He also said sometimes the pieces call to the space, and they forget they are no longer glued together." I hadn't thought about those conversations in a long time or how young I had been. "Anyway, imagine my surprise when someone finally told me Billy had been a freed slave and the church's first verger in 1855. They hadn't seen him in the flesh, like I had, but they knew him from the plaque that hung in the church tower in his honor."

The guys stared at me like I'd just sprouted a third eye on my forehead.

"Don't look surprised. I've always told you this was my life. You're in shock. I wish I could make this easier." I took another sip of shake. "Have I met another ghost like Billy who could talk, pick weeds, and hold my hand? I don't know. I haven't asked everyone I've met if they were alive or a ghost. All I can say is…what happened tonight…however frightening…is within the realm of possibility. We may not understand it, but there are lots of things we don't understand. The question is—now that we know, are we going to let that knowledge scare us?"

After a millisecond of thought, Gabe, Matt, and Josh all answered, "Yes!"

Seth kept chewing. He finished his burger and balled the wrapper into a tight grenade.

"What?" he asked as the rest of us stared.

"Um, a ghost just lit you on fire, man. Aren't you disturbed by that?" Matt's eyebrows were as high as they could go and still be on his face.

"The infrared caught fire, not me. I didn't let go of it fast enough. And yes, I had contact with an entity in a state of being that was unfamiliar to me. In my book, that's cause for celebration. Hence, the extra burger." Seth pointed to the last of the four grenades in front of him. Now Seth had the third eye. "Am I scared? Hell, yeah. But I'm excited too. Assuming nothing is wrong with the camera, we've got footage no other ghost hunters have. Until about thirty minutes ago, corporeal ghosts were a myth. I say we go back, collect the rest of our equipment, and have another look around."

"No!" was Josh's resounding answer. "We wait for

dawn." The group fell silent. I waited until the silence hardened into something that would trap us in its amber grip.

"So." I finally shattered the spell. "Where are you brave souls going to sleep?" I gave them an emasculating smile. I knew the answer. I was the only one with a blessed St. Michael's ward over my bedroom door. It protected my entire room from floor to ceiling, window to window. It didn't do much for the rest of my apartment or for the neighbors downstairs, but it helped me sleep. That and my CPAP machine usually saved me from listening to the partially materialized soldier ghost in my building moan for half the night. "I hope you brought sleeping bags."

Chapter Three

Bathed in tar and oil and fat; she burns forever in our hearts.

Seth was clearly trying to prove something by stretching out on the sofa while the rest of us cowered in my bedroom behind the ward. He was a brave guy. They all were, but I had the feeling that Seth was trying to prove something to himself.

I'd give him until three a.m. when my soldier friend usually arrived. I made a pallet for Seth on the floor next to my bed just in case.

I'd changed into my most modest pajamas, a faded blue tank top with a large owl on it and matching shorts with the words Night Owl scrawled across my butt. My breasts had stretched the owl's already big eyes into a look of absolute surprise. I couldn't help it. All the women in my family had big breasts. I'd also inherited a slender ribcage, so from the waist up, I looked like a pin up girl. From the waist down, I had a more athletic look. The result was a top-heavy hourglass with a well-used gym membership. I wore a minimizer bra all day long—I wasn't going to sleep in one too. The guys would have to deal.

Deal they did. When I stepped out of the closet, everyone found something else to look at. Josh focused on the glowing display for Camera One. Gabe resumed scrolling through texts on his phone, and Matt pulled his book closer to his face.

We'd shared sleeping space together before. The guys knew the drill. I was raised Episcopalian, so they weren't shocked when I knelt at my bedside for prayer. A couple of them even whispered "Amen" at the end.

We occasionally traveled far enough on ghost hunts to get hotel rooms, which we shared to keep costs down. They'd gotten used to my bedtime routine and the white noise of my CPAP machine. I hated to put it on in front of anyone. I had a top of the line Dreamgear mask that fit under my nose instead of over it. I'd waited months on a reserve list for it. The nose piece was much smaller and stream-lined than the old fighter pilot masks. Still, I felt like I was climbing into a cockpit every time I put it on. No one was sexy hooked to forced air. But it kept me breathing throughout the night.

I climbed into bed and slipped the head gear on. Air flooded through my nose and into my airways. I clicked the light off on my nightstand and whispered good night. You might think that, with a sleep disorder, it's hard for me to get to sleep, particularly after almost being abducted by a menacing ghost. Actually, with narcolepsy, my sleep latency time was about thirty seconds. What that meant was, within half a minute I was usually in Stage One sleep and halfway to dreamland. Getting to sleep was not the problem. Surviving sleep was.

Dreamland, for me, wasn't filled with rainbows and unicorns. The landscape of my dreams was the same night after night. The Apocalypse. Mostly I was in familiar settings. My beleaguered neighborhood. My crumbling city. Sometimes I could see farther across the land and sea, watching sickness and destruction spread.

A few times, I'd risen high enough above the planet to see darkness spreading, consuming farmlands, devouring mountains, poisoning oceans. From that vantage point I could see the whole world and the sources of the corruption.

Great black maws of evil yawned at God with indifference. There were seven of them. Always seven locations on the spinning globe beneath me. Seven points of infection spewing evil across the globe. Portsmouth, Virginia, my beautiful hometown, was ground zero for one of them.

Most nights, I was home in my dreams hiding behind the shredded protection of my Saint Michael's ward. I'd sit and wait most of the night, watching the mayhem unfold around me until the Shadow came. Then I'd use the ensuing wave of adrenaline to wake myself up. It was my biochemical escape hatch whenever the Shadow was near.

Other nights, I'd join the fray, kicking and bashing my way through twisted creatures whose forms I could barely remember after waking.

Portsmouth always seemed important somehow. Flash points of battle came and went over the city, but there were specific places—cemeteries, historic battlegrounds, places layered with old blood, violence, and despair. Those were the true frontlines. That's where the shining people were.

On my bravest nights, I followed them—men and women wrapped in glowing armor and swinging weapons made of searing light. Some were the size of a regular human, but others were much larger. A few were so out of scale with the rest that they only focused on one thing...the foe of equal size. I tried to stay away from those fights. It was a good way to get trampled.

The giant warriors were mostly on other continents; but once, fairly recently, I'd seen one here. I let myself float deeper asleep as I remembered that night. In that dream, I'd climbed to the top of the roof of my apartment building. The highest point was the tower, located above my bedroom. My apartment was in the older part of the building, which had once been the lavish home of a wealthy industrialist who liked the gothic look. The tower was round and pointed like a turban with a covering of aqua blue corrosion streaking down its copper facing. I usually sat on the wrought-iron widow's walk wrapping its base and watched the devastation with my adopted cat, Bouguereau.

In waking life, Bougie was a giant, black tomcat who belonged to the whole building. Mrs. Edmonson fed him in the morning, and the new guy in 5B gave him an afternoon snack. I'd seen Bougie leaving both apartments with a guilty slink to his step. I'd never complained. I didn't mind as long as he slipped through the tear in my window screen at night and curled up with me.

That night the dream had been different. A pulsing glow lit the horizon. I slid down the crumbling side of the building again and bounded through the city streets. I caught the attention of creatures as I passed. Some left the victims they were tormenting to chase me. Others continued pillaging. If given the chance to build speed, I was usually uncatchable in my dreams.

The hum of my CPAP machine carried me deeper

as I remembered the dream. I saw the glowing light again. I followed it to the far end of the downtown, across sleeping neighborhoods to the edge of the whispering river.

Midway along the eastern branch of the Elizabeth River was Craney Island. Originally a real island, now it was engulfed by a manmade peninsula of lifeless dirt attached to the shoreline using dredged materials from the murkiest depths of the channel. No one was allowed on Craney Island except birds. Nothing grew on the strange square of protruding dirt. No one treaded on the reconstituted ground except the Army Corps of Engineers who oversaw it. The light radiated from there.

I followed the shifting glow through shipping container yards, passed the wildlife preserve, picking up more and more speed until I reached the edge of the peninsula. An invisible barrier wavered in the still night air between a sprawling parcel of heavily forested land and Craney Island. At the southwestern corner sat a facility housing construction equipment where the boundary was thin. I leapt over the eight-foot fence with dream-powered ease and sprinted toward the melee.

I shielded my eyes from the blinding clash of light and darkness until they adjusted. I squinted at the swarm of moving bodies. A mindless battle raged on the far end of the peninsula. Dead-eyed soldiers in tattered uniforms clustered along the banks of the peninsula only to be swept away moments later by giant writhing tentacles. Those who survived stopped fighting to watch the main event.

Wraith-like soldiers in Union and Confederate

colors alike cheered as a giant man in starlit chainmail dealt a thundering blow to the head of a serpentine leviathan with coiling arms. The impact of the shining man's hammer rang from the iron skull of his foe. The shockwave of it knocked me from my feet and flattened the fence behind me. My ears went dead as I sat up and looked around at the paralyzing scene.

The creature had fallen. A giant, oozing crack split the top of its riveted skull. The details of the creature's body were indiscernible, almost as if a safety feature inside my mind wouldn't allow me to take it all in at once.

The shape of its distorted face and head was an abomination before God. Flesh and iron had twisted together to form a ship with cannon eyes. The boxy metallic vessel had few identifying elements other than one large central smokestack that belched charcoal-colored vapor into the starless sky. Several poles hoisted tattered flags, and tiny lifeboats clung to the slimy slopes of the ironclad's sides.

Horror still tingled along my scalp as I looked at the CSS Virginia, formerly the Merrimack. At some point, I'd made the connection between the battle of the Monitor and Merrimack and the later destruction of the rebel vessel in the waters off Craney Island.

Old men still teared up at the mention of the ironclad and its sorrowful demise. That ship alone had saved the port city from a Union invasion. All the hope and salvation men and women instilled in it burned to ash in 1862 when she was scuttled by her own men. They'd burned her to the water line to avoid capture by the Union's second wave. I'd seen an illustration of it once at a local diner. Under the sun-bleached print someone had scribbled, *"Bathed in tar and oil and fat; she burns forever in our hearts."*

A hissing replaced the silence in my ears. I could almost feel the sound soaking every human soul on the narrow peninsula with crippling woe. Wails rose from Confederate soldiers, and Union soldiers backed away.

I turned to run, but despair riveted my feet as though the island itself were made of iron sadness. I watched helplessly as the giant, glowing knight from somewhere else in history kicked the creature back into the water with all its might. Once the last of its poisonous tentacles had slipped back into the river, the towering man turned and thundered away.

I broke free and followed. I'd made it to the tree line when the hissing stopped.

A collective gasp was followed by a heart-rending explosion. I tumbled forward then looked behind me. The beloved CSS Virginia, twisted and warped by so much pain, was in flames once more, lit by the slow fuses of Confederate men long ago. The demon which had formed itself around that bitterness and loss burned too.

The sound of moaning dragged me from my dream into the groggy hypnopompic state. It was basically the same as the hypnogogic state but on the other end of sleep.

I opened my eyes, and my ceiling fan morphed into a giant hand. I took a deep breath and waited as the hallucination slowly dissolved. It was three a.m. The soldier had arrived.

I'd been warned there was a "Civil War ghost" in the building when I'd moved in last year. Mrs. Edmonson on the first floor had offered the information as soon as she'd realized I was a member of Ghost Towne Investigations. She'd never seen, heard, or even sensed him, but that hadn't stopped her believing in the possibility of his existence. To some, the idea of a spirit roaming the darkened corners of their homes was exciting.

Our resident ghost wasn't from the Civil War era. His uniform looked like those the local American Revolution reenactors wore—red coat, white vest and pants. His legs weren't fully materialized, but I'm guessing he'd worn dark boots. Lately he'd been wearing a dark triangular hat.

As a non-responsive, he wasn't a candidate for Ghost Towne Investigations. A non-responsive ghost can sense me or someone like me with hypnogogic brainwaves, but they can't zero in enough to make contact. Basically, I was wasting my breath on spirits like him.

That sounds harsh.

I feel for the guy.

Something was obviously holding him here to the material world, but even if he were fully sentient, so much time had passed since his life, it was doubtful I could help him.

I took off my CPAP mask and covered my ears with my pillow. I watched him hover in the open doorway. He couldn't cross the threshold, even though the door with the ward above it was open. He just floated in place like he did most nights.

Sometimes his vocalizations came close to speech, but he didn't seem to have what he needed to push through to this plane of existence.

His wasted face looked young. Had he lost his legs

on a battlefield, or had they been taken by a surgeon?

As usual, my patience ran out. I snatched the pillow from around my head and launched it at the ghost. It sailed through the doorway and wafted through his chest. A small cry sounded from the hallway. I sat bolt upright as Seth darted into the room. The last of the hypnopompic state faded, and I came fully awake.

"You okay?" I dragged my other pillow toward me.

"A cold spot manifested in the living room," he squeaked and held up the temperature gauge.

"It's okay. It's the soldier."

"What soldier?" Josh was awake and sitting up. The plush owl blanket I'd given him to fend off drafts beneath my windows had slipped to his waist. The light from the gas lamps outside revealed taut skin stretched over hard muscle. Josh drove a forklift at the cargo yard during the day. You'd think he lifted the cargo containers by hand. I'd never seen his legs. Josh didn't do shorts. I had no idea if the bottom half matched the top half, but I was willing to bet it did.

"He's a non-responsive vestige linked to this site. I can't make contact."

"Why am I…we…just hearing about this now?" Josh squinted in the low light. He had glasses but rarely wore them. He looked good either way, so I didn't understand why he struggled to see in low light without them.

"I don't know." I sighed. If I told them about every spirit I encountered, I'd talk of nothing else. "Maybe I don't want to talk about ghosts all the time." I spoke too sharply. I stared at my coverlet for a moment then yanked it back and swung my legs over the side of the bed. Everyone was awake now and looking at me.

What did they see?

Did I still look like a scared little girl who saw things no one else could? Did I look like an overly emotional basket case alienating her way to a lonely spinster life? I jammed my feet into my owl slippers and stomped out of the room.

I didn't give a shit what they saw.

I headed off to take a shower.

****

I swayed in the warmth of the streaming water and let my thoughts float. Lack of sleep threatened to drag me back into the hypnogogic state. I tried to fight it, but the water was soothing, and my body ached with exhaustion.

I thought about my life. My family. Growing up military had shaped my sense of belonging into a small sphere that included only my parents and little sister. Cities came and went. Some places held more appeal than others, but I'd never felt like I belonged to any one community or culture. Three years in India, Germany, Japan. Everything was ephemeral—friends, homes, schools. Seeing the world at such a young age set my perspective on life to a healthy width, but I'd never really had a hometown until now. Putting down roots was nice. Putting down roots with someone special would be even better.

My mind drifted to Josh and all the things between us that were unsaid. What was I waiting for…a man that had taken up residence on the fence? Was I supposed to wait forever while he made up his mind how he felt about me?

Maybe there was someone else out there that wouldn't have to think about whether he wanted to kiss me or not. Sometimes, I could almost feel him, my mystery man, drifting just out of reach. He was warm and passionate and commanding and not at all confused about his feelings for me.

In quiet moments, I almost pined for him as though he were a real person and we were only separated by a moment or a mile or a misunderstanding. The thought of being loved by someone, truly loved, spread an ache through my heart. I wasn't exactly an ideal package, but I liked to think it was still possible.

The image of my shadowy, blue-eyed mystery man had almost materialized in my mind when another presence entered the bathroom.

My body flushed. Had I looked at Josh before I'd stormed out of the bedroom? Had I tugged on the cord that bound us together? Thoughts of my imaginary lover vanished. Maybe Josh had finally made up his mind about me. Maybe he would put aside whatever misgivings he had and step into my shower. I staggered at the possibility of his hands against my skin…water pouring over his chest.

I sucked in a breath as I realized I was suddenly not alone in the shower. The soldier's hollow face hovered before me. I froze. Stray droplets of water tore at his visage as he drifted closer. The moving water was literally tearing him apart, but still he gravitated toward me.

"What?" I whispered. "What do you want?" I must have slipped back into the hypnogogic state.

His eyes were caverns of lost thoughts. He was melting into pieces before me. Soon, the water would corrode his apparition, and he would be a presence only, a prickle on the back of the neck…lost. I reached behind me and turned the water off. As much as I hate having my personal, naked space invaded, I couldn't watch this self-destruction. Not when I might be the cause.

"What!" I shouted as the soldier faded from sight.

In a flash, Josh was at the door calling me. I didn't answer—one more thing unsaid.

Chapter Four

Coat hangers and plastic cups are a dead giveaway.

I sat on the hard examining table with its crinkly paper covering and tried not to move around too much. I'd sat on enough of those tables to know that just a few squirms would leave a butt print the size of two boulders.

I was in the smallest of the examining rooms, the one at the end of the hall and right next to Dr. Suni's office. I called it the "usual suspects" room because the only patients I ever saw coming out of it were the sad sacks like me who were under constant supervision.

Bright watercolor prints of tropical flowers hung in colorful frames on two of the walls. The third wall, the one with the door, had a bio-hazardous waste box for needles and a poster of a flayed man with his lungs bisected in blues and reds. The illustrator had also dismembered him at mid-bicep and just below his diaphragm. His head was turned to show his trachea and nasal cavity. The remaining wall had a small sink with a mirror over it and a covered trash can with a pedal for opening and closing.

I caught a glimpse of myself slouching like a child in the mirror. I straightened my back, which added a few more years to me, but I still didn't look my age. I was twenty-seven and still was carded when I attempted to buy wine at the grocery store. People, cashiers mostly, misread the small amount of pastel colors in my white streak as an adolescent experiment meant to break a few rules.

Really, I was just a sloppy painter with a general lack of hair ties. Running my fingers through my hair as I paint often transferred whatever color I was using on the canvas to the strands that framed my face. Today, my temples were violet and blue. I'd pulled my hair into a braid, mixing the colors through my dark hair. Actually, as I looked at it, the blues contrasted agreeably with the amber of my eyes, turning the darker brown edges of my irises to a warm sienna.

Note to self—try blue eyeshadow.

The door opened and in walked Dr. Suni. A mirthful look rode her smooth caramel features. She'd swept her long, thready dreadlocks into a regal topknot, leaving just a few tendrils to snake down around her face.

"Hey there, Z," she greeted me in standard, cheerful fashion. Z was short for Zebra, which was her nickname for me. She'd given it to me when I'd first started coming to her, just after the great flare of 2015. Neither of us had known what was wrong with me. I was pretty sure it was something bad. Nobody's lips turn blue overnight unless they'd been on a Hawaiian Punch Blueberry Blast binge.

It was then that Dr. Suni gave me the horse versus zebra speech. She explained that even though my symptoms were pretty strange, it was best not to jump to the conclusion that I was facing something serious and unusual. As she'd said, *if you hear hoof beats outside your window, think horse not zebra.* With that, we'd started the year of tests that eventually ruled out all hope of there being a horse attached to those hooves. I was not only a zebra, I was a purple polka-dotted zebra, but that was too long for a nickname, so she just called me Z.

"I had a chance to look over your latest MRI results, and the lesions in your hypothalamus haven't increased in size." She stopped and smiled for effect. I returned the plastic, wind-up, chattering teeth smile. We both knew it was good news, but not necessarily cause for a party.

"Well, what's it gonna be? Up your steroids or marshal on?"

I rolled my eyes. "You tell me. You're the doctor."

"As if you'd take my advice that easily."

"Well, maybe I've evolved." I smirked. "Let's pretend I have. What would you recommend?"

"I would recommend shrinking those lesions, increasing your stimulants, and taking up a productive hobby like gardening."

"It's the ghost hunting thing, right?"

"I'm just saying," she began, with her hands up in mock surrender, "feeding that much energy into your hallucinations isn't going to tighten your grip on reality."

"Well, it ain't daisies hovering over my shoulder all hours of the day and night, and it sure isn't shrubbery climbing into my shower and invading my personal, naked space. As soon as the flower beds start whispering to me and asking me for help, I'll oblige, but for now, I have to deal with what's in front of me."

"The shower? Really?" She winced.

"Yeah, he's a relatively new one. He's not a very good listener."

Dr. Suni shook her head slowly as she wrote on her pad. "Let me know when you're ready to try a quick run of intravenous steroids. It'll take a few days, and we'll back you down to your regular dose in no time. Here's a scrip for a stronger stimulant. It's new. Just try it. Annie will be in to give you an oxygen treatment, and then you can go."

"Thanks." I smiled and took the prescription. I didn't have the heart to tell her that increasing my meds wouldn't make the spooks go away. I wished it would, and I could tell by her eyes she wished it too. Having narcolepsy with a side of central sleep apnea was bad enough, but narcolepsy plus a couple of decades of central sleep apnea can equal something much worse. Dr. Suni called it a hypoxic brain injury, but I called it by its more practical name, Dead Head. "Dead" meaning the collection of neurons in my brain that had gone on strike for lack of oxygen and were now, in essence, deceased, and "Head" meaning the place inside my brainpan where all the ghosts in a ten-mile radius had set up their summer home.

She jotted a note on my chart, opened the door, and winked. "Happy hunting," she chimed and whisked out of the room.

****

I ran the length of the art gallery from the front door I had just locked, through the studios, across the classroom, and let my body slam into the back door. No one was chasing me. The building wasn't on fire. I wasn't bleeding to death, and I still had a good fifty seconds to exit the building before the alarm kicked in.

The gallery's alarm was positioned next to the front door, which had to be locked from the inside. That left the closer for the day to make their way through the darkened building to the back door and out in less than sixty seconds. It was my day to close and the countdown had started.

I'd watched the other artists go through the process of locking up in a calm and worry-free way. They'd flick the lights off in the front gallery, saunter past the studios, take a moment in the classroom to gather their things, yank patiently on the sticky back door, and then glide into the parking lot as though they didn't have five seconds left before the alarm sounded and the police came.

On the days when I worked late, they'd find me politely waiting for them in the parking lot clutching my hair with a look of horror on my face. I had to fight the urge to assume the fetal position when they cut it even closer than that. I could stare down an angry ghost, but I couldn't bear the thought of screwing up the alarm so the building manager had to call down and give the police the password. She lived right above the gallery, so it wasn't that much of an effort, but still, if you're going to do something, try to do it right.

Plus, there was something exhilarating about running in an art gallery. Priceless sculptures, still wet canvases, jutting display racks—we artists practically tiptoed through the place during work hours. It was fun to break a small rule, as long as I had the safety net of racing the alarm as my excuse if I tripped and broke something. It was nice to stretch my legs.

I grabbed my tote bag, yanked the heavy metal back door open, and spilled into the late summer heat. I circled back to the front of the gallery just as the five o'clock ferry whistle sounded. I stepped out of the way as a set of tourists whisked by. They had five minutes to make it three blocks to the foot of High Street or the ferry would leave without them. They'd never make it.

I set a more leisurely pace, making my way past the Commodore Theater and cutting through Trinity Church's park-like churchyard. It was always a good ten if not fifteen degrees cooler under the mammoth magnolia trees. The downtown was mashed up against the city's historic Olde Towne neighborhood where two-hundred-year-old magnolias reigned supreme, but the downtown proper was a sweltering maze of office buildings and storefronts. One did well to chart a course that wound through as many parks and churchyards as possible.

The far entrance to the churchyard spilled me onto Court Street near the Confederate monument. I walked another half block to the library and took the stone steps two at a time. I pushed through the heavy glass doors and was awash in air-conditioning again. I've lived a lot of places, but coastal Virginia was by far the most humid. You don't walk anywhere in Tidewater without utilizing the shade.

I dashed past the reference desk, motored through the periodicals, and made a bee line for the elevator. The Local History Room was on the basement level, and I wanted to catch it before it closed.

The elevator's ancient metal door clanked open, and I stepped into the 1950s sarcophagus with its flickering ceiling light and peeling posters. I stabbed the B button and watched the door to the tomb seal me in.

I drummed my fingers against my thigh as the cranky cables ruminated over my request. I stabbed the B button again, and the elevator lurched with displeasure. A century later, the door opened onto the basement's gloomy book sale stacks. I leapt out and followed the glowing dinosaur footprints lacquered to the floor as they wound through the book sale maze. On the other side of the stacks, the footprints zigged toward the back entrance of the Children's Library. I zagged around the staff lounge and arrived at my destination. The lights in the Local History Room were still on, but when I tried the glass double door it didn't budge. I knocked, waited, and knocked again.

At last, a head wrapped in a halo of cotton candy hair poked around the rare books display. I waved my hand and was met with a warm smile. The older woman pushed away from her desk and stumped toward me. She leaned over stiffly, released the floor bolt, and the doors swung open.

"I thought I'd had my last visitor for the day." She smiled, and her blue eyes sparkled. She ushered me in. "How can I help you?" she asked in a friendly, well-worn way, as though it was the phrase with which she started most of her conversations.

"I'm looking for images of Reverend Braidfoot, the second priest of Trinity Episcopal Church," I explained hopefully. The older woman's eyebrows lifted.

"No small task." She contemplated it a moment. "The Reverend John Braidfoot lived before cameras were on the scene."

"Hmm." I knew it couldn't be as easy as one trip to one library.

"Well, don't give up." She patted my hand with

warm, feathery fingers. "There are a few illustrations from that time in the church's history. I know of at least one that caught Braidfoot's likeness." She led me to a bay of file cabinets in the rare books section. "These are the church files." She pulled open a drawer and thumbed through the archival folders until she found one labeled "Trinity Church."

"May I ask why you are searching for such an old image?" Her eyes glittered in the protective, low light.

"Oh, I've been commissioned by the church to paint a portrait of Braidfoot for their parish hall."

"How wonderful," she chimed. I looked at her name tag. It read "Adeline Spruill" in shiny, gold letters. Spruill was an old Portsmouth family name. She helped me sort through the contents of the folder in an unhurried fashion. There were bulletins and clippings, directories and memorial dedications. We traveled back through time as the fashions in the photos changed and the church grounds transformed. The church's structure shrank as additions disappeared. Eventually, the photographs gave way to black and white drawings. We reached the end of the folder, and she gave my hand another pat. Her soft skin was warm and filled with strength.

"Don't worry. Like I said, I know of one image. It's not detailed, but I think it might help. Are you up for a little walk?" Mrs. Spruill tilted her spun-sugar head and winked at me. I couldn't help but like her.

I waited as she closed the Local History Room, and then I followed her out the back door of the library, down the Middle Street pedestrian mall, and into the dripping pink crepe myrtle tunnels that lined the sidewalks of Olde Towne. She gave me impromptu bits of history regarding certain buildings and parks as we made our way through the neighborhood. The relaxed pace let me enjoy the dappled, late afternoon light. When we finally reached our destination, I looked up and smiled.

****

The coat hangers dangling from every doorknob told me all I needed to know. As did the plastic cups that balanced on the edge of almost every table inside Mrs. Spruill's home.

I cast a reevaluating look over my shoulder at the sweet old historian. I'd followed her to the sprawling Queen Anne next to the dog park on the corner of Glasgow and Middle Streets. I passed this house almost every morning on my way to the coffee shop and wondered about its occupants the way I did with all the towering antique homes in Olde Towne.

The house's interior was as impressive as its façade, but the mix of authentic Victorian furniture and delicate chinoiserie didn't exactly blend with the frat-house keg-party décor. I caught the edge of an empty cup with my hip and grimaced as it clattered to the floor. The hollow sound stopped the librarian in her tracks. She spun around and scooped the cup up before I could retrieve it.

"I'm sorry." I felt more and more like a bull in a china shop with every step I took.

"Oh, don't apologize. I'm just a messy old lady." She smiled graciously but broke eye contact with me when she lied.

Mrs. Spruill led me into the parlor where sunlight flooded in from the park. It was the best room I'd ever encountered. Tall, double-width windows welcomed the slanting light, passing it from mirror to mirror in a Rococo dance of glowing golds. The striped wallpaper was a pattern of gilded paisleys that glimmered behind an arrangement of carved wood furnishings. She gestured toward a crushed velvet couch with a pair of matching cushioned chairs.

"Please, have a seat. Would you care for a lemonade? Tea? Soda?"

"That's very kind of you, but I'm already feeling guilty about taking up your time."

"Nonsense. I'll just grab a couple of sodas and the photo album we need. I'll be right back." She whisked through the doorway in a rattle of coat hangers and disappeared down the hallway. I stood and walked to the hangers. I trapped the vibrating wires between my fingers and held them until the hangers went still. Either Mrs. Spruill had run out of closet space and was sharing her home with a fraternity or she had a ghost problem.

I crossed to the bay windows and stood watching a pair of Weimaraners play tug of war with a brightly colored chew toy until my hostess returned. Mrs. Spruill slipped back through the swaying hangers, and I rushed from the windows to help her with the heavy album, but she handed me the cola bottles instead. I took the drinks and joined her at a card table near the window that was clear of plastic cups. She thumped the heavy load marked Trinity Episcopal Church onto the wobbly table. The album was less a book of photos and more an archival box with an acid free lid and pages. Mrs. Spruill handed me a pair of white gloves and slipped a pair on herself.

I watched she thumbed through decades of church directories and parish registers. Just like the library's church file, pictures changed from color to black and white. Dresses lengthened and shortened and lengthened again. She occasionally paused to show me a diagram for each new building phase for the church. The parish shrank through time to a small, one-room building with a barrel-vault roof and only a small cross in place of a steeple.

"Wow, it's so small, and there's so much room around the church. I had no idea the downtown had been so spacious." I marveled at the rural setting.

The historian giggled, and her bright eyes shone. "The land is the same size, but the buildings have swelled."

"And there are more of them."

"There's more of everything." She smiled brilliantly and pointed to an old illustration of Portsmouth. "This intersection—" She pointed to the site of Trinity Church on the western corner of Court and High Streets. "—this was named Church Square by the town's founder, Colonel Grayford." Her white-gloved fingers fanned through the ages, stopping finally at the last page. "This," she whispered with adoration, "was Colonel Grayford."

Grayford—that name seemed always in the air. I'd seen the statue of Portsmouth's founder down by the river, but it looked nothing like the handsome man who stared up at me from the faded edges of a long-ago moment. The masculine lines of his lightly sketched face seemed familiar as though my fingers knew each dip and curve. I tilted my head sideways as I studied the sepia sweep of his eyelashes. They cast seductive shadows across the shallow seas of his eyes.

"Blue," I whispered. Maybe it was the artist inside

me always tinting the world to my liking, but I could almost see the phantom freshwater blue of his irises. I leaned forward, caught for a moment in the dark rings that edged his irises. The inky circles were so crisp and definitive as though they were put in place to contain the man's fathomless thoughts. "Blue ice."

"Pardon?" I heard Mrs. Spruill ask. She'd leaned in close too, as though Colonel Grayford's portrait held its own gravity and we were both slowly and willingly falling into his orbit.

"Oh, uh...his eyes." I blushed a little at my reaction. "The contrast of light and dark. They must have been blue...you know that kind of frozen blue..."

"Like inland seas," she offered.

"Or mountain lakes," I finished. We nodded, drinking in the otherworldly rendering a moment longer, and then Mrs. Spruill turned the last page. I was sad to see him go.

Something stirred the air in the hallway just outside the parlor. Mrs. Spruill looked up from her images. A heartbeat later, we heard a plastic cup clatter to the floor. My hostess went very still. A breath later, another cup fell and rolled slowly to a stop. My eyes lowered to the older woman's hands. The faintest of tremors shook the page she held in her fingers. Strong woman, strong hands. Something was very wrong.

I held perfectly still in the slanting light and waited for her trance to lift. Mrs. Spruill's eyes turned slowly to the open doorway and the two wire hangers that hung from the clear glass doorknob. A moment passed and then another. No other sounds met us from the gathering shadows of the hallway. Finally, a nervous smile spread across the historian's face, and I returned it perhaps too quickly.

"These old houses," she began, clearing her throat, "they certainly are drafty." I looked down at my own hands and found that the soft, white gloves held a slight tremor as well. I pulled my hands from the table and placed them in my lap. Clearly, my nerves had not yet made a full recovery from the events of last night.

"Yes…well, I won't bore you with any more city history. I believe Reverend Braidfoot's portrait is here." As Mrs. Spruill folded the last page away, she pointed to an envelope attached to the inside of the back cover.

I reached hesitantly and unwound the string that held the envelope's clasp in place. Carefully, I slipped the contents of the envelope onto the table. There were several faded images on copier paper.

"A few years back, I conducted an inventory of historic portraits of Portsmouth's prominent citizens. I was able to make copies of several daguerreotypes, tintypes, and a handful of illustrated portraits from a few of our oldest families."

I studied the faded faces of Loyalists and Patriots alike as Mrs. Spruill relayed a brief bit of history about each one. She pointed out those who were related and how their families were ruined by the need to pick a side in the war. My heart hurt for those fathers, sons, and brothers that found themselves separated from their loved ones by the Revolution. Their experiences had aged them.

At last, we came to a wrinkled illustration half-faded into ghost light and dreams. Beneath the man's work-weary hands someone had scribbled *Rev. John Braidfoot, Second Priest of Trinity Parish. A year before his death—1784. Buried at the Glebe. Reinterred in Trinity Churchyard.*

I lost the wistful smile I'd held while looking over the drawings of wizened soldiers. Each of those pictures were different. Some men held a cane or a sentimental item. Others held their memories, numerous and dear in the lines of their faces. Reverend Braidfoot's drawing was different. His face was young and brash. Even the gray copier ink couldn't steal the fervor in his eyes. It was clear, even to me, more than two centuries later, that this man's heart was caught up in the revolutionary beat of a raw and desperate time.

"So young," was all I could say around the lump in my throat. Mrs. Spruill nodded, and I looked up to see her own eyes shining too much.

"There's an interesting story attached to Braidfoot, you know," she said, casually brushing a tear from her eye. "I don't know that this will help, but it's said that Reverend Braidfoot was visited by a ghost who foretold the evening of his death." As I gaped at Mrs. Spruill, I found myself reevaluating her yet again. "Not everyone likes a ghost story, but I'm guessing you're used to this sort of thing." I shook my head in amused confusion. She smiled and said, "I recognized you from your videos."

"Pardon me. But you're not exactly our demographic. Do you surf videos on the internet often?" I quirked a sassy smile at her.

"A good historian knows everything that pertains to her city, past and present." She returned the sass. "Now that I live alone, it's a little hard to get to sleep by myself. The internet keeps me company."

I had the impression she was just commenting on the current state of her life and not soliciting sympathy, but I felt it for her anyway. Mrs. Spruill was fast becoming one of my favorite neighbors.

"Would you like to hear the story?"

"I would."

"It was Braidfoot's granddaughter who first recorded the tale that had been told to her about the night of the Reverend's death. The story goes that some months before his death, the good Reverend was visited by a spirit that relayed to him the fact of his dwindling days. The ghost even told him the exact night he would depart this world for the next.

So, on that fateful date, Braidfoot's wife threw him a great dinner party and invited all his friends. They celebrated late into the evening with lots of wine and many courses. Just before the dessert course, the Reverend excused himself, and when his wife went to check on him…he was dead."

"Wow." I wasn't sure which I'd enjoyed more, the story or the way Mrs. Spruill told it.

"Stop by the library tomorrow, and I'll make you a copy to keep." She smiled.

"Thank you so much for going out of your way to help me." I took the gloves off and shook her strong hand.

"It's been a pleasure," she replied as we stood. She showed me to the door, but as we passed through the parlor's wide doorway I paused. I rested a finger on the wire hangers and looked back at the beautiful room.

"I noticed the humidifier in your parlor," I mentioned casually.

"Why, yes, I have one in almost every room. My sinuses aren't what they used to be. Dry air can be a problem."

"I'm sure it's not my place, but may I offer a little advice?" I pointed at the humidifier. "It's widely believed in paranormal research circles that ionized water molecules create a type of energy necessary for manifestation. The right kind of humidifier can literally feed a ghost. The stronger the ghost, the more it can disrupt the physical world." I tapped the coat hanger causing it to clang into its neighbor.

I met the historian's shimmering eyes, only now there was too much white circling them. She knew who I was yet hadn't asked for my help about her obvious issue. Some sentient ghosts can actually avoid things like bells and motion sensors. Mrs. Spruill had clearly figured that out. Light-weight objects, like cups, that tip easily in a breeze or casually placed hangers that clank when disturbed are a good work-around. I hated to think of my new friend alone and afraid in a big house with "drafts."

"Thank you, again." I smiled and slipped into the early evening heat.

Chapter Five

Just so we're clear…I don't do poltergeists.

The infrared was toast. I mean a giant slice of Texas toast that had gotten stuck in the toaster and left for dead. I thought I'd find Seth in tears, but when I walked into Matt and Josh's garage, he was anything but.

"What's going on?" I shouted over the death metal blaring from Seth's sound system.

"Seth got some new toys," Josh shouted back and stormed over to the stereo. "Infrared guns with laser thermometers. He's making holsters for them." Josh found a button and jabbed it until we could hear our thoughts again. Seth's wall of high-fidelity equipment was intimidating to say the least. I was amazed Josh even knew where the volume was in all the levers and buttons. Seth poked his head around the van with a "why are you touching my stuff" look on his face. He saw me and waved his soldering iron in greeting.

"Was that the infrared I saw next to the trash can?" I asked Josh as we stepped out into the driveway.

"Yep. She's a goner."

"Did anything else burn?"

"Nope. Everything was just as we left it. The lawn care service moved a couple of our crates and cables to the side before we got there, but other than that, all of the equipment is accounted for." We shared a look of relief. Among the five of us, we'd each sunk a lot of money into this business endeavor. The equipment wasn't cheap, and even though we were making money on our web channel now through advertisements, we still had a long way to go toward solvency.

"So..." I gave Josh the look. "What's the footage look like?"

He took a deep breath and blew it out slowly.

"You should see for yourself." He swept his arm toward the front door, and we headed inside.

Josh and Matt lived just off Smith's Creek in a quiet neighborhood of mostly retired couples. The houses were small and looked even smaller under the towering pines that had, no doubt, been planted when the houses were new. It was the type of neighborhood where you could always hear a lawn mower churning or a leaf blower humming, no matter the season. The old folks might not have a lot of money, but they certainly had pride, and it showed in their pristine yards.

I followed Josh to the back of the house where the windows looked out onto a shaded yard that sloped down into a ravine. At high tide, the creek fed water into the small ravine, but at the moment it was dry. I missed having a back yard. Josh had put in some birdfeeders at my suggestion, and two months ago I'd talked him into a hammock. I guess I'd still been hopeful two months ago that I'd find myself in the hammock with him. I didn't blame Josh for the mixed messages. I was a mess. Who would want to date a girl like me?

"It's ready to go." Josh pointed toward the little den off the kitchen. I followed him in and took a seat on the edge of one of the loungers. The den was much like the garage, covered in electronics and large snarls of cables. I'd purchased zip ties to bundle the cables, but no one seemed to notice the mess but me, so they'd gone unused.

"I haven't done any editing yet, so I'm just going to skip to the time stamp." Josh sat in the lounger next to me and fast-forwarded to the Weeping Angel.

"Matt's not home yet?"

"No. They changed his shift at the Shipyard, and he's going fishing after work," he answered distractedly. Josh's long legs were near enough to brush mine in the cramped space. I liked it when he was this close.

"Okay, look at Seth's monitor when I swing the camera toward him. He's got it pointed at the people that came up to us." Josh hit play and the scene unfolded before me, but this time without the fog of the hypnogogic state. It had been disturbing the first few times I'd watched myself on camera lumbering along. It was particularly unattractive when my jaw unhinged and hung from my face like the undead. Well, maybe it wasn't that bad, but it wasn't cute.

Josh hit a button on the remote control and slowed the video down as the camera swept toward Seth.

"This is the first time I turned to him." Josh pointed at the video.

Seth was saying something in slow motion, and then the display on the infrared came into focus. I saw myself on the screen glowing a bright yellowy orange and violet. Beyond me the tombstones glowed a yellowy green. Blue trees and bushes reflected back their lower heat signatures, and in front of me a black hole drifted. Beyond it were smaller black holes that kept merging with the empty sky.

"That's the first thing we caught." Josh pressed the pause button and pointed at the flat screen again. "We've seen these black holes before, but look up at the top right corner." I squinted at the confusion of gray pixels as they blended into one another. "Do you see it?"

"See what?"

"There. That's a hand and what looks like an arm with lace or something hanging from the cuff."

Once Josh pointed it out, it was unmistakable. The riot of pixels had clearly taken the shape of a woman's upper torso.

"It's only there for a second and it's high on the screen, but it's moving in a line away from where your hand had just been. Here, watch it at regular speed." Josh rewound a few seconds and started the video again. I heard his voice on the video saying, "What's going on, Mel?" and then I saw it. I sucked in a breath and Josh grinned at me. I was amazed. Truly amazed. Not at the ghost—I remember her. I remember the cool touch of her hand and the sense of panic about her. That's not what amazed me. What shocked me was the fact that she'd shown up on the camera. There she was, caught in a snare of moving pixels.

Josh looked at me with an intensity I'd never seen before. He had finally seen what I see. Every ghost I'd ever seen was just empty air to the rest of the world. Up until this very moment, there was still the possibility that I was just crazy. I didn't know what to say.

"Wait. There's more." Josh fast-forwarded the video to the point when we first saw the woman in green and her companions at the back of the cemetery. My skin began to crawl. He pressed play just at the moment that Gabe pointed across the graveyard. I saw the bobbing light and counted the number of figures moving through the lantern light.

In the video, Josh counted "...five, maybe six." Then the Josh sitting next to me slowed the video and pointed to each figure. "Six...but look at the infrared."

The video bounced with Josh's steps as he positioned himself behind Seth. I could see myself. I could see the woman and the five other people with her. I could see the two lanterns they carried glowing like golden stars against the night. Then I saw it. The camera dipped, and Seth's display came into the frame. Two orange heat signatures swayed between the lanterns.

"Oh my God." The words flew from my mouth. I shot a glance at Josh. He stared at me intently. My eyes darted between him and the video. There were only two flesh and blood people standing in the group.

"And the lanterns." I pointed at the flat screen. The spinning play of light and dark inside the lanterns was causing a garbled effect that wasn't visible anywhere but on the infrared. I'd never seen that before.

The video shifted as Josh moved the camera to a nearby headstone. My heart thumped against my ribs as the small group moved closer. I could see the edge of my arm as I swayed in and out of the frame. A lock of my hair had escaped the bun and trailed down my shoulder.

"I...I can't watch." Anxiety surged inside me as the woman moved close enough for me to make out her perfect lips and the languid line of her lashes.

"Well…" Josh pointed to the screen, and the recording faded into static. "That's all we have…of video at least."

Tears blurred my vision, and I swallowed hard against a scream building in my throat.

Josh turned to me, and his face shifted to shock. "What's wrong?"

I felt like I couldn't catch my breath. I shook my head and waved that everything was okay. I just needed a second to get a grip on myself. Josh had turned his whole body to face me. Our legs entwined. I didn't want him to see me like this, but I didn't want him to go.

I took a deep breath and said, "It's okay." I willed the tears not to fall, but seeing the concern on Josh's face didn't help. "I just wasn't prepared to see her again, I guess. It's okay…I'm fine." Josh reached for me, but his hands stopped midway to my arms. Instead, he turned back to the static on the flat screen. He looked from me to the television and then to me again.

"What?" I asked.

"It's nothing." He reached for the remote.

"Josh…what?"

"Well, that's all we got on Camera One. Gabe had gone to get Camera Two, but it was around then that Seth caught on fire." Josh pointed the remote at the TV screen and started clicking through menus. "He never even got the chance to aim the camera, so I had no idea that he'd even turned it on." A new video came up, but the night-vision light wasn't on, so all I could make out was a dark strip of sideways grass and gravel. I turned my head sideways until I made out the base of the Weeping Angel.

"He must have pressed the record button because we've got some audio." Josh looked over at me with an assessing look.

"I'm fine," I assured him, but I wasn't. He hesitated a moment, then pressed Play.

I could hear voices, but they were hard to make out over the shuffling of feet in the gravel. Clouds of dust obscured the video further. I heard Seth yelp, and light flared for a moment in the dusty lens. Gabe's voice was strident but muffled as the two men wrestled through the loose gravel. A moment later, I heard Matt swear, and then Josh was calling my name. "Time to wake up," he shouted, and then I heard it.

"Beautiful dreamer wake unto me...Starlight and dewdrops are waiting for thee."

I screamed, and I thought the scream would never end.

****

"Now's a pretty good time to lay down some ground rules," I said from the comfort of my blanket cocoon. Josh dragged a chair next to the hammock and sat in it. There was enough room in the hammock for both of us, but I didn't blame him for wanting some distance from me at the moment. My words slurred a little, and my head still jerked as my neck fought for muscle control. The rush of fear at hearing the woman in green singing had triggered a nasty attack of cataplexy.

I remember screaming, and then Josh and Matt's lumpy brown carpeting rushed at me. Luckily, Josh caught me before I hit the floor. I usually did a better job of dulling my emotional responses, but that one sneaked up on me.

I'd stopped shivering ten minutes ago, but I kept the blanket just in case. Seth apparently heard my scream over his music and had come running. He stood with his back to the ravine, and his arms crossed over his chest. He looked like something out of a paranormal Wild West movie. He'd made a waist holster that reached down to secure around his thigh. As much as I hated to admit it, the leather, metal, and Velcro contraption was kind of sexy.

"Just so we're clear...I don't do poltergeists. I don't do demonic possessions, and I don't do evil, singing ghosts that pick me up and try to carry me away."

"Fair enough," was Seth's only response.

"So Oak Grove Cemetery is off the ghost-hunting map for now," Josh said. I gave him a look. "It's off the map indefinitely," he corrected.

"We have a two-week cushion on the videos. We can take a week to...regroup," Seth offered. "I can get started on the post-production and interviews for the Oak Grove footage while Mel takes a break."

"Do you need an interview from me?" I asked.

He frowned as he thought about it. "I'd rather have it and not need it, than need it and not have it."

"Fine." I didn't want to think about the encounter anymore, but with the bulk of our footage missing, we'd have to do a really good job at describing what happened or we'd lose credit with our subscribers. "Just one request." I looked at them both. "We don't use the audio from Camera Two."

They both looked at each other at the same time.

"How about this," Josh revised. "We use the footage from Camera One as a build into the audio from

Camera Two. But when we play the audio, we cut it off at my voice telling you to wake up. It just stops there, and we end the show with a message that says the audio on Camera Two was lost, leaving the rest of the encounter unrecorded."

"We can advertise it as a special edition with extra interviews and behind-the-scenes footage." Seth's wheels were turning along with Josh's.

I could tell that a rough sketch of the show had already played out in their minds. "Okay," I reluctantly agreed, "but can we just get my interviews over with? I've got to get back and feed my cat." I threw the blanket off and stomped back toward the house.

****

Josh looked over the questions he'd jotted down. He took his glasses off and rubbed the bridge of his nose. The camera was already rolling. I waited. I wasn't thrilled about the fact that the guys had asked me not to wash my face. The mascara streaks had dried into tight lines on my cheeks. This was definitely not professional. I must have looked more pitiful than I realized because Josh began to shake his head and reached to turn the camera off.

"No." I blocked his hand, and our fingers touched. I watched him watching me. Then, slowly, I turned the camera to face him.

"What are you doing?" he asked.

"I'm going to ask you some questions."

He rubbed his face again. I looked at him for a long minute.

"What are you thinking?" I asked him finally. He paused for longer than I'd expected he would. Thoughts spun behind his gray eyes.

"I'm thinking I don't want to do this. Not right now."

"You're upset." It was more a statement than a question.

"Yeah."

"Why?"

Josh thought about my question for a second, then put his glasses back on. "That...wasn't good...what happened."

"No. It wasn't." I waited for him to say more, but his face was just blank.

"Everyone was affected by what we experienced," I said, and he nodded his head in agreement.

"You got the worst of it." He fixed his storm-cloud eyes on mine.

"What was it like to see...what happened to me?" I chose my words carefully. I still wasn't sure how much of our encounter we were ready to share with the world, when we didn't have the footage to back it up. Josh exhaled a pent-up breath and pursed his lips the way he does when he's trying to keep something from me. I waited while he made the decision to share or not to share.

"What do you think it was like? You were not responding, and then...she...took you." He looked down at his hands, then rubbed them nervously through the long waves of his hair. "It's not like anyone is going to believe us." He gestured toward the camera. "There's no reason to record this."

I blinked slowly and then continued. "Then what happened?"

"Then," he started and stopped. "Then, my heart stopped because I thought I was seeing things. Mel, I don't think you realize the danger you were in." His eyes widened, and he shook his head back and forth. "I think I'm with Gabe. I think we need to…reassess. I mean, don't get me wrong. I love what we do. There's more to this life than what we can see and hear and touch. I'm sure of it. I was sure even before you joined us. But now that you're here…" His voice trailed off.

"Now that I'm here…?"

He looked at me again with that intensity that he kept a lid on so carefully.

"Now that you're here, it just confirms that we were right all along. There is life after death. We've answered the unanswerable question, Mel." He blinked wide eyes at me. "But it's also clear that we might be in way over our heads. I mean, don't you feel that way sometimes? I watch you casually reach for these…pieces of souls…remnants of people…without any clue as to whether they are just peaceful echoes or something worse. I can tell that this encounter scared you. I've never seen you so shaken, but I guess my question is…why aren't you always that scared? I know, I know, you've had a lot of time to adjust. You've been dealing with the unexplained for a long time because of your disorder." He threw his hands up and shook his head some more. "I don't know, Mel. I just don't know where to go from here. I want to keep going. If anything good came of last night, it's that at least we…our team—" His finger lassoed the air above our heads. "—at least we know that we're not nuts."

Suddenly, he leaned toward me, resting his arms on his knees. "You're not nuts, Mel. I'm so sorry you've had this burden keeping you separate from the rest of us. I'm so sorry if I've ever doubted you. I'm so sorry I couldn't stop that thing from grabbing you." His eyes were too wide and too shiny. His handsome face hovered before me, and I barely understood what he was saying to me. No one had ever said those words to me, at least not said them and meant them. He didn't think I was crazy. In fact, he now knew beyond a shadow of a doubt that I wasn't crazy.

I'm not crazy.

I must have whispered the words because he scooted to the edge of his chair and reached for my hands.

"You're not crazy," he whispered. Tears fell from my eyes, washing my stained cheeks. I leaned toward him. His hands slid up my arms.

And…he hesitated.

I could see it in his eyes—there was so much more. I know he cared for me. I know he wanted more. His lips parted, and his pulse jumped beneath his ruddy skin. What was holding him back? I needed him to touch me. To kiss me. To let me feel desired. At any given moment, I was trapped behind a wall of disembodied voices. The fingers that grazed my skin in quiet moments were cold reminders of the connections I couldn't seem to make with warm living people. I was alone with their lost thoughts. How could he leave me to them? I wanted to wrap myself in someone's warm embrace.

Anyone's.

And there it was.

I'd hoped with all my heart that the door had finally opened between us, but I watched his face as it closed. A fresh stream of tears washed the last of my mascara away.

The door had closed for me too.

His fingers slipped from my arms, and he turned the camera off.

Chapter Six

"Stick to what you know" and other useless advice.

Thank God for my day job. I'd actually gotten some sleep. No ghosts were abducting me. I didn't have a bunch of guys stretched across my floor snoring. Bougie had stood watch most of the night at the foot of my bed. He wasn't one of those needy cats that had to be on my pillow or worse, my face. He was satisfied with a small piece of real estate at the bottom corner of the mattress. Sometimes, I even forgot he was there. I was actually surprised when I woke to morning light. The soldier ghost hadn't made an appearance all night. I even felt halfway human today.

The art classes had gone by so quickly. I'd just finished my last afternoon class. It was made up of older kids who needed far less instruction. Today's lesson ironically was *Shadows, what color are they really?* I washed my brushes and waved goodbye to the last student.

I loved the way each child interpreted the color of the pear and the shadows it cast on the tablecloth. I hung their canvases to dry on the classroom wall and went to my studio to prime my canvas for the Braidfoot portrait. The gallery was quiet today, which left with more time inside my head than I like.

I'd chosen a four-foot canvas with back-staples and

a thick, untreated canvas. I opened my can of gesso and dipped a wide-bristled brush into the thick liquid. I brushed the first layer on with quick, crisscrossing motions. I let that dry, then I went over it with long vertical and horizontal brushstrokes to even out the texture of the paint.

My thoughts wandered inevitably to Josh and our missed connection. It might not be Josh's fault. I'd never really put myself out there. Josh was a good man, and I was...damaged goods.

My mind drifted to the only place that gave me comfort—my mystery man. The one I could never scare off because he wasn't real. He was tall and handsome and came to me whenever I needed him. I could never fully see his face. He was nebulous like the man in the graveyard who'd worn the shadows like a disguise.

The front door chimed, and I walked to the gallery to greet the new guest.

"Welcome to the gallery. If you have any questions or if I can help in any way, please let me know," I offered cheerfully to the potential customer.

He turned to me, and I froze. I locked eyes with the sweaty man from two nights ago. I opened my mouth to speak, but zero words came out.

"Hello," he said tentatively. He shifted nervously from foot to foot but didn't make any attempts to move closer. "It's Melisande, right?" He pointed to the wall of paintings that held my signature. I started to nod, but my head only made it halfway.

"I'm Ben...Martin." His hand lifted out of habit, but he realized quickly that I wasn't going to shake it, so he dropped it to his side again.

"Mr. Martin," I whispered in response. "What are

you doing here?"

"I felt…well, I thought that I…may I explain about the other night?" he asked, looking around to see if there were any other artists in the studios behind me.

"We're alone." I instantly regretted saying that, but nothing about his demeanor changed with that information. The last thing I wanted to do was get nearer to this man, but the shock of seeing him had triggered cataplexy in my legs so violently that if I didn't sit down, I was going to fall down. So I gestured to the bistro seats next to the brochure rack and we sat.

"I can imagine that the behavior of my companions was kind of a shock the other evening."

"You could say that."

He studied me for a moment, then said, "I work for the Olde Towne Business Association, so I'm familiar with Ghost Towne Investigations. We…like the work you do. It's actually boosting tourism." He smiled politely. "The videos are good—very different from the other paranormal shows out there. They are—" He searched for a word. "—authentic." He was trying too hard or stalling. I wasn't sure.

"So, Mr. Martin…"

"Ben, please." Another habit, I guessed.

"Ben, what is it that you'd like to say to me?" I asked in a surprisingly calm voice.

"Well…off the record, of course…there are some residents who have requested you find other sites for your investigations that are, perhaps, outside the city limits."

"But you just said that the city is happy with our work. Have you had complaints about our production?" I hoped for a disgruntled report from the guy who ran the storage facility next to Oak Grove Cemetery. He'd tried to have our van towed once because we'd parked for a few minutes on the service road between his property and the graveyard. But something told me I wasn't going to be that lucky.

"Of a sort," he continued.

"Would this sort be of the living variety?" I asked, and he laughed a humorless, nervous laugh.

"Well, see, that's the thing." Mr. Martin looked around the gallery again, then attempted to straighten his lop-sided tie. "As I might guess you already know, not all of our residents are, in fact, of the living variety." He gave me a look that one gives when they expect to see the person they are talking to suddenly go heels up down the rabbit hole.

I stared back at him with a look that said the rabbit hole was my weekend getaway spot. "Attacking me isn't the way to get me to do something," I informed Mr. Martin with very little quaver in my voice. In fact, I was a little pissed, and pissed, for me, was usually one step before reckless.

"Melisande…Miss Blythe." He shook his head. "The people I'm referring to don't operate the way you or I do. They hold to a different code of ethics."

"Are you threatening me?" I asked. My legs were still weak, but I was in complete control of my thoughts, and my thoughts were telling me to punch this guy in the throat.

I watched as genuine southern-style shock changed quickly to a numbingly certain fear. That fear was clearly not for himself…but for me.

"Please understand me. This is the only warning you will get."

"So, it is a threat," I said more than asked. I watched as Mr. Martin struggled for a way to get through my hardening resolve. He seemed desperate, which worried me.

"How can I convince you that it's in your best interest and the best interest of all the people at Ghost Towne Investigations to work outside of the city proper?"

"What was she?"

"I can't discuss it."

"What about the other three? The man in the red vest, the other woman...the other man?" For some reason I hesitated to speak of the last man. I waited for an answer, but he just shook his head. I nodded to indicate that I saw where this was going.

"Melisande, if I were you, not only would I work outside of the city, I'd live outside of the city too. Like, way outside of the city. I understand Canada is nice this time of year." It sounded like Mr. Martin was being facetious, but his face was pale, and he'd started to sweat again.

"If these people are so scary, what are you doing with them?" I had to ask.

"Trust me, it's not by choice," he answered too quickly for it to be a lie. Suddenly, I was less worried for me and more worried for him.

"It seems like your concern is genuine. I thank you for the warning, but you do realize what I do for a living?"

"Yes, you're a talented artist. I also serve on the Arts Commission that helps fund this gallery." He lifted a superior eyebrow. I think Mr. Martin realized right away that he'd just played his hand wrong. He must have read it on my face. He mopped his head with his sleeve and tried to backtrack, but I stopped him. Threats and innuendo were not his thing.

"You should stick to what you know," I recommended and stood. Mr. Martin stood too.

"And you should think about sticking to teaching art classes," he parried. "I've done what I could," he said as he turned for the door. I followed him and held the door for him as he stepped out into the heat. He turned on the sidewalk and leaned back toward me.

"She's taken an interest in you. If you get off her radar now, you might be okay." He held my gaze for one imploring moment then nodded and walked away.

****

I closed the gallery early and headed over to the library. The Summer Reading Club had just let out for the day, and young families flooded the check-out desk. A line of baby strollers stretched back to the elevator. I tried to maneuver my way through the stacks to the back of the library, but it was just too crowded. Instead, I made a U-turn next to the business section and slipped behind the periodicals display. I'd almost made it to the front stairs, which led down to the basement level, when I felt an icy stir in the air.

I peered out at the general reading area through the clear, acrylic display next to me. Beyond the chattering children and tired moms, I saw a few high school kids sitting at the study tables, staring numbly at their tutors as they prattled on. There were a few retirees perusing the new releases. I looked behind me at the business section, but all I saw were the usual homeless folk—Jerry, the Grapefruit Guy, who always carried a crucifix jammed into a grapefruit; the Preacher, who was oddly quiet as he stared intently into a corner; and Silent Mack, the gentle giant with the broken glasses.

Though he never spoke a word, Mack was pretty good at keeping an eye on the empty gallery for me from the bench outside whenever I went next door to grab my lunch from the bakery. I liked sharing my cronuts with him in silence. It was pressure-free dining. We usually got by communicating with nods and waves. It wasn't in-depth conversation, but it got the job done. I lifted my hand in greeting, but Mack didn't respond. He turned away from me to stare at the same corner that the Preacher faced.

Something wasn't right. I hooked my fingers through the magazine rack next to me and let a piece of my brain go to sleep. Images from the day washed against my mind's shore like flotsam on the tide. Mr. Martin handed me a pear, and in the shadow of the pear was a warning. I fought past the Stage One wanderings and focused on the scene before me.

The library's business section was pretty small. In fact, it was basically an alcove with three chairs and a few stacks, which held legal manuals, stock market ratings, and a wall of how-to books for people looking to start a business. Officially, it was there if someone needed to look up a specific executive from a corporation or figure out what business was a subsidiary of another business. Unofficially, it was a cool, quiet place for the unemployed to take a siesta.

On this long, hot afternoon, the tiny space was at capacity with one addition. A crawling mass of vapor twisted and knotted itself in a shadowy corner of the windowless alcove. My thigh and calf muscles tensed to compensate as my knees went limp. The left side of my jaw unhinged as I gaped at the roiling mass. I watched in horror as the Preacher stepped closer to the clenching coil of madness.

The only humanoid features the seething cloud seemed to possess were two glowing white orb-like eyes and a wriggling mouth that squirmed and puckered in an unceasing way. It was whispering softly to its captive audience.

I felt my fingers loosening. I was losing my grip on the magazine rack.

"Mack," I called to the big man. My zombie mouth slurred the word, but I'd said it loud enough for him to hear me. Still, he didn't turn back to me.

I took a wobbling step toward him, which put me that much closer to the thing. I let go of the magazine rack and took another uncertain step. A child giggled from the other side of the periodicals display, and the juxtaposition of the sweet sound so close to this twisting nightmare sent shivers down my spine. The high-pitched, gleeful sound fractured into shrill hallucinatory bird song.

I braced myself on the top of the business directories shelf and pulled along it until Mack was within arm's length. I waved my hand in his peripheral vision, but he didn't respond. I looked back at the Preacher's rigid form. His thin arms hung loosely at his sides, and his Bible dangled from bloodless fingers.

I heard the whispering. It was soft and incessant and filled with a million questions. I tried not to listen, but the words wormed through my thoughts, scattering them. There were so many questions. I couldn't possibly ponder them all. I couldn't even work on one. The sheer volume of inquiries threatened to short circuit my brain.

I looked from Jerry the Grapefruit Guy to the Preacher to Silent Mack. They were all lost to the endless cycle of contemplations that whispered from the specter's warbling mouth. Contradictions swirled. Doubts loomed. The Preacher mumbled as he tried desperately to find a line of thought that would lead to escape.

I fought the onslaught of queries until I'd made enough room in my mind to think. This thing was no longer a remnant in the normal sense of the word, but it was still a ghost. I could feel its human origins wrapped up in the DNA of its memories. Maybe I could reason with it.

"What do you want?" I whispered. I shot a glance behind me at the check-out line, but no one seemed to be looking our way. I looked back at the thing, and the swinging motion of my head made the library spin around me.

Once my eyes agreed to focus again, I saw that the apparition had moved. I took a staggering step back as the myopic orbs of dull white light fixed on me from just a few feet away.

I sucked in a breath as the confusion narrowed in on me. Questions spun around me, but they were no longer random disjointed things. The questions were about me. The closer it drifted, the more I could feel the press of its aberrant aura of energy. Its curiosity filled my head.

How did the elderly man standing in the Ganges know my name? I hadn't asked that question since I was a child living in India.

Why did I get narcolepsy and not my sister? A

painful question, but again, one I hadn't asked in many years.

Did I choose the right major?
Did my dog really run away like my parents said?
Why does the Shadow chase me?
Did that guy put something in my drink that night?
Are my art classes making a difference?
Am I unlovable?

I felt myself falling deeper and deeper into a miasma of uncertainty and self-doubt. I'd lost sense of anything else but the questions and the orbs of sightless wondering. I flung my arms out in the suddenly empty space of unknowing and someone caught me. One last question whispered through my mind.

Am I really this weak?

I hung from Mack's arms like a ragdoll until my legs agreed to work again. I turned my head to see several mothers look quickly away. I gripped Mack's hands until I was sure the cataplexy was under control. Then, I stepped away.

"You shouldn't look in corners. Sometimes bad things hide in corners." Mack's voice was gentle and low and hoarse with disuse. I stared at him in shock. I wanted to ask him about what had just happened. Where had the entity gone? Had he encountered it before? How had he broken free? I had a million questions, but there'd been too many already. I'd never heard his voice before. I didn't know what to say. I wished he'd say something else, but it just didn't feel right to force a conversation. What little he'd said felt like a gift.

"Thank you," I finally said, and he nodded his acknowledgement. The Preacher peered at me with his usual mistrusting eyes. Jerry the Grapefruit Guy got up and wandered away. I straightened my T-shirt and turned away from the checkout desk. I slipped my foot back into my flip flop and headed for the stairs. Most libraries had ghosts, but that thing was something else. I'd heard of thought-bending entities called Murmurs, but they usually haunted asylums. Maybe this one had gotten lost. I gave a nervous look behind me then rushed down the stairs as quickly as I could.

****

Mrs. Spruill's glittery eyes held the shadows of sleep loss, but they were shining nonetheless. She'd scanned the illustration for me and, even though she hadn't been able to locate any further images, she'd found a few entries that made mention of Reverend Braidfoot. The entries were short but described a man of zeal and purpose. He was an ardent patriot and served as chaplain for the Second Virginia Infantry Regiment when the Revolutionary War broke out.

In one account, he was described as coming home from the victory at Yorktown and ringing Trinity's church bell with such fervor that it cracked. That victory marked the end of the war for independence. I could only imagine the swell of emotions Reverend Braidfoot felt when he gripped the bell's rope knowing that, after eight years, his entire country was finally free.

"It's moving to make a connection with someone from such an exciting time in our history, isn't it?" The historian smiled. I could tell that she searched my face to see if I'd been infected like she had. I agreed. I'd never realized how connected Tidewater, Virginia, was to major events through time.

As if reading my thoughts, Mrs. Spruill explained that our lands were a nexus of activity even before the first explorers arrived. Tidewater had once been the site of a great community belonging to the Chesopian Indians. I could listen to Mrs. Spruill talk all day, but new patrons had come in and I'd taken enough of her time. I thanked her again and headed back up the front stairs. It was my first time not feeling at ease in the beautiful library.

The trio of homeless men had left as well. I wondered if they had fallen prey to that particular entity before. Was it localized to this site or did it seek out people whose minds had convenient cracks for it to slip through? I thought about the last question the ghost had dragged from my mind.

Am I really this weak?

I hadn't dealt with my feelings about what had happened in the graveyard, but then processing feelings wasn't exactly my strong suit. I pushed through the heavy glass doors and the mid-July heat washed over me. I placed my photocopy in my purse and headed home.

Chapter Seven

Nobody likes a bloody chick in a bustier.

I'd chosen a magenta eyeshadow with a dark purple liner for my eyes and I'd twisted my lavender streak into a braid. The blue and violet shadows we'd painted in class earlier wove through my hair, leaving my streak a pale rope of shimmering lilac. It worked with my mood. I felt like being flashy and conspicuous.

I'd changed my mind about Oak Grove. I wanted to go back, but the guys outvoted me. No cemeteries tonight. I'd added a little red to my already bluish lips which blended to a grape kiss. It looked good with my black bustier and knee-high boots. The guys were thrilled. I didn't usually show this much skin. It was hard to find a bustier in my size. My waist wasn't a problem, but my bust certainly was. I'd picked this one up at a Renaissance Faire because it had detachable shoulder straps with sturdy grommets to hold them in place. The bustier gave my athletic hips a more feminine curve as well.

I looked out at the buzzing night. This was almost certainly a mistake, but I didn't care. It was a warm, muggy night with lots of ionized water vapor in the air. This should be easy. All I had to do was latch on to a spirit stream and hold it long enough for the guys to catch a video or audio trace and we'd be done. Besides, this was my stomping grounds. I paid rent and taxes. Why should I be the one to leave?

"Okay, we've all got the plan right. The theme tonight is—A Ghost Hunter's Guide to Finding Neighborhood Ghosts." Josh tried to sound certain, but his mood was sedate at best. In fact, everyone but Seth looked as though they'd be happy if they never hunted another ghost as long as they lived. "Mel has already scouted a few hot spots for us. Matt, you're with Gabe. You two will go ahead of us and prep the stopping points. Here's the map." Josh unfolded the Olde Towne brochure with the best map and circled our three sites.

"We'll start at the Gall House with the Headless Judge and then walk over to Glasgow Street to the Sea Captain haunting. From there we'll cut through Middle Street to North Street and end with the old lady in the rose garden." He closed the brochure and handed it to Gabe. "Seth, Mel will be in the hypnogogic state the entire time we are walking between sights. If she senses something, we'll stop and give her time to relate whatever she gets. When she's not talking, I want you to describe the various pieces of equipment and how to use them."

"Got it. I'll walk in front of her and call out trip hazards." Seth gave me a wink. "What if the Shadow shows up?"

"Mel and I have that worked out. She won't be too deep while we're moving. I can pull her out." Josh seemed confident about his ability to yank me out of the hypnogogic state quickly, but he'd never seen the Shadow. No one had. Only I knew how quickly it moved. I pushed the thought from my mind. Nothing was going to ruin my night. This is what I do, and no ghost was going to scare me away.

"Eyes on the ground, girlie." Gabe pointed to his eyes and then the ground. He gave me a brilliant smile and headed off through the shadows to our first site, lugging the portable floodlights.

"See you in a few minutes." Matt picked up the boom and rushed after Gabe.

It was a beautiful night on the front stoop of my apartment building. The gas lamps flickered in the thick evening and heat lightning flashed over the river. We started out walking parallel to the water, only catching glimpses of the sea wall at the end of each cross street as we passed. One more block and we'd lose sight of the river, but I could feel its moisture hanging in the air around us.

There was something else in the air too…anticipation. It was always exciting just before filming. If I could keep my fear at bay, I could convince the guys that we were safe. Portsmouth, Virginia, was one of the most haunted towns in the Unites States. Ghost Towne Investigations had been referred to over and over again as the "river ghost guides" because of our work here at the mouth of the Chesapeake Bay. The Elizabeth River, the James River, the York River—we'd investigated hauntings along all the major waterways and creeks in Tidewater. This was our town.

Josh walked so close to me, I thought he'd bump into me. Seth's head swiveled as he scanned the darkened neighborhood. He closely scrutinized every person we encountered. I hadn't told them about my run-in with Ben Martin, aka the Sweaty Man. I had every intention of telling them about the warning right after filming, but I needed to prove to them first that we had nothing to worry about.

"Coming up on the Civil War Hospital," Josh announced. "You ready?" I nodded and took a deep breath. Entering the hypnogogic state was easy when part of your brain was always tired. I just simply stopped fighting it. My muscles relaxed, and I tipped forward as my sense of balance left me.

"I forgot to check…is Bougie following us?" I slurred my words a little. My cat, Bouguereau, liked it when I was outside. Sometimes, he followed me on the sidewalk. It made me nervous when I crossed busy streets, so I always chased him back home when I got close to the downtown. If I turned around now to look, I'd probably lose my balance and fall on the chipped brick sidewalk. Nobody likes a bloody chick in a bustier, so I asked Josh if he would check.

"Nope. Coast's clear."

"Thanks." Nevertheless, I had that strange itch between my shoulder blades that I get sometimes when I think someone is following me.

I stopped in front of the first of two apartment buildings that had once been used to house injured soldiers during a few of the local Civil War battles. I had no idea how renters tolerated the ambient sorrow that still permeated the two structures.

"Sounds." I turned to Josh. He held his hand over the red light until my eyes adjusted, then he focused the lens on me.

"Can you make out words?"

"Not really…well, yes…someone is crying for help."

"A wounded soldier?"

"No…a nurse, I think."

Seth climbed the front stairs and pressed the button on his electronic voice phenomena recorder. He looked to me, and I nodded.

"When recording around live structures, you want to use a simple hand-held EVP recorder. A GEOPhone/recorder combo won't help you because of the vibrations produced by other people walking around in the structure. This is also not the time for sophisticated listening devices. You'll pick up too much ambient noise. Plus, it's kind of rude to listen in on private conversations. So be a polite ghost-hunter and don't spy on your neighbors." Seth grinned as Josh cut back to me.

"Any visuals?"

"Sorry." I shook my head. I wasn't all that sorry, though. The souls that lingered in that building were trapped in a misery I didn't want any part of. I'd tried once to make contact with the ghost of a young boy I'd seen on the porch, but he'd run from me.

We moved on. Middle Street was a little more active. Cold spots drifted through the muggy air, and twice we picked up voices. While we walked, Seth gave a brief tutorial on how to catch real time EVPs using tandem recorders. He also showed off his more discreet one-touch voice recorder pen, which happened to catch a bit of disembodied laughter as we walked.

The Gall House, our first stop, was a two-story tax-dodger with a slate shingle roof and humble façade. Gabe was careful not to shine the flood lights in my eyes or into the windows of the home. Matt gave a brief description of the resident ghost who, in life, had been a hanging judge. As the story goes, his punishment for sending so many innocent men to their deaths had been the loss of his own head. Seth gave another ethics lecture on pointing cameras and other devices like infrared at an occupied residence. Infrared can't see through walls. It just reads the heat signature bouncing off the exterior, but the residents might not know that. When in doubt, as for permission first.

We'd had success in the past catching shadows in the house's windows, but without access to the interior, none of the images could be substantiated. In fact, one photograph had been so tantalizing that it had made it to the cover of *Paranormal Quarterly*. The picture had been taken at twilight and had clearly caught the outline of a headless figure in an antique night gown. The Headless Judge was a favorite on Portsmouth's Annual Ghost Walk. This site was usually good for at least a few chills down the spine, but tonight the property was quiet. I wasn't even picking up a galvanic skin response.

I took a wobbly step over the front hedge and sat on a wrought iron bench beneath a frilly crepe myrtle. Seth whispered to the camera that I was demonstrating exactly what not to do when ghost hunting in a residential area. But I was in my bad girl boots, so a little trespassing was to be expected. I listened to the cicadas crackle in the trees of the tiny front yard. Frogs chirped in the puddle below the mossy downspout, and grasshoppers sang their summer song beneath the heat lightning.

The night was filled with life, but I knew just beneath that layer of pulsing energy was a cold harbor for transient souls. I reached for its icy surface and felt the soul stream stir. I waited, but REM sleep clawed greedy fingers at the edges of my consciousness. If I sat much longer, Josh would record me snoring and not much else. Josh called it. Gabe killed the floods, and he and Matt moved on to site two.

I climbed back over the hedge, and we continued on to Glasgow Street. The next house was an English Basement style home with tall windows and a large, second-story porch. This haunting was tricky. Josh explained the cold spots and orbs that we'd caught here on other nights, but this was a sporadic haunting.

In the 1980s, the Jaffos family members were the first residents to report the spectral activity to police when, one night, the top floor had come alive with the sound of a man pacing. The booming steps then left the attic level and descended the stairs. Mr. Jaffos had gotten his wife and two daughters out of the home, but police never found the intruder or any evidence of forced entry. Since then, the sound of a man's voice has been heard on occasion along with heavy footsteps, but the incidents were so spread out that recording the events are practically impossible. Nevertheless, the Sea Captain, as the ghost has been nicknamed, is a part of local history and permanently on file with Ghost Towne Investigations.

Josh gave the background on the home this time while Matt filmed. We'd contacted the family ahead of filming and gotten permission to enter the backyard. Gabe reached over the tall gate and unlatched it. The alley between the Jaffos House and its neighbor narrowed as we walked until the thin passageway echoed the click of my boot heels off the painted brick walls.

Seth took the lead and called out uneven spots in the walkway. I made it to the backyard without tripping, and we fanned out.

Seth extolled the virtues of night-vision binoculars to sight distant orb activity while I searched the back of the yard for energy signatures. Again, the night crackled with a pent-up expectation. I couldn't describe it any other way. The trees held their breath as something stirred the thick air. The busy pond at the back of the yard iced over with silence.

It wasn't until the crickets in the flowerpots stilled that the guys took notice. Everyone froze. I heard Seth's recorder pen click a millisecond before a barely audible sigh drifted down the alley behind us. Pale light flooded from Gabe's ovilus as he scanned the opening to the alley. This was a talky ghost, so we'd brought our verbal communication devices for better results. Seth explained to the camera that the ovilus allows an entity to select words from a database for display on the ovilus' screen.

Matt positioned the ghost box, but I waved a hand to stop him. This was a good haunt for the ghost box. It had been reliable in the past. It added the opportunity for a presence to communicate through radio waves. The device constantly scanned the FM and AM bands so that a spirit might have more opportunities to select and combine words. The downside was that the device was noisy and would block out what I normally could hear.

Something crunched along the oyster-shell pathway on which I stood. I felt the unmistakable vibration of footsteps. I caught a flash and then another as something darted through the trees.

"I'm getting words," Gabe whispered. Josh swung the camera his way. "P-r-o-t-e-c-t," he read the ovilus display. "L-e-a-v-e."

"Fireflies?" Matt whispered. He took the night-vision goggles off and pointed Camera One in the direction of the flares. I shook my head and moved toward Camera Two.

"Galvanic skin response." I lifted my arm so Josh could focus on the tiny hairs standing up along my skin. "Hello?" I called gently as the glowing orbs drew wiggling lines through my altered field of vision.

"They are mine." A voice echoed out from the direction of the potting shed, and a rush of wind rolled toward us. "Go away!"

"Mel?" Josh called.

"A voice. Male. It wants us to leave." My legs went a little weak with the prospect of another ghostly confrontation, but I held my ground. "Why are you upset?" I asked to the night air.

"Leave us alone," the voice whispered close to my ear. "I will protect them." A flowerpot tumbled off its stand next to Gabe. The big man turned and calmly headed back down the alley without a word. The cracking sound of the terra-cotta pot triggered an auditory hallucination of a crashing wave, and the yard began to roll and sway around me. A second later, the ground stilled and the bubble of tension around us popped. The crickets struck up the band again, and the pond came alive with frog song.

"That was great!" Seth cheered. "We can use the audio on Camera One as a baseline and check my recorder pen for electronic voice phenomena."

"I definitely heard something." Josh smiled. He was caught up in the excitement of the hunt once more, as were Matt and Seth. Poor Gabe was still not back to his old self, but all things considered, the evening was going well.

****

The third site was a piece of cake. The Glencoe Inn was a grand, late-nineteenth-century home built for a family of Scottish immigrants but now served as a lovely bed and breakfast. We set up on the wraparound porch, which doubled as an outdoor dining area, and waited for the last of the evening's foot traffic to die away. Ever since Ghost Towne Investigations reviewed the Glencoe for the Haunted Inns website, the B&B had been booked solid. The proprietor had no problem giving us the porch for half an hour. She even left us a basket of muffins, which the team set upon like ravenous wolves.

This time, Matt introduced the location and gave a brief explanation of an EMF detector. We'd gotten high readings for electromagnetic field radiation in and around the Glencoe in the past, so that would be our tool of choice for zeroing in on one of Olde Towne's favorite spirits.

"It's widely believed that a rise in EMF not attributed to electrical wires or devices can indicate the presence of a non-corporeal awareness." Matt's bright hazel eyes drank the light from the floods as he explained. "The living brain passes information from synapse to synapse electrically, creating an electromagnetic field. When we die, those physical pathways deteriorate, but the electromagnetic field does not." A wide smile spread across his handsome face. "Paranormal researchers have found that some ghosts not only consist of this EMF, but they can manipulate and collect electromagnetic energy."

For all his flightiness, Matt was a natural public speaker, and he really did enjoy the job. If I didn't know him as well as I did, I'd be as confused as everyone else over the fact that Matt was thirty and not yet married. When he entered a room, he was usually the best-looking guy in it. He had a friendly, robust personality and was gainfully employed. It didn't make sense until you peeled a bit of his onion and found that he was still searching for a part of himself. Only complete people find complete love, and Matt still had pieces missing.

I wandered the front garden of the inn, letting my mind drift through hypnogogic cerebrations. Mental musings came and went in a long stream of consciousness that never made sense. It was difficult to explain dreaming with one's eyes open. It was almost like looking behind the curtain of the universe and seeing the true chaotic nature of existence.

Then, the smell of roses wafted through the open window of my mind. It was almost cloyingly sweet, the way roses must have been a century ago. I turned to the guys as the overpowering scent slid over the garden and rolled up onto the porch.

The Glencoe ghost had arrived.

She was a friendly remnant of a past family member, not at all scary. I saw her outline in the moonlight drifting among the roses. I knew I could get her attention, but I waved Gabe over first.

"Come here," I called to him, but the muscle-bound man held his ground.

"She's not malicious." I promised. "She's...sweet." I could see his thoughts warring. He was as infected as the rest of us by curiosity about the afterlife. He was a good investigator. He'd just been thrown by a bad experience and needed to get back on the horse. I waved to him again, and he reluctantly joined me in the rose garden.

"Stand right here." I pointed to the space right in front of me. Gabe squeezed his bulk into the small garden with me. "Now wait for that cloud to move." Moonlight spread through a crack in the clouds and poured into the small garden.

"Do you see her?"

"No."

"Are you looking there by the trellis?" I pointed.

"Yes."

"Wait...she's moving."

"Oh my God...I see movement." I felt Gabe's entire body tense.

"Don't look directly at the movement. Sort of unfocus your eyes."

"Are those hands? Those look like hands moving through the leaves."

"She's tending her garden." I smiled. "Not all ghosts are scary." The moon slipped behind a cloud again.

"I can't see her anymore. She's gone." His voice was filled with amazement as he stepped back toward the porch.

"She's still there," I said. A faint outline of the elderly woman's face, torso, and hands were still visible to me, but to anyone else, she'd likely just vanished.

"Do you want to attempt contact?" Josh asked, but the ghost had already turned toward me.

"I think she sees me," I whispered as the woman's eyes found mine. She smiled, and the smell of roses filled the air once more. Her mouth moved, and I lifted my hand to Seth. He holstered his infrared guns and grabbed the tandem EVP recorders.

I let a little bit more of the waking world slip from me so I could hear her gentle voice. I closed my eyes and breathed in the sweet aroma around me. I heard a whispered sound, but the words were quick and high as though she was frightened. I opened my eyes and was shocked to see her lovely face pulled into a mask of horror. *What have I done?* I must have startled her.

"I'm so sorry." I stumbled over my words in a rush to apologize, but she shook her head. She raised a bony hand and pointed to a spot somewhere behind me. I frowned in confusion and turned. Standing on the sidewalk only feet from me was the woman in green and her male companion in the bloody vest.

Chapter Eight

A howling melee in B minor

"If it isn't my beautiful dreamer." The woman's voice floated on the air. Moonlight flashed in her predatory eyes as she smiled at me. The man standing next to her lifted the lantern toward the gentle spirit in the roses. The lady in green laid a delicately gloved hand on his, and he lowered the lantern to his side. I thought its greasy light had attracted fireflies, but as I looked closer, I could make out orbs zigzagging in the lantern's corona. As I stared at the light, I felt a gentle pulling sensation and the faint echo of screams.

"I see you've dressed for the occasion." Her perfect lips pulled at the corners of her mouth flirtatiously, and her hooded gaze raked my skin. "And you've brought me a gift." Her attention slid to the shimmering outline of the elderly woman cowering behind the trellis. "How thoughtful," she cooed as she drifted toward the vanishing apparition.

With cobra-like speed, the woman in green snatched the terrified ghost and dragged her misty form through the rose bushes and onto the sidewalk.

"It is my birthday after all," she whispered to the struggling apparition as her jaw unhinged. I fell backward into Gabe, and his giant arms locked around me. My skin crawled with multi-legged hallucinations and my knees buckled.

We could do nothing but watch in frozen horror as the woman's beautiful mouth distended into a long, gaping, black maw. A shriek pierced the night as the woman in green clamped giant, shark-like teeth on the helpless ghost and shredded her head and shoulders.

A cry escaped my own mouth as Gabe and I tried to back away. Josh shouted at Gabe, but our feet wouldn't work. Cataplexy swept across my muscles and I drooped in his arms. I heard the last whimpering sobs of the poor spirit as the nightmare in flowing green velvet devoured the remnants of her earthbound soul.

"Melisande!" Josh shouted my name, but I couldn't respond. All I could do was focus on my diaphragm.

Just keep breathing.

Just keep breathing.

Air slid shallowly in and out of my lungs.

Gabe's arms began to shake. I knew it wasn't from exhaustion. Gabe could bench press my weight over and over without tiring. Something else was loosening his arms.

"Come along, Miss Blythe. We shan't be late to the gathering." The woman's voice purred along my skin. A shred of ethereal nightgown hung from the corner of her ruby mouth.

"No!" Gabe shouted as his arms slowly pulled apart. I slid from his straining grip into the icy, cold embrace of the man with the bloody vest. He hoisted me across his shoulder as the Glencoe disappeared from view. I stared mute and wide-eyed at the antique bricks of the pockmarked sidewalk as panicked voices rushed away from me. Touch hallucinations slithered across my skin as we launched into motion. In a blur of movement I could barely register, the red-vested man sped down North Street away from the B&B. My gut lurched as we whirled around the corner onto Court Street, heading toward the river. Gas lamps flashed by in a nauseating blur. Buildings flitted past. I saw my own apartment in the rush of pavement markers and carved stone.

Finally, we slowed as we neared the river. I gulped at the briny air in an attempt to breathe. Ropes twanged against boat masts at the marina, and waves thumped against the boardwalk.

As I got my bearings, I realized we were at the corner of Court and Water Streets. The red-vested man rearranged me on his shoulder with his bloodless hands, and as he turned I saw the majestic, old Water Street Estate spread out in front of us. Its warped glass windows looked out at the restless bay. We'd covered nearly four blocks in the blink of an eye.

A damp ichor spread from the man's vest. It soaked into my bustier where his coat opened. I tried to squirm away from it, but my muscles were still paralyzed by sleep. I recognized the metallic smell of the oozing material.

Blood.

I needed to wake up. If I could just push myself free of his grasp, the fall to the sidewalk would wake me. The more I struggled, the farther the paralysis spread. I tried my adrenaline escape hatch, but it wasn't working either. There was something confusing my emotions.

Music filtered through the air as we drifted toward the sprawling mansion. Candlelight glowed through the windows revealing a glimmer of ghosts inside. Half-corporeal figures in antique evening wear wandered the shadowed grounds. We glided through the open gates and up the curved stairs to the wide porch.

Dead eyes fixed on me as we moved past. We slipped through the grand foyer and into a giant hall. All around hung the trappings of faded grandeur. Molding velvet curtains swayed, and tarnished candelabras flickered. A wide staircase wrapped along the outside wall and climbed into darkness. The furnishings were the finest, yet the embroidery was faded. The chandeliers dripped with crystal, but the facets were dull with dust.

We moved past a large parlor where a grand piano stood on three ornately carved legs. Its yellowed keys fluttered under invisible fingers, and its slightly off-key notes echoed through the hall. Spirits waltzed unperturbed through the walls of the music room, spinning into the great hall and back again. To the left, through a set of pocket doors, I caught the glint of silver and china spread meticulously across a long banquet table. The dining room sparkled with crystal stemware and hungry eyes. Everywhere I looked, from the depths of gilded alcoves sets upon sets of voracious eyes fixed on me.

I tried again to uncork my fear as the horror of the moment played out around me, but something was twisting my emotions, syphoning them almost before I could feel them. The cataplexy would wear off eventually, but I was trapped in the hypnogogic state until something triggered a glandular response. Where was my adrenaline?

We came to a stop at the far end of the hall near the entrance to the music room. The man with the bloody vest held me at an angle so I had a better view into the dining room. Fresh flowers bloomed from oriental vases, and beneath the heavy petals piteous things squirmed on silver trays. Like an answered prayer, green velvet obscured my line of sight. Suddenly, my captor's moonstone eyes looked down on me.

"Give her to me." Her words caressed like a mother requesting to hold her newborn for the first time. The bloody-vested man spilled me into her steely embrace. I could feel my limbs, but they jerked with impotence as paralysis stole through them. I was nothing more than a rag doll. The image made me angry, but it was a flaccid, feeble feeling.

The shifting from embrace to embrace tugged at my clothes. I was more than thankful I'd attached the straps to my bustier or much more of me would have been on display than was decent. Yet as I took in the partygoers around me, I realized decency was not high on their list. The dancers' attire was formal, but their behavior was anything but. I tried to avert my eyes from the enraptured grasps and lewd touching, but there was something about the writhing spectacle that was intoxicating.

Movement caught my eye as a tall, hastily dressed figure made its way down the long staircase. Rumpled Stiltskin fixed me with a loathing look that matched the one he'd given me two nights before in the cemetery. His not-so-royal-blue tie was replaced with a wider gray one. He looked down his pencil nose at me and cocked his wavy head. Maybe he was trying for aristocratic disinterest, but his eyes lingered too long on my breasts for that. His deep scowl conveyed open disgust. I believed I was the victim in that moment, so I wondered what the hell he had to be mad about?

"Isn't she lovely, Maynard?" the woman in green cooed. From every angle, lascivious eyes stole across my body, but Maynard barely glanced at me again. "Look at these lovely curves and her skin—" She took my hand in her frozen fingers. "—so supple."

"If you like that sort of thing," Maynard sneered. I could tell, even in my mesmerized state, that the woman in green was displeased. Her fingers dug into my skin like jagged shards of ice.

"I can make you like...that sort of thing." Her voice dipped from a purr to a growl. Maynard's face went blank in an attempt to hide his distress, but the creature holding me could likely smell his fear.

"It's my birthday, Maynard," she barked. "I would like a treat!"

She turned back to me, and her hand brushed my hair, then my shoulders, and then the curve of my breast. A warm tingling washed over me and desire flooded through my veins. I liked this man even less than he liked me, but at that moment, all I could think of was his mouth on my neck and his hands pulling me against him. He wasn't unattractive—the look of disdain was, but not him.

"Edwardia," he whispered, "please." I couldn't tell if he'd just made a huge mistake by revealing his vulnerability in that moment or if he'd found something inside the monstrous woman to appeal to. Her moonstone eyes bore into him. Was sex with me that much of a hardship? Then I saw it—hidden at the back of his slate blue eyes. He loved this woman. This evil, velvet-wrapped nightmare, whom I now knew went by the name Edwardia, had inspired love or something like it in another person.

I couldn't help but stare at the tortured man. How could he feel anything but revulsion for this sadist? I squirmed a little as lust began to chase the paralysis from my muscles. He caught my subtle movement the way any man would, but again his face grew cold and dispassionate. That's when I put two and two together. It wasn't me that turned him off. It was the life in me that did. Maynard had a bad case of necrophilia. My stomach swam.

With the jerking movements of an infant, I turned away from him and stole another glance at my captor. Something sparked across her elegant features. There was a brief moment where Edwardia's thoughts looked as though they danced on a razor's edge. Did she want the pleasure of torturing him, by forcing him to have very public sex with a woman he did not desire? Or was there something even more delectable to be had from the moment? His soul seemed to be bare, and I'd seen what she did with hapless souls. The private musing flashed across her face, but it was gone before I could fully read it.

"My love," a voice whispered at her ear. "Perhaps we should open the invitation to our guests." Edwardia whipped around to face the man in the bloody vest. He wore a wicked grin. Unmentionable sins burned in his eyes, sins they clearly liked to share. The ferocity in her eyes banked to a smoldering hunger. Her lids lowered and a corner of her mouth quirked.

"An excellent idea." She gripped my neck with the icy noose of her fingers and pulled my back against her. Her breasts pushed against my shoulder blades, and her bony hips cupped my buttocks. She wrapped her other arm around me, and I clamped my teeth together as her hand slid down my front.

"So beautiful and yet so broken." Her voice trickled through my senses. "I know how lonely you are, Dreamer. How desperately you want to be touched...cherished...invaded...desired...consumed." I felt the wet warmth of her tongue cascading down my cheek. "But no one will play with you. How sad." Her voice filled with merry malcontent. "Let's see if one of our gathering finds you tantalizing. Who knows...you might prefer our attentions to those of the living." Edwardia tittered, and the feminine sound sent vibrations down my skin.

"Honored guests," she addressed the spirits crowding into the hall, "we are gathered here tonight to celebrate the senses." Her fingertips teased along my cleavage. "We gather to drink from the light of souls and remember."

I watched in horror as Edwardia's companions brought forth the two lanterns they'd carried with them in the cemetery. I felt the gravitational pull of the flickering lights, and over the thundering of my heart I heard the sorrowful wails of the orbs trapped within their flickering prison.

The bloody-vested man closed his fingers on a latch and swung the door to his lantern wide. Howling filled the air as desperate souls fought free of the light.

Maynard reached for the latch on his lantern and set loose the souls from his light. Glowing orbs danced in the air. Some bounced along the ceiling while others sought a path through the crowd. I gasped as, one by one, the faces around me transformed. Delicate skin peeled from bone and carefully coifed hair fell lank on moldering shoulders. The orbs raced through the air in a desperate bid for freedom. I saw one streak for an open window only to be caught in the boney fingers of a blackened corpse. I heard the shuddering cry of the ill-fated soul as it disappeared down the throat of the rotting man. Ligaments snapped and popped over the floating music as he chewed.

A cluster of lights scattered across the floor, but fleshless mouths dipped hungrily toward the Venetian rugs, sucking the screaming orbs into their fetid maws. All around me lurched creatures from wordless nightmares. Fingers sharpened. Limbs elongated.

My muscles contracted in a cascading motion as my body fought my brain to keep what little control I had gained. I knew it was the wrong thing to do, but I couldn't fight the urge to flee. I dragged my tingling hands to my throat and pulled weakly at Edwardia's fingers, but my struggles only tightened her grasp.

I clenched the muscles of my neck against the pressure of her hand, and the room began to spin. Slowly, she loosened her grip. Her fingers caressed my bruised skin. Her arm coiled around my waist like a vise. She spun me in a circle so I could see every stomach-churning angle of the beastly event. In the end, I could do nothing but squeeze my eyes shut.

The howling melee whirled around me in B minor as my mind raced. There had to be a way out of this. I prayed to St. Michael, but my thoughts splintered.

Finally, the terrible feasting slowed. The last of the orbs were devoured, and the guests slipped back into their lovely disguises. They laced up their hair and buckled their skin. All had returned to normal except their eyes. Each pair of irises glowed with a brimstone light. With so many red eyes, the room took on a different tint. A lilting waltz spun to life on invisible woodwinds, and the guests began to sway.

"What would a birthday party be without dessert?" Edwardia's voice rang with laughter as she gripped my arm and danced me around the hall. She spun me past the parlor, twirled me into the music room, and tilted toward the dining room. She brought us to a stop before the crackling fire at the far end of the banquet table.

The back of my brain had lost all track of right and left or up and down. It took a moment for my eyes to focus, but when they did, I saw a familiar face. The Sweaty Man. Ben Martin stood next to the tea service table doing his best to blend into the wallpaper. From the look on his face, it was a wonder that he hadn't climbed behind the curtains completely. We locked eyes, and the babbling desperation of my thoughts quieted.

Somehow, the fact that there was a living witness to all that befell me made it that much more real and horrifying. Before I knew he was there, some part of my brain had explained this all away as a nightmare. I'd had plenty of nightmares this bad before, so it wasn't that hard to believe. Now that I knew he was a part of this ghastly gathering, my skin began to crawl anew.

I knew he saw the desperation in my eyes, and it looked as though he had no plans to help me. The certainty of it froze the marrow inside my bones. I shivered against my captor, and she purred in my ear.

"For those of you that might still be hungry, we have a special treat tonight." Edwardia whirled me in front of her, then spun me back into her arms. "Come now, my darlings, don't be shy. My Dreamer needs a partner. See how she yearns."

Edwardia's voice stretched, deepening into a bestial growl. Her last word echoed in my head, and the suffocating fear melted away. Sounds softened, and for one elongated moment I thought she was pushing me into sleep. If I began to dream, the Shadow would come, and I'd suffer the same fate as the orbs. I couldn't let that happen, yet as I fell further under her spell, the less I cared. There were more important things to think of...like my aching skin. I suddenly burned to be touched. With each breath, my nipples rolled against the fabric of my bustier, sending pinpricks of pleasure through my upper body. I reached a shaking hand to the laces to loosen them.

Eyes smoldered with desire as they drank in my movements. I saw both lust and hatred fanning the flames equally as they drew nearer to me. Did these remnants still feel desire without the help of Edwardia's enchantment? Was I a painful reminder of what they'd lost? From the look of it, we were all pawns in her fantasy now, willing or not.

Edwardia's eyes searched the gathering, sizing up the more corporeal of the guests. Her mouth curled into a vicious smile, and I followed her gaze as the crowd parted.

A tall man in white trousers, billowing shirt, and a long olive vest separated from the shadows at the far end of the dining room. I immediately recognized his darkened brow and the icy blue treasures it hoarded in the shadows of his face.

"Colonel Grayford. So glad you could attend my humble soiree." Edwardia dipped her head in greeting. I felt more than saw her two companions step closer.

"I was delighted for the invitation." He bowed, and the chocolate length of his bound hair fell across his shoulder. His voice was a siren song of masculine promises whispered in the dark. Had I heard it before? Edwardia released her grip on my waist as the man stepped forward to look at me.

"A decadent dessert indeed." He smiled, and something inside me snapped into place. I couldn't say for sure what it was that had been misaligned, but the straightness of it had suddenly rewritten the stars and refolded the land. The very air felt redirected and almost as if on cue lightning forked outside, flashing through the windows with its new pattern of fractals. I looked around at our spectral audience, but none seemed to have noticed the shift.

I'd heard Colonel Grayford's name mentioned a hundred times as a side thought or a tangent in conversations about other things. But here he was, standing before me, in the flesh—and there was nothing peripheral about him. His face seemed familiar. His eyes seemed to know just where to look. His mouth toyed with me in a knowing way.

"Blue," I whispered in a voice gone breathy and soft and all wrong for this situation. I remembered the sketch from Mrs. Spruill's album. The man with the blue eyes. "I was right," I muttered to myself as I watched the exquisite sweep of his head and arm as he bowed low before me. He held the polite pose for a suspended moment as I tipped and swayed before him, and then his face turned slowly toward me.

He kept his eyes locked on mine as the room swam. Crystal clattered, and china shrieked. I tore my eyes from his long enough to see Edwardia rake her velvet arms across the dining room table. When had she let go of me? She looked like a mad woman sweeping silver platters to the floor and tipping over candelabras. Tiny, night-eyed creatures tumbled from their prisons and skittered to the safety of the shadows.

Before I could turn back to the handsome stranger, he'd stepped so close that not even a breeze could move between us.

"I'm sorry for this," he whispered so low that I could barely be sure that I'd heard him speak. The room had dimmed with the loss of so many candles. Oily hurricane sconces still burned along the walls, but all that lit the center of the room now was the strobing light from the windows.

Figures shifted in the corner of my eye as I stared at the man before me. His luminous eyes held a spark of the hellfire that burned in the watchers around us. I was distantly aware of Edwardia hovering in the air above us. Her loosened hair writhed against the ceiling like snakes. Something told me not to look at her again.

A yearning swept over me, and I closed my eyes as my blood rushed to all the right places. When I opened them again, he slipped his hands around my waist. I waited like a caged animal for his lips to touch mine. He bent close in the flashing light, and the scent of summer-ripe fields spread through me. His fingers tightened. A tingling spread across my mouth followed by a hungry pressure. His mouth closed ravenously over mine, and I pressed into him.

My movement sent a tremor through his body, and he clutched me close. His lips crushed against mine until my jaw forced open. His tongue filled my mouth. I thought I would suffocate as he forced his way to the back of my mouth. My untamed gasp of pleasure fought for release, but it was trapped. He tore his tongue from my mouth long enough for me to take a staggering breath, and then he plunged between my lips again.

I'd never been kissed like that before, if kissing is what it was. It felt more like a claiming of my flesh. He'd taken my voice, my breath, my strength, and I opened for him willingly. Someone moaned over the thrumming chords as the spectral waltz picked up tempo around us.

I reached up and clamped my hand around the long curls of hair twisting together at the nape of his neck. His head yanked back, and a deep groan rumbled through him. I released his hair, and he fell upon my neck with hot breath and sharp teeth. He spread his amazing tongue across the bend of my neck, and a small cry escaped my lips. He bit me quickly and sharply, then licked me again. My legs shook, and he locked his arm against my back.

I couldn't tell if the pain had woken me up or if I was still in the hypnogogic state. Spirits crowded around us in the wavering light. Some looked solid while others shimmered like fevered dreams. Their faces begged. Desire hung on their flicking tongues and grasping fingers.

The music played, and the room spun. I winced as he pressed his teeth into the muscle that sloped to my shoulder. The ache spread through me, and I yanked his head back again. The ice in his eyes melted into azure lakes, and a wicked grin unfurled across his hungry mouth. I couldn't have dreamt of a more perfect face. His strong jaw squared perfectly with his sharp cheekbones. His aquiline nose made a masculine T with his lush aristocratic brow line. The liquid roundness of his eyes was the only softening to what was a perfectly balanced face.

I reached for him. I ran my fingers over his features. He closed his eyes. I pushed to my toes, leaned my face up, and kissed him gently on the side of his chin. I could barely control the urge to lick his rugged mouth. My lips parted. My teeth raked the stubble along his jaw line. I pressed my lips to the pulse in his neck, but there was no flutter beneath his warm skin. I sucked in the air as pieces of reality pricked at my awareness.

What was happening?

I had the sense of something horrible hovering over me. I looked up, and my eyes tried to help my brain make sense of what I saw.

The tangled pieces of Edwardia swarmed across the ceiling as her impossibly wide mouth hung over us. Eddies of shimmering energy poured upward from my skin in tiny tugging sensations. Edwardia was drinking my life-force.

"Avert your eyes," he commanded and trapped my chin in his steely fingers, forcing me to look at him. Behind Colonel Grayford, I saw Ben Martin clutching his face in horror.

"No." I pulled my head free, which made the room tilt.

"If you stop now, she will drain you all at once. Just a few moments more," he promised tenderly. "There is still a chance to survive this." The enchantment swam through me, calling me back to his mouth. But I also felt the truthfulness of his words. He had the same hungry look as the other guests around us, but there was something more to him. That's when I realized he was not under Edwardia's spell. He was in complete control.

He lowered his face to mine and reached for my legs. One arm cradled my back as the other swept my feet from the floor. I clutched at his vest as he carried me to the table. He placed me on the polished wood and spun me to face him. Slowly, he slid his hands between my knees and forced my legs apart.

He leaned down, kissed me on the head, and whispered, "We must make a good show of it." My heart missed a beat. I searched his face for any sign of a lie, but there was none. He was the honest portrait of a man about to take a woman because he desired her.

My lethargic brain struggled to keep up. Maybe this wasn't the way I would die. I was surrounded by death, but there was still hope. I studied the man that had stolen between my legs. His clothes weren't the overt fashions of the Victorian period. They reflected an even earlier time. He had a proper look about him, but there was a hardworking reality to his stance and demeanor the others did not have. His hands said he was a man of action, and his eyes held plans within plans. He was different from all the other faces in the room.

"I know who you are," I gasped. "You're Colonel William Grayford...the town's founder." For decency's sake, I tried to put a few inches between us, but he placed his hands on my hips and dragged me against him.

"I am." He lowered his face to mine. Again, the forceful press of our bodies seemed less an invitation and more a claiming. His muscular mid-section held my legs apart. I tried to ignore the proof of his arousal, but he'd broken all barriers between us when he'd pulled me to him. I hadn't realized how much I needed to feel a man's attraction to me until that moment.

Edwardia was right. I was lonely. I did yearn for human contact...even if it didn't have a heartbeat. I'd become so isolated by my disorder I'd begun to feel unlovable...undesirable. Colonel Grayford might be acting out a plan to save me, but there was true craving in his touch. There was no uncertainty like with Josh.

Josh.

Oh, God.

"I...was with others. We were separated," I whispered against the soft tendrils of hair that had slipped from Colonel Grayford's tie when I'd pulled his head back.

"One thing at a time, Miss Blythe," he soothed, and the sound of my name on his lips was musical. I didn't even question how he knew my name. He gripped my arms and pushed me to the table. The muscular frame of his upper body pinned me in place. Movement caught my eye, and I sucked in a breath as I looked upon the nightmare above us.

Pieces of Edwardia still clung together in a hellish portrait of human remains, but the rest of her had stretched and twisted like the edges of a lost thought.

"She's distracted," Grayford explained quietly. "She's forgotten to hold her form together." I couldn't respond. I couldn't catch my breath. A scream climbed up my throat.

"Help me give her what she wants. Help me distract her further." His fingers dug at my flesh, and the pain distracted me. I looked back at him. "It's our only chance." He lifted his hand to my eyes and closed his fingers over them. "She can affect your limbic system. Let it help you. Think only of me," he whispered against my skin. He pressed against me with the swollen reminder of his desire.

I was caught beneath him, unable to see. The ghostly music whirled around us, and I couldn't help but feel every inch of him that lay against me. His mouth lowered to my trapped breasts. His strong tongue fought my cleavage and plunged beneath the straining fabric of my bustier. He searched the rolling mound of my breast until he was rewarded with the hardened treasure of my nipple. He cherished it with the wet heat of his tongue. I cried out, and my aching pleasure drifted up to the ceiling.

Moans of pleasure echoed around the room as he fastened his teeth on the laces that held the fabric tight against my breasts. He pulled at the silky bow and the laces loosened, giving him easier access to my other breast. I sucked in a breath as his tongue delved beneath the fabric again. He found the other hidden gem and rolled it against his tongue. I gave a breathy cry and wrapped my legs around him. A quiet growl of delight escaped his lips.

As he shielded my eyes, his thumb brushed my lips. I licked its length and then sucked it into my mouth. I could tell that he was losing concentration. He shifted, and his loosened hair fell against my shoulders.

"We must act now," he whispered urgently. His breath had quickened, and his missing heartbeat wasn't missing any longer.

Heat lightning flashed soundlessly against the windows. He kissed me softly, longingly, holding his lips to mine in a way that froze time. "Go to sleep now, and I will take you away from all of this."

"W—what?" I asked as he took his hand from my eyes.

"It is time to sleep." He smiled, but his shoulders had tightened in defense. "I need you to call the Shade." My eyes went wide.

"No, no, no," I chanted as thin, blackened fingers stretched down from the ceiling. How did he know about the Shadow?

"You must. A Shade is the only thing they fear."

"No, I can't do that." I pushed at him, and panic stole the softness from the moment. "It will kill me. It will kill you."

"I will protect you. Trust me. I have a way out. Go to sleep." For once I wasn't sure if I could, but then I looked up at our hostess. It was like staring at the end of all things. Edwardia had unraveled in the air above us, and every shivering piece of her fought the other parts to drink us in. But our fountain of pleasure had dried up. She appeared to bubble as her organs desperately searched for a way through her transparent skin. Her backbone writhed at fractured angles, and her tortured limbs twisted against each other.

A noose of freed intestines dropped toward Grayford's neck, but he yanked us up and off the table.

"Bring the Shade, Melisande." Grayford's voice was low and intense. The dining table shook violently. As he shielded me, a loud crack filled the room. The only thing I could imagine that could make this situation worse was the Shadow.

The air closed in on us as ghostly faces swam near. I felt an icy hand tear at me and then another. Grayford gathered me in his arms and whispered, "Sslleeeep." My head sagged, and I began to drift. Voices rose in haunting shrieks, and something thundered above us. I stood on the shore of REM and let the tide take me.

"*I. See. You.*" Its words never made sense. It didn't always speak, but when it did, it was like tuning to a radio channel from another world. I opened my eyes as Edwardia's ruined dining room faded from view. Spirits stained the air as their sins leaked from them. They tried to flee, but the weight of their wrongs held them down. The Shadow tore their souls in two as it searched for me in the wreckage, but I was moving away. I always wondered what it was that I had done to make it hunt me so. It didn't matter now. All was black and calm and quiet.

Chapter Nine

Those who prowl about the world seeking the ruin of souls

"Wake up," an impossibly intimate voice whispered through me. "Melisande, we are away. Wake up." The voice was closer to me than my own thoughts. "Please, you must wake up now." The voice had taken on a commanding tone. My eyes fluttered, and I took a shaky breath. I recognized the framed print that hung on the wall opposite me. It was *Orestes Pursued by the Furies* by William-Adolphe Bouguereau, my favorite painting. I was in my apartment.

My hands clutched cloth. I straightened and pushed away from the person who held me. Ever since I'd had my first sleep attack as a teenager, I'd been waking up in strangers' arms, though waking up wasn't always the correct term. If I was just having an attack of cataplexy without a sleep attack, I was often wide awake and could hear everything people were saying around me as I lay paralyzed. "*Is she drunk?*" they'd ask, or even worse, "*Is she dead?*"

Anyone suffering from type one narcolepsy with the accompanying cataplexy was afraid of waking up in a body bag because someone thought they were dead. It has happened, but thankfully, not to me. That's why I wear a medic alert bracelet, not that everyone will check for that, but it beats tattooing the words, *I'm not dead, just narcoleptic*, across my body.

I gave the man in front of me an extra shove. Sometimes guys were a little handsy when they pulled me to my feet. The distance helped me regain control of the situation. I looked into his luminous eyes, and the events of the evening rushed back into focus. "Colonel Grayford!" I winced at the lingering pain in my neck where the memory of his teeth still throbbed.

"William." His voice caressed me from the inside out.

"What happened?" I clamped the palms of my hands to my temples and tried to ease the pounding. "What did you do to me?" I felt wrong, which in my body meant something was way off. I also felt a little guilty for snapping at the guy who had probably just saved my life.

"I removed you from the situation," he said, and the tender tone banked my temper a little.

"Thank you," I finally managed. He bowed his head as best he could in the cramped space of my hallway. We stood just outside my bedroom doorway. I looked at him again. Really looked at him. He seemed so solid…so real. "How is this possible?" I asked, touching his hand. "How is any of this possible?" I turned his hand over in mine, searching the creases of his palm for the answer. "I've only met one other corporeal ghost in my life, but I was so young. I've never really been sure that I didn't imagine it."

"I wouldn't know where to start." He shook his head, and I could hear the colonial accent in his words. It was similar to the accent the local reenactors used, but smoother. "Time is short for me this night," he whispered. Again, his words seemed to form in my mind before he even spoke.

"I feel strange."

"Most of it will wear off," he assured, but that just made me worry more.

"What will wear off?"

"The Joining." He looked over his shoulder at my darkened apartment.

"What joining?"

"Melisande...Miss Blythe, there was no other way. You must believe me." A howl cut through the night outside, or was it my head cracking open? I wasn't sure. I clamped my palms to my head again.

"Get behind your ward, and remain there until morning. Do not step out before dawn. Promise me." His liquid eyes were intense. His hands gripped my ribcage.

Something huge slammed against my front door. I jumped out of my skin as something thick and viscous pulled through the wood of my apartment door. An impossibly long hand grasped through the air and latched onto the light fixture hanging over my dining room table.

The tiny, antique chandelier bent, and plaster fell in a cascade of white dust as the hand used it as an anchor. I watched in horror as the rest of the twisted body pulled through my door with a wet, stomach-turning slurp. Green velvet and black lace pulled and knotted over a misshapen body. The warped visage of Edwardia stood in my dining room looking at me and then Colonel Grayford.

Her other hand seemed stuck in the wood of my door, but she pulled and it came free. Something hung from her clenched fingers that my mind refused to focus on. My gaze slid from the gray, rotting skin of the severed head she gripped by its white fringe of hair.

"Thresholds won't bar her, but your ward will. Go!" he shouted, but I couldn't make my feet work. Colonel Grayford gripped me under my arms and lifted me into the air. My stomach clenched as he tossed me through the doorway of my bedroom. I sailed through the air and landed on my bed in a tangle of arms and legs.

A voice thundered down the hall, and I saw the Colonel backing toward my room. His boots thudded against an invisible barrier as though my door were closed instead of open. I watched as Edwardia drifted down my hallway holding the severed head before her like a lantern.

"Colonel William Grayford," a voice boomed from the rotting head. "You are called before the Ghost Fleet on the evening next for the charge of indiscipline acts." I felt light-headed as I listened to the air sucking through the specter's shredded trachea. "You may choose to address these charges of misconduct visited upon one Edwardia Landry personally—" The head took a sucking breath. "—or you may bring counsel. The Fleet is Law. The Law is unrefutable!"

Edwardia lowered the cackling head to her side and glared past the colonel at me. Grayford bowed at the waist and faded from sight.

My mind went numb with terror. He'd left me alone with her. I drew my legs up in front of me as she drifted toward my bedroom. Thick oozing ropes of matted hair licked at the air around her. Her face was as gray as a gravestone, and the whites of her eyes had putrefied to slick black orbs. All that remained of the beautiful woman I'd met in the cemetery were the shimmering moonstone irises.

I clutched my face with maddened fingers. This was all too much. I'd had nightmares with indescribable horrors, but in the end I'd always woken up. Why was I not waking up?

I looked to the St. Michael's prayer that hung above my door. Edwardia's snaking hair slithered along the invisible barrier. What if Colonel Grayford was wrong? What if she could pull herself through my ward the same way she'd forced herself through my front door?

Panic pinned me in place as her eyes burned into mine. I felt the familiar twitching that meant paralysis was setting in. I did the only thing I could think of.

Holy Michael, the Archangel, defend us in battle.

Be our defense against the wickedness and snares of the devil.

May God rebuke him, we humbly pray, and do thou,

O Prince of the heavenly hosts, by the power of God,

Thrust into hell Satan, and all the evil spirits,

Who prowl about the world seeking the ruin of souls.

Amen.

Her laughter trailed through my mind as she vanished from sight. I'd leave in the morning, I thought. I'd go west to the desert. I'd always wanted to see the desert. I closed my eyes and slept.

****

Josh wouldn't let me out of his sight, but I had to

take a shower. The sun was up. The police were gone. I don't think they'd bought the whole "just a spooky prank" story, but when they'd seen me in the flesh only slightly worse for the wear, there was nothing left for Portsmouth's finest to do but remind us not to disturb the peace. I didn't blame Josh for calling the police, but abduction was a serious charge. Had I not turned up unharmed, Josh and the guys would have been prime suspects, regardless of the fact they were the ones that reported my sudden disappearance.

"I'm going to take a shower," I said, not asked.

"Well, leave the door open," he ordered. I looked from him to the other guys crowded into my bedroom. "Unlocked...I meant unlocked," he amended.

I smirked and pushed past Gabe to the restroom.

In my head, I told him if he wanted to guard me so badly, he could take his clothes off and climb into the shower with me, but I didn't have that kind of confidence. It was just as well, because the wind was kind of out of my "romance with Josh" sails at that moment. I guessed being ravished by a sexy ghost kind of does that to a girl.

What I felt for Josh was more than friendship, but that didn't mean that we were meant to be more. I liked him. I liked everything about him. Even his grumpy, negative world view didn't bother me. I liked the way he always thought of me but tried to play it off. I guessed what I didn't like was the subterfuge. I valued honesty, and sometimes it felt like Josh was lying to me when he hid his feelings.

I reached a hand to my neck where the faintest twinge of pain still pricked at my skin—a reminder of Colonel Grayford's all too clear intentions.

I turned on the water and waited for it to heat up as I undressed. I gripped the towel rack as the memory of Grayford's tongue sliding over my breasts came rushing back to me. I kicked out of my clothes and stepped into the cascading water. I lathered up and let the suds slide slowly down my body. I could still feel Grayford's hands on me. It was like a connection had been made between us, and no matter how I tried to hang up the phone, all I had to do was lift the receiver and his presence crackled to life in my ear.

I had a choice to make. I could pack my bags and head down to the bus station or stay and attempt to process what I'd experienced last night. Processing things was not exactly my forte.

Fuck it.

I couldn't take a chance with Edwardia. I was leaving.

I rinsed the conditioner from my eyes and wiped my face with a washcloth. I opened my eyes to see another set of eyes staring back at me. I sucked in water and air at the same time. The face that floated before mine was sunken and shredded at the edges. Water beat off my shoulders, tearing holes through the soldier's chest. He was out during the day and standing in running water again. I watched as he practically melted in front of me.

For God's sake!

"WHAT?" I screamed with all my might. I screamed with every ounce of my body. It was the kind of scream where you have to close your eyes or they'll pop out of your skull. It was the kind of scream that equaled twenty stomach crunches. Yes, the scream was meant for him, but it was also a scream that was meant for Edwardia and the bloody-vested man and every cruel-eyed spirit at the party last night.

I coughed droplets of water from my lungs and grabbed the soap dish to steady myself. The ghost backed away from me. He no longer stood in the shower. He hovered over my bathmat looking at me, but this time with recognition. He looked as though he'd heard me. I blinked in amazement.

Josh stormed through the door so forcefully the doorstop tore from its base and clattered to the tile floor.

"What's wrong?" he shouted, ripping the shower curtain the rest of the way open. I stood in the beating water naked from head to toe. Josh stared. His mouth hung open. I thought to pull the curtain around me, but...again, fuck it. He was the one that barged into my shower. If he didn't like what he saw, he could turn away.

He clearly liked what he saw. He couldn't stop staring at my large, round breasts, my narrow waist, my sloping hips. There was no minimizer bra to tame my curves. I was perfectly waxed. I wanted to scream at him, "This is what you've been afraid to pull the trigger on. Take a good look!" Instead, I held my hand up and waved him off.

I kept my eyes on the soldier as I stepped from the tub. I didn't turn the water off. I didn't bother with a towel. Josh saw my intense look and backed off.

"Wow," I heard Gabe say from the doorway.

"Lord," came from Matt behind him.

No doubt Seth was getting a good look too.

"You heard me." I pointed at the soldier and he looked at my finger. "You've never heard me before." I stepped closer to the spirit, but he backed away. "What's changed?"

"Mel, can you give me an update here?" Josh asked, handing me a towel. I took it and wrapped it around me.

"It's the soldier. He's normally a non-responsive. A pain-in-the-ass non-responsive who can sense me but not hear or see me. Now, suddenly he can do all of those things." I glared at the ghost who was quickly turning translucent in front of me.

"Oh, no, you don't!" I shouted at him and reached for his arm. My fingers met cloth. I yanked my hand away as the soldier's eyes went wide. His battered mouth hung open in surprise. He lifted his hand in front of him, and I reached for it. Our fingers touched. It was a cold wispy touch like the hands of the ghosts I'd touched in the cemetery so many times. We both drew our hands back in shock.

"Why are you here?" I asked, and for the first time his eyes filled with understanding.

"I need to find her," he whispered. I could barely make out his words. My heart sank as realization dawned on me. Like so many soldiers, the man had probably left his love to fight a battle he'd likely not wanted to fight. He was so young, but maybe marrying age. I swallowed hard as I searched for the right way to handle this. "You can help me find her. You are different. You are here." His voice traveled from such a long way, but if I strained, I could understand him. Was he having the same trouble hearing me?

"Mel," Josh spoke quietly, but compared to the soldier, he was shouting. I jumped then glared at him. "How are you doing this?" It seemed like a strange question from the guy who hunted ghosts with me for a living.

"What do you mean?"

"You don't appear to be in the hypnogogic state," he explained. I frowned, then looked back at the ghost.

"You're right," I said more to myself than him. "I'm not." I lost my mental footing as my mind reeled. The soldier began to fade. I reached out for Josh, and he clamped an arm around me.

"Please," the ghost whispered and was gone.

****

Something was definitely wrong. I felt altered, but I couldn't tell how. I'd had extreme exposure to some pretty strange stuff last night. My mind kept going back to what Colonel Grayford had said about "the Joining." Why had he seemed so nervous...no, guilty? What was this Joining, and how had we made it all the way back to my apartment?

Unfortunately, Colonel Grayford was the only one who could answer those questions, and he had disappeared into thin air.

I thought about my parents. It would be great to see their smiling faces and feel their arms around me, but they couldn't help me with this. Neither could my sister. I yearned for the comfort of being with them, but they were safer if I stayed away. Just thinking about them made me nervous. And...what if they could tell I was different?

I did my best to dress and do my hair for work. I'd slept without my CPAP which meant I hadn't slept well. It was the weekend so the guys could rest, but I still had to cover my share of the hours at the gallery. It would give me a few more hours to mull over the bus ticket. There was still time to put distance between me and Portsmouth before nightfall. I just needed to make sure that's what I wanted.

Every time I thought I'd finally gotten my mind off Colonel Grayford he snuck back in.

*If I could just speak to him again….*My sense of self-preservation slammed the brakes on that thought. Interacting with corporeal ghosts was contraindicated from now on. But still…he had risked so much to help me. Why had he done that? I'd never encountered remnants like those party-goers last night. They weren't normal ghosts. They were vicious, corrupted things. The same predatory light that had shown in all their eyes had shown in Grayford's as well. Was he guilty by association only or was he a monster too?

It seems his guilt would be determined by someone else. I tried not to dwell on the memory of that severed head and the sucking sound that came from its neck when it spoke. I'd seen a lot of bad things in my dreams, but that was among the worst.

"Matt, you know that collection of decommissioned ships moored together in the bay? Isn't that called the Ghost Fleet?" I asked. I'd heard my parents mention it once or twice, but I'd never seen it.

"Yep. Good fishing around those ships, but the Coast Guard usually shoos us away before we can hook anything big." He went back to bundling extension cords. "Why?"

"Not important. I'll see you guys tonight for the video upload," I said, but in my mind my suitcase was already packed. "Don't close my window. It's the only way Bougie can get to his food," I called over my shoulder as I headed out the door. Business as usual, I told myself. Nothing is wrong. Just enjoy the day and sell some art. Piece of cake. I got this.

****

It was raining biblically by noon, and apparently, the ensuing floods had washed all the tourists into the river and out to sea. I'd had more time to think than I'd expected, and those thoughts hadn't gone in a good direction. The rain tapered off, and the afternoon wore on until finally I picked up the phone.

"Matt? Change of plans. Want to go night fishing?"

Chapter Ten

Indian's breath

Josh flatly refused to let me on the boat. Technically, it was Matt's boat, so it didn't matter what Josh said. It did matter that he was physically blocking the way, though. I'd told him and the team I wanted to search the water near the Ghost Fleet. An overwater ghost hunt was on everyone's bucket list, but in light of recent events, the guys were less interested in the list and more interested in avoiding the bucket. Gabe, particularly. He was not okay with what happened in the rose garden at the Glencoe. None of us were.

Josh could tell I was hiding something. He didn't understand my vague motivations. Neither did I. I should already be on that bus headed west. He tried to forbid me from ghost hunting entirely until we could properly assess the danger. Josh didn't know the half of it, and I wasn't about to tell him. But if we did decide to go forward with Ghost Towne Investigations, I was their best tool. That, coupled with the fact that I don't recognize his authority, landed us in the Cedar Grove Cemetery for a little test. It wasn't Oak Grove, but it was a cemetery nonetheless.

"Okay," Josh said. "Put your money where your mouth is, girl. Let's see you 'handle' a ghost." He hoisted Camera One and hit record. I slowed my breathing, and my eyelids drooped. I hadn't gotten what equates to a good night's sleep last night, so it was too easy to slip into the hypnogogic state. I stumbled forward on the main path, heading for the circular walkway in the center of the graveyard. I usually hallucinated more in this cemetery than in any other because of the funerary art. Giant sculptures threw dramatic shadows, and hulking obelisks loomed overhead.

Josh swung from angle to angle behind me, trying to catch the lines of sight with the most interesting sculpture. We'd filmed a special edition video here last year entitled "Mausoleums and Who Haunts Them." It was our most viewed video yet, but I had a feeling that was about to change.

Seth had done a great job on the Oak Grove film so we'd moved it forward on the schedule. It aired tonight to what we hoped would be a record number of viewers. I pictured little Mrs. Spruill cuddled up in bed with her laptop, her dandelion hair glowing in the Internet's light. I hoped she would like it.

"Movement to the right," I called out just as we reached the central ring. We crept quickly along the path unencumbered by our usual equipment and staff. It was just Josh and me alone in the sweltering darkness. I told him that my experience this morning with the soldier had been different from all other experiences in that I'd felt like I was in control. He hadn't understood what I meant, and honestly, I wasn't one hundred percent sure about it myself. So, here we were testing the theory before he would let me go hunt ghosts in the middle of the Elizabeth River.

"It has a strong presence, but it's not very big," I

whispered over my shoulder. I didn't like to talk very much in the hypnogogic state. Sometimes internal sounds made my ears ring and that got in the way of hearing the faint sounds made by ghosts. Nonetheless, this was a video with sound, and Josh liked me to communicate with the living as well as the dead.

When I'd set out to show Josh I could control my interactions with a ghost, I'd been hoping for a challenging subject like a brigadier general or one of the many intrepid souls that had survived the yellow fever epidemic. There were lots of strong energies in this particular cemetery, but the one that presented itself was a child.

We came to a stop on the path while I listened. I let my mind drift as the little girl materialized a few yards away from us. She was thin like she'd died of a wasting disease, but then she turned to check her surroundings and I saw it. An arrow jutted from the center of her tiny back. Tears welled in my eyes. I must have made a sound of dismay because Josh moved a little closer.

"Are you okay?" he asked, keeping his voice low. He was careful not to touch me.

"Yeah." I nodded. "It's a little girl." That was enough said. No ghost hunter likes to encounter a child.

"Can she speak?"

"I'll check." I knelt on the path and waited while the remnants of the child's mind tried to make sense of the past and present. I saw her struggle. She seemed as though she could see me but couldn't quite reconcile me with the events of her own life.

"Josh, this is amazing. She's partly aware and partly residual. Her remains must be here in the graveyard or she'd be haunting the site of her strongest living memories."

"If she's still attached to her remains, then you should be able to talk to her," Josh explained for the purposes of the video, and I nodded in agreement.

"Hi," I said automatically, then remembered that not all ghosts are familiar with modern greetings. "How do you do?" I corrected, and the little spirit drifted closer. She glowed like the dawn against the evening's darkened backdrop. "She's really bright. Can you see anything?" I whispered to Josh. I heard the gravel crunch as he moved a little closer.

"Pray, madam, would you like to be friends?" Her tiny sparrow voice quavered on the night air.

"Aye, indeed." I smiled and meant it. Her accent was heavy like William Grayford's. This soul was so pure. It was invigorating just to be near her. She inched a little closer. I waited patiently while she negotiated the physical world with her incorporeal body. Sometimes her tiny feet slipped below the gravel as she lost sense of the ground between us. She stopped moving when she'd made it close enough to feel my aura. I already sensed the icy chill of her spirit stream.

"Can you feel a chill?" I asked Josh.

"Yes!" he nearly sang.

The little girl with her lank blonde locks reached her small hand in my direction. This was it.

"Okay," I whispered to Josh. "Here goes." I reached my hand toward hers, and we touched.

My fingers brushed her memory, and it was a living thing slithering across my hands, coiling around my wrists. She tugged me across time and space, skipping like a stone across the landmarks of her soul. She showed me her favorite tree, the one she'd found leaning over the creek bed. The vines that twisted and hung from its ancient branches were perfect for swinging. She placed me on the lowest vine, gave me a push, and I was drowning in her reckless abandon as our feet flew out across the water. My stomach swam with butterflies, and her laughter burst from my lips.

Suddenly, we were rushing again across the countryside away from the winding river, over the pine forests toward tiny bald spots where people bent and tilled the earth.

"Tobacco," she beamed, and we raced down the rows of quickly growing crops. We ran until we felt the cool stretch of forest shadows at the edge of the farm.

"*STOP*," she shouted and wrapped her arms around me. "Not that part," she warned. "That's where they come to watch us." My scalp tingled with her fear. Fog rolled under the branches of those trees. "Indian's breath," she whispered, and the scene changed again.

Now we were inside a small building. A church. It was so little, but the walls were made of sturdy brick. High windows let in the light. It filtered down, warming her lap. She wiggled her dirty fingers through the sunbeams, then hid her hands beneath her Bible. She'd forgotten to clean them before they'd left for church.

We watched her older brother beside us as he indicated when to kneel and when to stand. We didn't know, and we didn't really care. We were just happy to be with him. Church was the only place he didn't frown.

"He's relieved," she explained. "This is the only place where we are safe. The wooden door is thick oak, and their arrows bounce off the brick. We stay here all day.*"* She handed me a cloth and unfolded it in my hands. I felt her stomach growl as we reached for the bread. My mouth watered as I tore into the smoked fish and hard cheese.

"Are you thirsty?" she asked, handing me a cup. "It's fresh from the swamp." She smiled, and my stomach turned. With a sickening jolt, I slammed back into my own body. I blinked my eyes against the light mist rolling in across the graveyard. I hadn't noticed when it had started. How long had I been with the little ghost? It felt like only moments, yet my heart ached from years of laughter, love, fear, and belonging.

"What's your name?" I asked as the tiny slip of a spirit began to melt into the mist.

"Petal." She smiled and kissed me on the cheek. I lost sight of her through my tears.

****

"I'm not convinced." Josh wiped the camera down and fit it back into its case. "If anything, that experience just proved my point. You're a plaything to these ghosts. How can you hope to control an angry apparition when your mind is wide open to them?"

"By making those ghosts wide open to me." I climbed into the van. Josh just stood there with his arms crossed and his glasses covered over with droplets of mist. His glasses slipped to the end of his nose, but he refused to push them up. He was too busy being obstinate.

"How do you propose to do that?"

"I don't know how to explain it, but something just feels different in here." I tapped the side of my head with my finger. "When I was talking to the soldier…I could tell that my will was affecting our interaction more than his. He wanted to leave our encounter, but I stopped him."

"You said he was a non-responsive, a weak ghost with a fading tie to the material world. That's not what we've been up against lately. That's not what grabbed you on the street and dragged you off. If you don't start being straight with me about what happened last night and what's given you this miraculous new power to control ghosts, then I'm not taking you anywhere." Josh spread his feet and readied himself for an argument. I know I said that his stubborn, difficult ways don't upset me, but right then…they annoyed me.

I got out of the van and stomped toward him. I walked a few inches past where he was expecting me to stop and put my face in front of his. Thanks to my heels, that put me almost eye to eye with him.

"You seem to be laboring under the misconception that you are in control of me. You are not responsible for me. You are not my bodyguard, and you're not my parent."

"Mel, you are less than defenseless when you are in the hypnogogic state. You're going to get hurt!"

Anger rushed through me. I tried to throw some water on it, but I must have reached for the gasoline. My peripheral nervous system had taken a beating with all the negative emotions of late. It took all my effort to keep the paralysis from dropping me right in front of him. I wasn't going down like that.

"Look at you! You're shaking. Mel, let me take you home."

Something snapped in my head. It was a tiny fracture, but it grew. I knew what he saw. It was the same thing Ben Martin had seen last night in Edwardia's dining room…a helpless girl. It's what all the ghosts had seen last night when they looked at me. Screw that.

"*NO!*" I shouted with all that was within me. The giant hand of narcolepsy tried to drive me to my knees, but I fought it. I raised my hands to my sides and called forth the pieces of the night that hid from human eyes. I could always feel them. They were always there. I'd spent my whole life trying to wish them away, but not anymore. I breathed in the permafrost of their spirits as their streams passed through me. I clenched the chains of sorrow that held them to this world and wrapped the links around my fists.

I felt my will roll out across the cemetery, and in its wake spirits stirred. I sucked in a misty breath and exhaled frost. My body shook violently, but as I breathed, I gained more and more control. At last, my muscles stilled, and I opened my eyes. Josh stood in front of me with his hands over his mouth. For a split second, I thought to laugh. He looked like the monkey that spoke no evil, but then I saw the set of his eyes and the blanched pallor of his skin. He was terrified. Guilt washed over me as I realized the extent of my emotional outburst. He and I had our disagreements, but we were a team and maybe even more than that. I'd just taken all my frustration from the last week out on him.

"I'm sorry," I whispered, but Josh shook his head slowly back and forth. That's when I noticed he wasn't really looking at me. His eyes were fixed on a spot somewhere behind me. I turned my head, and ice crackled in my hair. My eyes fell upon a blood-chilling scene. Ghostly faces hovered in the mist behind me. Some wavered in the drifting water droplets while others held their forms with burning determination.

I saw men and women, priests and slaves. Some wore uniforms and others wore scraps. There were ladies in lace and feathered hats and men with muskets and haunted eyes. They glared at Josh and, to both my surprise and horror, Josh gaped back at them. Power crystalized through my veins. It poured forth from my clenched hands in the form of frozen chains. I stared in shock at the manifestations wrapped around my knuckles. Vapor rose from the icy lines that trailed through the muggy air toward each of the assembled apparitions. I smelled ozone on the mist around me.

"Josh?" I turned to him and raised the shimmering links.

He lowered his hands slowly, and his mouth fell open. I waited desperately for him to say something. It took a few tries for him to get sound to come out of his mouth, but finally quiet words rumbled out.

"T—tell them that everything's okay." He placed his palms in the air. "Tell them to go back to w— wherever they came from." We both knew this situation was way out of hand, but I appreciated his attempt to treat this dilemma in a calm manner. Just a misunderstanding at the office. All in a day's work. Nothing to see here. Move along.

I turned slowly back to the ghosts.

"Thank you," I whispered. Their grave-light eyes turned to me. I felt the power rising off me in motes of frost. "Rest now," I soothed and squeezed the icy chains in my hands until they crunched. Frozen shards splintered beneath my fingers, and I watched as the souls slipped their bonds and vanished through the mist.

Josh fell to his knees.

"I'm sorry," I whispered. I didn't know what else

to say. I stared at my hands where the last sparkling traces of frost still clung to my palms. I was cursed. "I'm sorry," I whispered again. Nothing would ever be the same between us, and I was so, so sorry.

Chapter Eleven

Twenty-three giants emerging from the mist

We climbed onto the skiff just as the mist turned into a light net of rain. We all pretended as though we weren't ensnared by the silence that rolled off the river. Fog dampened my thoughts until I could barely hear them. The only thing I could still hear was the ringing. It had started when I'd screamed and the ghosts had appeared. I bent over and held my head between my hands as we pulled away from the dock.

"So…are you guys going to tell us what happened?" Seth asked tentatively.

Josh and I hadn't uttered a word since we'd returned from the cemetery. The motor chugged quietly as we cut through the waves. I had nothing to say, and I feared what Josh might have to say. I heard him shuffling behind me as he shifted his weight on the shelf seat. Gabe had stayed on shore with most of the equipment so that we had more room in the skiff. Even so, it was still cramped.

"We contacted the remnant of a little girl. She was a residual entity attached to the location of her remains." He paused as if searching for the right words. "Mel appeared to catch the child's attention, and they communicated."

"Communicated with a residual?" Matt questioned.

"Yep…I got it on tape."

"That's amazing!" Matt's voice floated up an octave. "So, what's changed, Mel? I mean…you've gone from limited communication with sentient spirits only to chatting it up with whatever presence drifts by." I heard him shift as he looked from me to Josh. "I don't get it. What's with the long faces?" The silence was as thick as the fog.

"That's a good question, Matt. Mel, what has changed?"

I was almost relieved to hear Josh's voice directed at me even though his words stung. I cradled my head and didn't look up.

"I feel like we're missing something," Seth said.

"Be glad you did," was Josh's only reply.

"Okay, this is as far as we can go before the Coast Guard has something to say about it," Matt announced. I looked up from the cradle of my fingers. We'd left the small marina only minutes ago. How had we covered so much water in so little time? Fog had eaten the land. I couldn't see lights in any direction.

"It's super dangerous to be out here in these conditions, so let's turn and burn, missy," Matt instructed.

I looked around me. "Where is the Fleet?"

"About a hundred yards off the starboard bow." He pointed.

I peered through the whirling waves of rain and mist, but I saw nothing. Matt brought us to a stop in the rolling water. We bobbed in silence while everyone looked at me.

"We're not close enough." My voice shook.

"Well, you're not talking about actually trying to

get on one of the ships? Right?" Matt chuckled nervously.

I nodded.

"Could we?" Seth asked, and the daredevil in him reared its mischievous head.

"No," Josh barked.

"If we get too close, we could be arrested," Matt informed us.

"But it's so foggy out tonight. We could bump right into the Fleet without even knowing it. Wink, wink." Seth was clearly onboard, pun intended.

"I'd have to kill the navigation lights." Matt shrugged.

"You're not killing the navigation lights," Josh ordered.

"Seth, you'd have to hold this pole in front of us to keep us from ramming one of the ships."

"No, no poles. No ramming."

"Josh, if you're not going to help, then get out of the way," Matt commanded in a very authoritative voice.

We all stopped and looked toward the older brother. Josh stared at him incredulously, but then after some thought he got up and traded seats with Seth.

"Even if we do get usable footage, it's not like we can announce that we were here," Josh pointed out.

We all looked at each other for a moment.

"So, we'll fudge a little on the location. Or better yet, we'll call it an 'undisclosed location' and cut out any identifying markings," Seth offered optimistically.

"This is on your head." Josh glared at Matt. Matt nodded and steered toward the thickest spot in the fog.

****

I counted twenty-three giants emerging from the mist. It was an unbelievable sight. We sidled up to an abandoned cargo ship at the end of the first row of rusty-eyed leviathans. They seemed to be lashed together in groups of four or five. Colonel Grayford could be on any of them. There was no way to search them all. It would take all night.

"Light!" Seth pointed toward a small boat moving around the next row of ships. A beam of light scoured the corroding hulls of a few ships then disappeared. The boat moved on.

Matt steered us into a sheltered space between crisscrossing anchors. The empty hulks groaned and scraped against the night air. Their paint-chip protestations echoed overhead. A sense of foreboding filled that forgotten place. My heart beat a little faster, and my ears strained a little harder against the slurping and slapping of the waves.

"They're here," I whispered, and my words bounced off the creaking metal.

"You sense ghosts?" Josh reached for the handheld video camera. I nodded. I felt horrible about keeping my real reason for being here a secret, but had I told him, he would have deemed the trip too dangerous. It was too dangerous, but this was my only way to find the colonel.

I closed my eyes and lifted my hands into the swirling mist. The spitting vapor turned to rain again as I waited to feel the cool stirrings of the spirit world. They were here, but I couldn't say for sure just where.

"Not these two," I said finally, and Matt moved us on to the next two ships. We continued that way for long minutes as I searched the ships two at a time. It wasn't until we reached a decrepit old merchant vessel on the far end of the center cluster that the air filled with voices.

"Here!" I called out, and Matt eased up on the throttle. We glided next to the thin hull, and Seth searched the corroding metal for something to tie to. Josh whistled quietly, and we looked in the direction in which he pointed. Metal stairs hung in a diagonal line from the ship's port rail to the water's edge. We slid along the boat's side.

SCRAPPED.

The giant letters stretched above our heads like a mammoth tattoo. Seth reached out and shook the rickety staircase. It didn't budge. We tied to it and cut the engine.

"What now?" Josh asked, and I turned to look at him for the first time since the cemetery. I'd expected to see anger in his eyes, but I was wrong. I saw worry, maybe fear, and something else. Loss, maybe. I stood as the boat rocked. I was locked in a place in-between. Part of me faced my friends and searched for a way to explain why I'd dragged them out here to this floating land of the dead. The other part of me already raced up the stairs in search of a missing piece of myself that Colonel Grayford had taken. I knew that something awful waited on that ship, but I also knew that I couldn't leave him to it.

"You are right. Something did happen to me," I said finally. "You already know the basics, and I did a little research as well. The woman in green is Edwardia Landry, a prominent business owner from the late 1800s. She lived and died in Portsmouth and, for whatever reason, has found her way back." I bent my knees as the boat lurched and tipped in the unsettled water. "Apparently, Edwardia can tell that there's something different about me. I think that's why she took me to her home at the Water Street Estate." I shivered as I remembered the press of her cruel fingers around my neck. "There was a huge psychic concentration within the structure with a large number of corporeal ghosts. There were members of the living there as well. I barely made it out alive." I looked down at the drifting chunks of ice that had begun to form in the bottom of the boat in the middle of July.

"Another thing I didn't tell you is that I was warned not to ghost hunt within the city limits before we started taping last night. The Sweaty Man paid me a visit at the gallery and conveyed the message. I'm sorry I didn't tell you. I didn't think there was any…I didn't think." I checked their shocked faces before continuing. "I also didn't tell you that the only way I made it out alive was with the help of a corporeal ghost…Colonel William Grayford."

"Wait, *the* Colonel Grayford?" Seth quirked his eyebrow. I nodded.

"Colonel Grayford distracted Edwardia, and when the Shadow showed up and wrecked the party, Grayford got me out. I collapsed behind my ward, and when I woke up, I called you."

Josh stared at me in disbelief. "Why are we here?" Josh pointed his finger down at the bottom of the boat and the fathoms of water beneath it. The camera sat in his lap, but the record light still glowed red.

I took a breath and steeled myself. "There seems to be some system of justice among the sentient spirits. Edwardia pressed charges on Colonel Grayford for interfering with her plans for me. And now he's up there somewhere facing punishment."

"What?" was Matt's reply.

"This is insane," Josh interjected. "Matt, turn the skiff around."

"No! You can't. I have to help him."

"No, you don't."

"He saved my life!"

"Then we thank him for it, but Mel, he's already dead!"

"Matt, don't! I have to do this."

"Why? Give me one good reason why we should let you climb up those rain-slick steps onto a condemned ship with angry, possibly murderous ghosts on it?" Josh was practically apoplectic. I could tell he barely believed the words he said.

"Mel—" Matt shook his head. "—we saw how they took you. These things are too strong. You're my friend. I can't let you do this."

I covered my face with my hands. Invisible fingers clutched at me, pulling me toward the stairs.

"I can protect myself." I pulled my hands away from my face. "Josh, tell them." Josh stared at me for a moment then at his feet.

"What you did with those ghosts at the cemetery tonight…those ghosts weren't corporeal."

"Did you doubt their strength?"

"No."

"Then you doubt me."

"Do you even know how you did that? I mean, can you do it again?"

It was a good question, and as I stared into his deep gray eyes, I realized in a strange, new, and almost exhilarating way, that I had a good answer uncoiling inside me. I raised my hands to the misty rain and reached for the emptiness between all things. It was cold between the particles of reality, cold enough to freeze rain. Ice hissed against the skiff. Then moans echoed across the water's surface. I felt them trapped beneath the waves. So many souls drifted with the tide, unable to free themselves from the moving water. Matt and Josh looked nervously at the water lapping the boat. Something moved beneath the surface.

"Seth, hit the pen recorder," Matt instructed out of habit. Turbulence whipped the water into frothy peaks, and I staggered backward. Josh grabbed my hand, then drew back as frost formed along his fingers.

"Where's Seth?" Matt asked numbly. Josh whirled around. We heard the clank of tactical boots on aluminum as Seth stole up the stairs. A skeletal hand reached from the waves, followed by another. Josh pulled me down to the seat, but I pushed away from him. I scrambled to the bow and flung my leg over. The boat had drifted away from the staircase when Seth had jumped, so I stepped on the rope and we dragged back toward the ship.

"Mel!" Josh lunged for me, but the boat tilted wildly. Matt fell against the tiller, and the air left his lungs in a loud cough. I leapt for the bottom step and my heel slipped. I was still wearing my dressy sandals from work. My hands landed on the third step, and I gripped the metal hard. A wave slapped me from behind, and I used the force to get a better grip. I pulled my legs onto the bottom step, and the tall metal treads bit into my knees.

I got my feet under me and reached for the

handrail, but the combination of my poor balance and the movement of the waves made me grip the edge of the step again. I started to climb that way, with my body against the steps. I moved as quickly as I could, gripping each step until the water fell away and I could no longer hear Josh's muffled shouts.

I looked up but couldn't see Seth. I couldn't see the top of the ship anymore either. The fog had thickened right above me. I climbed for what seemed like forever. With each step, I felt more and more regret. A hollow clang cut through the mist above me. I froze. No other sound followed.

Slowly, I started climbing again. Fog closed in around me as I reached the last step. My hands slid out into empty air. I'd run out of steps. I pulled myself onto the platform at the top of the stairs and crawled onto the ship's deck. Paint chips cut at my fingers as I felt my way forward. Mildew assaulted my nose.

"Seth?" I whispered. I held my breath and waited for a response. I heard faint whispers in the fog over the ringing in my ears, but no one answered. "Seth, please."

Nothing.

Wind cut across the deck turning the fog into undulating curtains of gray. As more and more of the deck came into view, I gained enough confidence to stand. Before I even realized what I was looking at, Seth's face came into view.

"Seth!" I shouted in relief, but he didn't greet me with his familiar, mischievous smile. In fact, he didn't greet me at all. His face was red, and his eyes bulged. The misty fog unfurled around the woman in the frost blue evening gown. One delicate, gloved hand held Seth by the throat, while the other hand played with the long spill of his strawberry blond hair.

"I can't thank you enough for this lovely gift," the auburn-haired woman tittered. The insipid tones of her child-like voice echoed across the deck. "Oh!" She giggled again. "Did you want it back?"

I was struck dumb with fear as I stared into Seth's purpling face.

"Come and get him," she taunted.

Horror threatened to drop me. My muscles loosened as I staggered forward. Seth's mouth opened wordlessly as he pulled at the woman's porcelain hand.

This was not happening. The plan was to talk the guys into staying in the skiff while I climbed aboard by myself. My thoughts lost focus as panic swept over me. My knees began to buckle. My friend was suffocating before my eyes. I tried to remember how I'd called the ghosts in the cemetery, but cataplexy swept through my brain.

I saw the desperation in Seth's eyes. I fought the giant hand of narcolepsy pressing down on me. I took a step toward him and then another. The effort didn't seem to close the distance between us even a little. I tried again and again, but each time he drifted just out of my reach. Finally, a bright, blessed spark of anger lit inside me, and I used it to call the grave to me.

Waves crashed somewhere far below as my will sank through the rusted hull and leaked into the water. I was shocked at the sheer number of spirits I sensed below the waves. Their despair clawed at me. Memories of lives long gone spun inside my head, stirred by the immediacy of my call. It spoke to them of drowned desires and riptides of responsibilities. They remembered it all, but the water, in its flowing negligence, would not release them.

I pulled at the anguished souls, but the waves fought me. I pushed desperately at the heavy hand of narcolepsy as it closed over me. Seth's eyes grew distant. I let go of the souls trapped in the water below and reached for the one before me.

"Mine!" I shouted, and ice crackled from my hand. My will whipped out in a frozen streak, and I wrapped my command around her. The icy chain looped around her neck and dragged her toward me. A look of utter shock rippled across her face as she slid through the air. I reached for Seth's hand, but just as our fingers met, the woman in blue released her grip and Seth fell. Not to the floor. He fell through the air out of sight. A moment later, I heard a cracking thud. The mist parted before me so that I could see the open cargo hold below me. There were no rails around the giant hole where containers had once been stored. The floor just fell away in a giant square only inches from my feet. One more step and I would join Seth at the bottom of the hold.

"No!" I screamed and ice crystals formed on my lips. The sound of Seth's fall still rang inside the hold. Power rolled off me as I fixed eyes on the ghost. She turned her heart-shaped face sideways and smiled. I reeled as I took in the fractured teeth that peeked from her torn cheek. Her eyes burned black.

I slid my sandal away from the edge of the opening, but I knew it was too late. The specter laughed a dry, whispering sound and wrapped her fingers around the frozen links. I tried to let go of the chain, but it was too late. She yanked. With an icy snap, I fell forward into darkness.

Chapter Twelve

A place of forgetting

I was asleep and dreaming. In my dream, I sat on a sprawling porch that overlooked a wide river. The briny scent of the tide was raw on the air, and seagulls slanted through the morning light.

And there was nothing else.

No destruction, no death, no cataclysm, just a soft breeze rustling a nearby mimosa tree. I sat for a long time. I had the sense that there was no need to hurry. The Shadow wasn't coming. I wondered, distantly, if I was dead.

Cart wheels creaked, and horses' hooves beat out a familiar cadence behind the house, and I was suddenly aware of a town in the distance. A town I loved and a collection of people of whom I was deeply proud. The dream felt more like a memory, but it wasn't my memory.

"Melisande." My name was on the breeze. It tangled in the mimosa blossoms.

"Melisande," the seagulls sang.

"Melisande, wake up!" With a sorrowful sigh, it all faded away from me, and I was left in darkness and pain.

My heart hammered out a stabbing beat against what felt like one, maybe two, broken ribs. I tried not to take big breaths as I lifted my head. I opened my eyes, but I could only see through my right eye. I found my hand and lifted it to my left eye. It met a swollen mass with sticky tears. In fact, the entire left side of my face felt numb as though I were touching someone else's face. I tried to push to a sitting position, but my hip cried out with stabbing pains that shot down my left leg.

"Seth?" I turned my head, and the cargo bay swam around me. Nausea flipped my stomach. It was made worse by the pitiful sight of unmoving arms and legs next to me. Rose gold hair spread out across the rusty floor.

"Oh, Seth." My heart lurched. He was too still. Seth was never still. I brushed his hair away from his neck and checked for a pulse, but my hands shook. I was going into shock. I tried to find his pulse but eventually had to settle for the fact that his skin was still warm and his chest still rose and fell with shallow breaths.

How far had we fallen? I strained to see the top of the hold. The fog was clearing, but something sticky kept dripping into my eye. Anger was the first emotion to step forward. I would end that ghost. I'd shred her life force and feed her to the souls beneath the waves. I just needed to get my feet under me.

I knew that I should probably try to administer CPR on Seth or at least try to assess his wounds. He could be bleeding out beside me. But all I could think of was the woman in blue and how to bring her down. This was probably why I wouldn't make a good mother. If something injured my child, I'd likely step over the child in an attempt to confront the danger rather than tend to the little one's injuries. It's weird, the things we think of when we're about to die. I'd never thought of children before.

"Stay down," someone whispered off to my right. I squinted in the soupy grayness of the hold.

"Don't call attention to yourself," another voice advised.

"If you hold still, they may forget about you," a thin voice called from behind me.

It took forever for my eyes to adjust, but finally they did, and I was not happy about what I saw. The cargo hold we'd fallen into was less a hold and more a dungeon. The walls were lined with tortured souls clinging to the last vestiges of their sanity. Gibbering voices came and went. I peered into sightless eyes and watched as mouths twisted around missing tongues. Some ghosts hung by the only limb they had left, while others were left intact...on the outside. Their misery seeped through the crack in my brain, but I couldn't understand what held them to this realm of hopelessness. What were the bonds from which they could not escape?

Sleep tugged at my quaking mind, but going into the hypnogogic state seemed like a bad idea and strangely unnecessary. I fought the urge and looked up to the unattainable sky. It churned above me, mindless and gray.

Silhouetted against the misty night, several stories in the air, was a decaying wheelhouse with broken windows and weathered railings. I made out two bridge wings on either side of the wheelhouse with a narrow walkway connecting them in front.

Figures moved along the walkway. I spotted the

woman in blue instantly. She strolled alongside Edwardia, who, by now, had reconstituted herself to the very vision of feminine perfection. The ladies took up spots on the left bridge wing to either side of the bloody-vested man.

I wiped what I assumed was drying blood from my eye and focused on the right bridge wing. A man stood there alone, tall and noble in the mist. It was Colonel Grayford. I watched as he was joined by another. Colonel Grayford bowed to the man then took his hand. The other greeted him cordially. My heart threatened to crack another rib with its pounding.

"What is this place?" I turned to the entity on my right. He seemed to be sentient and aware of the events of the moment. He was dressed in a doctor's coat and antique head mirror.

"This is a place of forgetting...an oubliette." His lips spread across sharpened teeth in a vicious grin. His manifestation flickered through a sickening spectrum of putrefied greens and blighted blacks. His hands were in constant motion. I squinted at the medical tools that littered the dank space he occupied. My face slackened with horror, and he drank in my reaction.

"I am the Butcher of Hospital Point. I am pleased to make your acquaintance. Do you know my work?" His manner was erudite and fiendishly sharp, as sharp as the knife he was using to dissect his own leg.

I knew who the Butcher was. Anyone in the Tidewater area with an interest in the paranormal knew the story. The Portsmouth Naval Hospital was on the city's annual Halloween Ghost Walk, but because it was an active military compound, tours only made it to the front gate of the installation. The hospital was situated on a solitary slip of land referred to as Hospital Point. I knew the nature of the claims, but no paranormal investigation teams had ever been granted access. It had been a very active haunting until a few decades ago. Apparently, the source of that haunting sat right next to me.

I let my gaze drift slowly around the cargo hold. Each tortured soul had a darkness about them. Poisonous thoughts leaked from their minds into the ether around me. My skin began to crawl, and I reached behind me for Seth's hand. I felt a little movement in his fingers. I gripped his hand in desperate relief.

As much as I was loath to engage the doctor again, I needed information if Seth and I were going to get out of here alive.

"What are they doing?" I asked, pointing toward the wheelhouse.

"They are preparing for a trial, dear." The doctor's voice sent shivers down my spine, or maybe I was shocky from my injuries. Either way, I had to find a means of getting us out of that place before I fell asleep. There had to be a way for merchant seamen to climb out of these holds. I needed to get to my feet and search the walls, but I couldn't leave Seth so close to the doctor. If I could just sleep for a moment or two and recharge my battery, then I could drag Seth to the center of the hold. I lowered my head to my hands and covered my eyes.

"Do you not want to see the proceedings? I can take care of that for you." The doctor grinned again and produced a tong-like instrument. "We only need remove one eye since the other is swollen shut."

I fought to my feet and dragged Seth to the center

of the space.

There were no ladders, but there was a hole in the wall. It was a tall, narrow square-shaped hole opening onto blackness. Had I not worked up the courage to stick my head inside that darkness, I would have missed the rungs in the tiny square compartment. Had I not been paying attention, I would have missed the fact that there was no floor in the compartment. The space was actually not a compartment but a vertical shaft.

The rungs ran upward to a metal cover and downward into darkness. I dropped a small chunk of marine paint down the ladder shaft and waited for it to hit bottom. When it finally did, it was almost too far away to hear. What I did hear was moaning. Voices whispered up from the forgotten depths. Were there other holds in that blackness? How horrible were the crimes of the souls in those depths? How bad did you have to be in order to be consigned to such oblivion?

Come and see, the darkness seemed to whisper. *Come and see.*

I backed away from the shaft and checked on Seth. Now I knew that we had been lucky. We'd fallen into the belly of the whale, but luckily several levels of containers were stacked below us. If we'd fallen one more level it would have killed us.

From what I could make out in the dim light, Seth's color had gone from bad to worse. His skin was ashen and clammy. If the stairs only went up, then maybe I could try and pull him along with me. But knowing that one wrong move in the shaft could cause me to drop him farther down...I'd rather leave him with the devil I knew.

I scanned the hold. Souls lined the walls like

bubbling water stains. I wasn't sure what force bound them to this place, but I was about to change their sentences.

I started with the Doctor. He looked up from his surgery, which caused his mirror to flash dimly above his eyes. His pointed teeth glistened in the shadows. I willed the chains from my hands and took him first. Then I moved to the next, a bestial specter with almost no intelligence left in its face. It unfurled its twisted limbs and came willingly.

I made my way around the hold, claiming souls. With each capture, I stepped farther and farther away from the waking world. Mist drifted down into the hold, changing to a light pelting sleet. I took another step and the sleet softened to a floating dance of snow. It caught the fog's faint light until the chamber shone with an eerie glow. The air around me was charged with spirit streams. Some were so corrupted, I hesitated to draw on them, but I couldn't leave Seth alone with these fiendish entities.

Black dreams spun around me. Once I'd gathered all that I could from the ship's cargo bays, I reached for the portless sea below me. Its restless embrace held no calm harbors for the sailors it had claimed. I whispered promises to them. I offered a sheltering shore and the embrace of dry earth to those held so long beneath the waves. To the lost ones, endlessly moored to this floating gulag, I offered escape and revenge. And then I pulled them to me.

The power of the grave roiled around me as I tested the icy bonds. When I was done, frozen chains reached from every part of me. I felt the weight of hundreds of condemned souls as I climbed the rungs of the shaft.

Devilish apparitions exploded into the night air like frost-rimed nightmares as I pushed the heavy cover open. The metal clanged against the deck announcing our arrival.

I tipped and swayed on the narrow deck as I struggled to maintain my grip on so many frantic spirits. I felt their fear and rage threatening to tear them apart. Some had earned their imprisonment, but to my horror, some had not. For the drowned sailors I had collected, this was their first time above water in more than a hundred years. They strained against their restraints, stretching spectral limbs.

I heard what sounded like a wrestling match behind me and turned to see Josh and Matt rolling and slamming against the platform at the top of the aluminum staircase.

Josh pulled against the translucent hands that pinned him to the metal grate. Matt pushed at their steely grip as he fought to make it onto the deck. They called to me—my friends, their voices straining—but I needed all my concentration to hold the ghosts I'd collected. I wasn't in control of the entities with which they struggled.

I looked toward the bridge rail where Edwardia smiled down on us. Hatred, venomous and defiling, rippled through me. It traveled down the chains I'd manifested until it found what I needed. Now I knew what the lower levels of this rusting purgatory were reserved for. I found a psychic impression so vile that it floated alone at the end of its icy tether. Even the irredeemable souls that had somehow avoided a one-way ticket to Hell gave this entity a wide berth. I should probably have left this one in its lowest cell, I thought belatedly, but there was no changing that now.

I tested the links of the ghostly chain that restrained it. This small convergence of evil didn't really have a visage I could see—just a dark thickening of the air. It was more a collection of seething emotions and fragmented thoughts. I pulled at the tether, and its awareness responded. It was as I feared. I'd picked up a poltergeist. That should have been impossible considering a poltergeist requires a host, but this entity had a presence of its own. I hesitated a fraction of a second. "Waste not, want not," my mother always said, so without further thought, I pushed the building sense of foreboding aside and gave the festering congregation of violence a task.

Stop those hands!

It raced along the deck, dragging its chain through the mist and dissipating fog. Metal creaked and paint chips flung through the air. There was a ripping sound as some of the hands simply shredded in the air where they hung. Some were flung to the deck and crushed into vaporous tendrils, while others condensed into balls of quivering ether with an audible crunch.

I didn't have much experience with poltergeists. As a rule, I avoided them vigorously, but even I could tell that the level of damage this entity had just displayed was way beyond the regular spatial displacements of a typical poltergeist. This thing could target its malcontent. That wasn't a scattershot explosion of psychic pain. It had evolved.

I pulled on the link that bound it to me, and it recoiled, testing my strength. I yanked the chain hard, and it drifted back toward me through the mist. I wasn't at all confident that my will was what made it come back, but at least it had come back. I didn't want it anywhere near me, but I wanted it near the guys even less.

"He's down there." I pointed into the hold. Josh and Matt startled at my voice. It did sound strange, almost hollow. I could only imagine what I looked like. Damp hair. Bloody face. Frost-covered hands. I probably looked like the ghosts I dragged behind me. I spotted the entry to the six-story bridge structure and started forward.

"Halt!" A booming voice rolled over the ship, followed by the sucking slurp of severed flesh. I locked eyes on the head Edwardia had held clasped in her fingers the night before. It floated in the air, tinting the mist arterial red beneath it. My stomach twisted.

"There will be order in this court," it shouted. The sharp sound of a gavel hammered on the air. I took a step forward and felt the prick of sharpened bayonets. A line of spectral soldiers appeared in the air before me. The head floated up through the mist. It came to a stop just above the bridge walkway as if that was its bench. The red stain of its passing drifted over the cargo hold.

"This court is now in session," it ordered. "Plaintiff, state your complaint."

I watched as Edwardia bowed to the court.

"On evening last, at the celebration of my birth, held within my own estate, I was subjected to the indisciplined conduct of one William Grayford." Edwardia drew forth a handkerchief from the black lace bell of her sleeve and squeezed it tightly.

"Colonel Grayford displayed indecorous behavior in the midst of my gathering, thereby ruining the event. I suffered manifest damages both to my home and my person." The spectral crowd materializing around the bridge moaned in disapproval. "And my guests were exposed to his caprice yet again." She nodded to the crowd, and moans turned to gasps.

"How does the defendant plead?" the judge barked.

"Not guilty, Your Honor." Grayford's voice slid through me, and the ringing in my ears stopped. I drew in a sharp breath.

"The court will now hear testimony. Madam Landry, please bring forth your witnesses." The head rose to hover just outside the broken windows of the wheelhouse. I watched as a fan of apparitions spread out across the night. I recognized Edwardia's guests from last night. They still wore their evening fashions and smoldering brimstone eyes. The hairs on the back of my neck rose in the presence of so many predators. I pulled my ghosts close, but they didn't offer much in the way of comfort.

Voice after voice called out their testimony. Each accusation was wilder than the next as they described my abduction and torment as their rightful entertainment. The fact that they had been robbed of the opportunity to drink the full quantity of my life force was portrayed as a violation of some macabre hostess/guest contract.

"Who speaks for you, Defendant?" the head boomed, and a tall man in a beautiful red plaid kilt materialized next to Grayford.

"The court recognizes Sir Andrew Pratt, founder of the Gosnold Shipyard, Tory, and supporter of the British Royal Navy." The head chuckled through its exposed trachea.

Mr. Pratt bowed stiffly. "Though I was not present

for the doomed event, I stand witness to Colonel Grayford's character in many such situations." I was struck by the quality of the man's voice and demeanor. His Scottish accent was clear and commanding. Something about the way he spoke gave off an air of strength and moral correctness. The spirits hanging in the air above me turned to him as though he were the North Star.

"I see many souls here tonight that owe their freedom from the grave's confinement to Colonel Grayford. When first he found purchase in this land between, this man—" Pratt gestured to Colonel Grayford. "—sought to continue his life's endeavors by overseeing the health and well-being of this port. In life, he gave of his land for the city's annexation. He nurtured trade and commerce, and when he passed, he rose again to safeguard its movement through time." The man clutched his hands behind his back and began to pace.

"We are all aware of the dark and derelict decline that pulls at the fibers of this city. We are all, in fact, a reflection of its malady. Are we not?" His eyes scanned the crowd. "It is the duty of our kind to fortify the pieces of this land and invigorate our children. But look at us. We have fallen victim to the siren song of lust and indulgence. As we speak, our malice opens a door onto such evil…" Mr. Pratt hesitated. "Neither the living nor the dead will survive what waits on the other side." At hearing Andrew Pratt's words, Edwardia shot the judge a withering look.

"Do you testify, Mr. Pratt, or do you tell us a bedtime story?" The head chuckled. The gathering's amusement murmured on the mist.

"I do testify. I testify to the pure intentions of one Colonel William Grayford. I testify to his struggle to maintain the integrity of our realm. I testify to his unending war against the corrosive effect of Madam Edwardia Landry's actions on the natural world."

The gavel hammered. "Do not paint this man a saint." The judge's head floated toward Mr. Pratt. "Look at his eyes. We all know the improper acts he performed."

"Ms. Blythe has been called to the Battle," Mr. Pratt continued. "She is the only 'living' member of our forces. The limit of her power is unknowable. I charge Madam Edwardia Landry with impeding the Light by stealing Ms. Blythe and offering her for consumption."

The gavel cracked again.

At first, I wasn't sure what I had heard. Had the man in the red plaid kilt just used my name? What battle? I guessed it was good that someone was speaking for me, but I'd never met this man before. I knew nothing about his Battle or his forces of Light, and then my thoughts drew inward. Somewhere on the shore of dreams, I'd seen a battle. I'd seen many battles, in fact. I remembered the shining people and the darkness that spread across the land. I looked at my hands and then the vicious faces of the ghosts surrounding me. I didn't shine. How could I be a part of that bright army? Unless...the thought turned my heart into an anchor, unless I was on the other side.

"You cannot level charges, Mr. Pratt. You are defending." A cacophony of voices filled the air. The scene unraveled under a cloud of indignation and accusations. Josh and Matt dragged Seth up through the hatch and onto the deck. Their faces were white as they took in the parts around them that they could see and hear.

I saw the horror in their eyes as they looked at me. It was then that I realized I might very well be the most fearsome vision on the ship. My outstretched arms were clothed in frost, and my hands were frozen into fists. Chains of ice stretched away from my hands and tore from my body in all directions. At the end of each one of those chains was something that should not be looked upon. Yet my friends seemed to be able to see the collection of phantoms swirling around me. Maybe they couldn't see them all, but the ones that hovered nearest to me had an almost solid look to them.

"All that you offer, Mr. Pratt, is hearsay!" the judge's severed head boomed over the melee. I looked to Colonel Grayford and was shocked to see him looking back at me. It was the first time he'd even acknowledged my presence. Then, he did something I was not expecting. He smiled.

"I find the defendant guilty as charged," the festering head shouted, and the red-eyed audience raised their voices together as one raging beast. My ghosts stirred and thrashed against their chains. Dread drained the last of the warmth from my body as my feet left the deck. The swarm of spirits levitated into the air, taking me with them. I hung by the chains that bound them to me, and it became painfully clear that I might not have the control I thought I did. The more ground I lost to doubt, the more violently the chains pulled at my flesh. I clenched my teeth and tugged at the maddened throng.

"Stop her," the newly exhumed sailors cried, jabbing fleshless fingers at Edwardia. "He cannot be lost!"

The criminal ghosts seethed as well. They jostled the sailors, and fighting broke out in the air around me. Panic flooded through me. Blood loss and the stabbing pain in my head and side siphoned my strength.

The piercing tips of bayonets closed on me as I rose. I couldn't stop the levitation. The ghosts drifted out over the open cargo bay, and I was suddenly aware of the space between my feet and the floor of the hold. I was losing my grip on them. I hung in the air as the struggling spirits threatened to draw and quarter me. On the deck below, I made out Josh and Matt moving Seth down the aluminum stairway.

"Prepare for sentencing." The head sucked in a bloody breath. "Colonel William Grayford, you are here by convicted of criminal misconduct." I barely heard the judge over the howling court. The line of bayonets vanished only to materialize in a circle around Grayford. The ghosts shouted in my head.

Free us! Free us, and we will fight!

The chains pulled at my soul. I wanted nothing more than to loose the poor spirits of those drowned soldiers. Their sins had been taken by the tides long ago, but some of the prisoners were a very different story. I couldn't separate one from the other.

"It is this court's will that you be stripped of your holdings and diminished!" A wailing filled the air as first one then another of my spirits slipped their bonds. The words the judge spoke didn't sound worthy of the reaction that rippled through the court. I didn't understand the sentence of diminishment.

I clawed at the air as, one by one, icy chains snapped. I looked to Grayford, but the soldiers had taken him into custody. I gripped the tethers of my remaining ghosts, but I was sinking through the air. I caught movement to my left as Edwardia streaked toward me through the mist. Her hand curved into sharpened scythe-like claws. I reached down the frozen length of the chains, searching frantically. I found the doctor and gave him his order.

Like a tiny thread of lightning, his surgical knife flitted through the air, carving red lines across Edwardia's throat. First one then the other carotid artery opened. Even though her heart didn't pump blood, the memory of life's elixir floated from the second mouth that the doctor had opened below her chin. Her head tilted back as the severed tendons in her neck recoiled. I reeled away from her, pulling the doctor with me. My mind went to the posters in Dr. Suni's office. For one stunned moment, Edwardia looked like one of those medical illustrations. I cringed, and she took it badly.

She lifted her hands to her neck, and her eyes went wide. I didn't have many options. I could hang there in the air while she eviscerated me, or I could use the weapon I had. I whipped the doctor's chain out before me, and his bone saw blurred through the air. Edwardia rippled as the metal teeth passed through her. She materialized again. Her long, sickle fingers tore through the air. In the time it took her to cut through my tethers, the doctor had relieved her of several limbs.

I plunged. The dank air of the hold claimed me again, and I braced for impact. There would be no surviving this drop. My fall had started from way farther up this time. I caught a glimpse of Edwardia's rotting eyes as I fell, then the shadows swallowed me whole.

****

The doctor's arms felt like any other man's arms, strong and possessive. He was the only ghost to which I was still tethered. Even so, the question begged…why did he catch me? If he had let me fall, my head would have smashed against the moldy floor of the hold and I'd be dead. He would be free. He didn't strike me as the kind of guy that formed attachments. He did, however, strike me as the kind of guy that formed obsessions.

I was thankful that there was enough strength to his essence to slow my fall. I'd still hit hard, but only bruising hard, not brain viscera spread out around me hard. In fact, he'd not seemed very solid when I first met him. Yet, now he looked almost corporeal. Was there something about me that was changing these ghosts? The reality of my situation caught up with me quickly. I was back in the hold and in the arms of a particularly loathsome entity. The doctor's face hung above me in a mask of poisonous glee.

"It will take some time for Madam Landry to heal those wounds." The doctor grinned and smoothed a surgical glove over my hair affectionately. "We won't be disturbed now." Icebergs clogged my veins. The last bit of warmth I'd managed to hold onto floated from my skin and was gone. I thought it was fear that I felt spreading through me or cataplexy loosening my muscles, but as the tingling chill eating down my arms and legs turned to numbness, I realized it was anesthesia.

Through the thick metal hull I heard the skiff's motor roar to life. Relief washed over me. The doctor had stolen all other sensations. I waited to hear the boat pull away, but it didn't.

Please, for once, Josh, just cut and run.

I wished so terribly that he would assess the situation and realize that Seth's condition took first priority. As much as I wished he could help me, I knew he couldn't. I was beyond help now.

"So I see you have a neurological abnormality. I've had quite a bit of success with the leucotomy procedure. It is commonly referred to as a lobotomy." His waxy face split into a jack-o-lantern grin. The air left my lungs in a piteous moan. My eyes tracked his hands as he reached for his tools. His tether was gone. How had that happened? The anesthesia must have loosened my hold on the doctor. I tried to call a spirit, any spirit, to me, but my mind was quickly clouding over. The only thing I feared more than sleeping outside of the protection of my St. Michael's ward was losing consciousness altogether. I'd evaded the Shadow so many times, but not even my adrenaline escape hatch would save me now.

"First, we need to relieve the intracranial pressure," he explained in a ghoulishly clinical tone. The Doctor brought out what looked like a giant, hand-powered drill. Panic burned through the last of my conscious thoughts except for one.

My last thought was of Billy, the gardener, and all the psalms I'd learned from him when once we'd plunged our wiggling fingers into the cool, moist soil of the church's flower beds. One came back to me now clear and crisp. Psalms 18:39. *For You have girded me with strength for battle; You have subdued under me those who rose up against me*. I hated to close my eyes against the shining light that suddenly filled the cargo hold. It was so beautiful. I hated to close my eyes, but I could do nothing else.

Chapter Thirteen

Yes, you're fucked again.

I hovered over my body almost indifferently as I surveyed the horrifying tableau below me. The doctor spread my arms and legs wide and cut a thin line up the fabric covering each limb. He set my sandals neatly aside and combed my blood-soaked hair in a fan-shape on the corroded floor.

I barely recognized myself lying there in the first stages of death. I'd always considered myself curvy in a well-fed kind of way. When had I become so gaunt? *I should have eaten more*, I realized numbly. Sharing a can of tuna with Bouguereau once a day didn't provide enough protein for an adult. *Why had I done that to myself? I could have made time to eat. Bouguereau. Who would take care of Bougie?* My mind wandered on a spectral breeze as I prepared myself to exit this world.

I took a last glance at myself. *I was pretty*, I thought sadly as I focused on the side of my face that wasn't swollen and crusted with blood. I'd always liked the way my eyebrows swept up, delicately arching over my brow bone. They balanced my pouting lips and sloping cheekbones. It was a good face, strong but feminine. Light played over my bluing skin, casting long shadows from my eyelashes. It sparked along the knives and forceps the Doctor had so carefully laid out next to my head. He seemed so delighted to have a living specimen again, but the light was growing brighter.

The Doctor tilted his mirror away from my body and shielded his eyes. Several points of incandescence moved in the sky above the ship. He squinted up toward the top of the cargo bay as one of the human-shaped lights lowered toward us. The doctor fought for a look at the woman in shining leathers. Her black hair offered the only relief from the dazzling glow as it streamed out from her chiseled Cherokee face.

I drifted clear of her descending form and watched in amazement as she touched down in a dizzying blaze of colors. She whispered something to the doctor, and I watched a tragic look wash over him. The woman knelt beside my body and slipped her hands beneath me. She whispered again, but this time I heard her.

"Not yet."

Her words found me in the halfway place where my spirit lingered. She lifted my body into the air, out of the cargo bay, over the rusted edge of the ship, and laid me in the boat next to Seth. The boat pulled away to a fate I couldn't know.

****

I woke up in the wrong part of the hospital. I remember the Emergency Room. I remember a nice, young doctor checking me for a concussion. I remember the nurses wheeling Seth into surgery. I remember watching Josh warring with himself in the chair next to me. The part of him that I can't ever seem to walk away from must have won because the last thing I remember was his hand gently cradling my cheek and his fingers tangling in the dried blood in my hair. I must have fallen asleep in the ER, but I didn't remember any nightmares.

I looked around the hospital room in which I'd just woken. There were various signs on the walls. They pretty much all said the same thing, "CAUTION—Call Don't Fall" in as many languages as they could. But then, I couldn't read Arabic or Hindi. For all I knew, those signs read "Yes, you're fucked again. Stay in bed, or the nurse will give you an enema."

I was in the seizure ward. Not because I necessarily had a seizure disorder, but because there is no ward for brain-damaged, hallucinating narcoleptics. This was as good a place as any in which to have my cataplexy monitored, so I relaxed into the adjustable bed and waited for Gabe to wake up. His giant form was crumpled into an ancient recliner seat next to the window. It must have been his snoring that had woken me.

I stretched as far as the heart monitor leads would allow until I'd discovered the location of most of my injuries. The pain in my ribs overshadowed most everything else, but my head was a close second. I leaned forward on the bed until I could see myself in the mirror that hung over the tiny sink in the corner. My left eye was a shade of magenta I'd never seen in a bruise before, and my head was wrapped in bandages and covered in a gauzy hat. I pulled at the itchy chin strap that held the hat in place. I looked ridiculous. The top of the hat was knotted in such a way as to give me an overall sock monkey look. All I needed were some button eyes and a tail.

I raised my left arm to find a capped off IV protruding from the skin of my mid-forearm. It was a precaution for seizure patients to chemically abort grand mal events. Apparently, they hadn't looked at my medical alert bracelet closely enough. There was no aborting cataplexy.

"You're supposed to be lying down."

I jumped at the sound of Gabe's voice. I stuffed my heart back into my chest and gave him an exasperated look. "How's Seth?"

"Recovering from surgery." It wasn't exactly a detailed update on Seth's well-being, but something about Gabe's tone made me nervous to ask further questions.

"His leg?" I risked.

"A compound fracture and shattered ankle."

Tears pressed instantly at the swelling around my eyes. The pain almost took my breath away. Clearly, I needed an IV for aborting emotion. Gabe's voice was filled with a wrath that, luckily for me, had been beaten down by exhaustion. He braced his elbows on his thighs and leaned his head into his hands. I sank into the bed and went back to staring at the posters on the walls.

Some of the languages had recognizable letters, but many did not. I could read the French poster and the Spanish one. I knew enough about German to muddle through that one. There was an Arabic sign with its swooping series of fishhook Js and plentiful dots. I'd eaten at enough Chinese restaurants to correctly identify the Mandarin sign, but the rest may as well have been languages from another planet.

"Wow." I selected finally to break the silence. "Some of these languages are pretty wild."

Gabe looked up but didn't say anything.

"Look at that one." I pointed to a sign with words

that seemed to hang from a shelf. "Do you think they write upside down?" I chuckled in an attempt to lighten the mood.

"That's Hindi," Gabe murmured with barely a glance.

I looked from Gabe to the sign and then back at Gabe. My mouth curved around the word "how" and then switched to "where," then shaped at last around "when." "Since when do you know Hindi?"

"I know a few things, Miss Cultured."

Whoa, now it was biting sarcasm. This was a week of firsts for Gabe.

"Okay, Smarty Pants, what about that one?" I pointed to the weirdest sign I could find. Every word looked as though it were spelled out in coiling snakes.

"That's Lao," Gabe said tiredly.

My mouth hung open. I looked back at the walls. I found another one and pointed to it.

"Gujarati."

I was stunned. I pointed to another and another.

"Cambodian."

"Korean."

"Vietnamese."

My mouth was still hanging open when Dr. Suni came in and yanked the partially closed curtain aside. She nodded to Gabe and then eyed me for what felt like an eternity.

"Rescuing a cat from a roof?" She didn't even try to hide the suspicion in her voice.

I shrugged. "My cat likes to hang out on the widow's walk outside my window." I started strong. "He missed his step and was hanging from the gutter." My words trailed off when I realized they were making no impact at all.

"And your friend, he just decided to follow you out onto the roof?" I opened my mouth to deliver my not so carefully considered answer, but Dr. Suni just lifted her hand to stop me.

"And you." She fixed Gabe with her withering stare. "You were a part of this too?"

"No. Definitely not," he answered emphatically.

"Good man," was her reply.

"Listen." She whipped a pair of glasses onto her face and flipped through some papers on a clipboard. "Have you forgotten that you have a unilateral weakness of the balance center?" She turned her head and pointed through her ponytail of dreadlocks to the base of her skull where the balance center resides.

Again, I opened my mouth to answer and again she shushed me.

"You can barely keep your balance on a sidewalk, much less a roof, Z." She used my nickname, which meant that maybe she wasn't as angry at me as she seemed.

A nurse came into the room pushing a vitals cart. Dr. Suni handed the woman the clipboard and pulled a light pen from her pocket. She instructed me to look at her nose as she flashed the light in my eyes. Gabe left the room as she lifted my gown to check my ribs. I looked down at the dinner plate-sized bruise on my side and gasped.

"It's a doozy." She shook her head. "Two fractured ribs." As soon as she said it, the pain in my side doubled. "Unfortunately, there isn't much we can do for fractured ribs beyond pain management. They may heal faster than the contusion around your eye."

"Is that why I keep seeing double?" I asked, gently probing my swollen lid.

"Nope. That would be the concussion," she answered. I took a painful breath and blew it out slowly. The doctor gingerly checked my reflexes, then took the clipboard back long enough to make one more note. Then she turned a serious face back to me.

"Melisande." She took my hand in hers. "You are young, and your body is managing this autoimmune disease rather well, but—" She thought for a moment. "But we can't give your immune system any reason to react or it will attack you. This swelling—" She pointed to my eye. "This bruising—" She pointed to my ribs, then gently pulled my gown back down. "These are extreme immune responses that may trigger a full-on flare."

I shook my head. I couldn't face another flare. Not while ghosts were trying to kill me.

"And that means?" I hated to ask.

"That means you could lose what trace amounts of orexin you have left." My skin went cold at the mention of the neurochemical. Orexin is the chemical that paralyzes people when they sleep so they won't act out their dreams. It is also responsible for un-paralyzing people when they wake. A narcoleptic's immune system attacks orexin and the receptors that process it, causing sleep paralysis and cataplexy.

She gave my hand a gentle squeeze. "If you think your narcolepsy is bad now…it could get worse." Her words were soft, but they sliced through the last of my defenses. I felt my jaw loosen as fear ushered in a mild wave of cataplexy.

"You've got to be careful." She let go of my hand

and asked the nurse to take the IV out of my arm. I looked down to hide the tears welling in my eyes. I couldn't bear to think of my symptoms getting worse. I could take anything else but that.

"I'm going to keep you here overnight for observation, but you will need to take a few days to stay in bed and rest. It will take weeks to heal these wounds. Because of the concussion, you will be more of a fall risk than usual for the next few days. Have you got someone who can stay with you?" She blinked at me over her glasses. I blinked back.

"Yes," a rocky voice answered from the doorway. My left eye stung as tears welled again. My parents lived in Northern Virginia, and my sister was taking summer classes. I have lots of friends at the gallery, but they all have lives. I'm sure they would all offer to help if they thought I needed it, but I knew I wouldn't ask. I might not even have asked Josh, but that's the thing about a best friend—you don't have to ask.

"Okay." She smiled at Josh, who was still holding his position in the doorway. "The nurse will give you some home care instructions for concussions. You will need to stay with her and help her if she needs to get up. There will also be a checklist of questions to ask her every two hours. If she has difficulty answering the questions, then bring her back to the hospital right away."

"Will do. Thank you, doctor." Josh took a step in and shook Dr. Suni's hand.

"Have her call my office for a follow up in one week." Dr. Suni turned to me and winked. "Gardening," she whispered. "Just think about it." She smiled and whisked from the room.

Chapter Fourteen

Time is of the essence.

The next morning, I had my release form and was rolling my way toward the elevator in one of the hospital's wheelchairs. Seth wasn't so lucky. Gabe took me to his room in the critical care ward. Gabe explained that Seth would be there until tomorrow. Then they would move him to a regular room.

"They are watching for infection at the pin sites," Gabe explained. He had given me the update on Seth's leg last night, but when I saw it in person, it was much worse than what I had imagined. A metal carapace enveloped one side of his leg with metal rods piercing his skin at five gruesome points.

The critical care room was small and mostly filled with medical machinery. Matt sat in the only chair. We'd come down the back elevator, which allowed us to bypass the front desk. Otherwise we'd never have been allowed to visit Seth all at once. We crowded into the glass-walled room and listened to the doctor lecture us on how to call the fire department when faced with all things cat- and height-related. We also learned a few facts about falling that we hadn't known before.

Apparently, Seth's relaxed, feet-first body posture had saved his internal organs from injury. I couldn't say that it was lucky he'd been choked unconscious by a sadistic ghost right before the fall. I didn't think that would have been well received.

When Seth woke up, I couldn't have imagined his first words.

"Where is Lizbeth?"

I stared at him in confusion.

"Who is Lizbeth?" Gabe asked. The guys had filled Gabe in on most of the happenings last night, but no one knew who Seth was talking about.

Seth seemed to think about his question for a minute and then shook his head. "Never mind." Seth's voice was hoarse, and I could see the necklace of bruises circling his throat.

"Are you talking about the murderous ghost that nearly choked the life from you and then dropped you down a deep, dark hole?" I asked and stared at him in disbelief as Seth casually rubbed his eyes.

"I don't really remember. Are you sure that's what happened?" He stared back.

My mouth fell open.

"What do you remember?" I asked finally.

"I remember her perfume. She smelled like little, blue flowers. I mean, I could almost see the flowers in her hair. She was so beautiful...and her smile..." His voice trailed off.

"...was visible through the rotting hole in her cheek!" I finished his thought for him. Seth gave me a shocked look.

"Whoa," Gabe interrupted.

I didn't know how to react. I wanted to shake Seth, but I'm pretty sure that was not what you're supposed to do to post-op patients. "This is what they do! They...they make us all dreamy when we look at them!

171

They make us love them!" I turned to the others. "He's been—" I searched frantically for the right word, and nodded as I found it. "—enthralled just like me!"

Everyone looked at me like I'd lost my mind, but I hadn't. These corporeal ghosts had some sort of glamour that could turn us into doe-eyed worshipers. That woman had victimized Seth, but all he remembered was the smell of little, blue flowers. It was just the same as my first encounter with Edwardia. In the end, all I'd wanted to remember was her lilting voice and the song. I pushed the chords from my mind before they could take root again.

I pulled myself out of the wheelchair and stepped from the room. Surprisingly, no one stopped me. I was operating on very little sleep and even less self-control. My visual field glowed with afterimages, and my temper simmered at the edge of boiling. Those were two signs of fatigue that didn't lead anywhere good. I needed sleep. It was the only way I was going to heal, but I wasn't about to close my eyes until I'd made it behind my ward.

I sat in the nearest seat I could find and rested my head in my hands. I studied the tile pattern of the hallway floor for a few minutes while the guys talked. Someone with hospital socks that matched mine took the seat next to me. I assumed my good Italian wood-heeled sandals were still sitting in the cargo hold at the center of the abandoned Ghost Fleet. My work pants were now work shorts, and my dry-clean only blouse was now a tank top. I'd had to cut them off because of the slits the good Doctor had made in my clothing.

"Did they take your stuff too?" someone asked, and I looked up at the person who'd taken a seat next to me.

I was actually a little thankful for the afterimages the shiny floor had drawn across my sight. The young man was handsome except for the part of his head that was caved in.

"Car accident." He gestured, and I noticed that the fluorescent lights in the hallway passed through his hand. My heart began to pound, and it immediately made everything hurt. "Sorry to bother you, but I was asked to deliver a message." I blinked slowly as if it would reset my brain and I'd somehow understand what was happening.

"Colonel Grayford asks that you meet him at the Fresnel Lens at noon. He said it's urgent." The young man smiled, and I realized that he was younger than I thought, maybe not even out of his teens. I wanted to scream. I wanted to cry. I wanted to gather him in my arms, but if the nurses saw me do that, they'd haul me up to the ninth floor, which was reserved for psychiatric patients only. Instead, I nodded and looked back at the floor.

The young man stood to leave. I looked up at him again. "Thank you," I said. Before he could disappear, I reached out and took his hand. He stared at the place where our two hands touched. He felt almost solid.

"Is there anything I can do for you?" I asked.

He smiled sadly and then nodded. "Please tell them to have the brakes checked in the car. I wasn't driving recklessly. The brake pedal went soft." He pointed to a newspaper that had been left on the seat to the other side of me. It was open to an article about a deadly car crash.

I picked it up and gripped it in my hands. "Okay," I whispered, but he was already gone.

****

Josh escorted me home and made sure I was in bed before he left to fill my prescriptions at the pharmacy. It was almost noon, so after he'd left I pulled on some sweat shorts and did the best I could to tidy myself and get downtown. It was hot by the river. The pilings under the boardwalk radiated the odors of warm tar and fish brine.

The giant lighthouse lens at the center of the small seawall park threw rainbows in every direction as it turned on its pedestal. I didn't know much about the lens other than it had come from a lighthouse down river and now served as a historic marker. I waited in the heat, shielding my eyes from the rainbows. If the afterimages got any worse, I wouldn't be able to see. My nerves were frayed, my face looked and felt like I'd been in a boxing match, and I couldn't remember the last time I'd eaten. I sat on a bench and clacked my painting clogs together impatiently.

I kept my throbbing head down as people jogged by. Passengers loaded and unloaded at the ferry stop. The occasional dog walker passed by. It didn't feel right sitting out in the open like that.

I ran my hands through my tangled hair. What if it was a trap? Maybe the young ghost at the hospital had been ordered by Edwardia to mislead me. I stood to leave, and that's when I saw him. He wavered through the spectrum of light, appearing somewhere between blue and violet. He was an indigo dream. He bowed, and I floundered into a jerking curtsy. I shrugged my shoulders, and he flashed a very genuine smile.

"Thank you…" he started, but I talked over him. We chuckled nervously and tried again. This time he gestured for me to go first.

"How did you get away?"

"The battle went badly for Edwardia and the court. Thank you for your assistance, but maybe we should start with the evening previous." Colonel Grayford swept his hand toward the bench and waited for me to sit. I clamped an arm around my fractured ribs and lowered myself awkwardly. He perched, straight-backed, on the edge of the bench without leaning back.

"I think the extent of your injuries must be more than you are letting on, Ms. Blythe." The light of day brought a formality to his countenance that seemed natural to him and at the same time wrong for our acquaintance. The lush curve of his brow bent in sympathy as he took in the left side of my face. "It was a monstrous thing which happened to you," he whispered hotly.

"I'm fine," I assured him, but nothing escaped his notice.

"I must say, I was taken aback when I saw you at Edwardia's gathering. I had not known her to take prisoners before that night. When her intentions became clear, I could not stand idly by." He looked down at his hands.

Touch her. Kiss her. Take her.

"What?" I searched the space around us. I'd just heard something.

Grayford's eyes shot up, but his face was still downturned. The almost ashamed tilt of his head fought the eager searching of his eyes. "It is nothing. An intruding thought." His gaze lingered on my lips and then dropped lower.

"What do you mean?" I shook my head in

confusion.

Tear the garments from her flesh. Devour her.

I pushed to my feet so quickly, I fell forward. Grayford was there in an instant to stop my fall. His hands gripped my sides, and I felt the pressure of his fingertips as they slipped beneath the hem of my T-shirt.

"I'm so very sorry. It is my fault."

"What's your fault?" I looked into his handsome face.

"The Joining…when I took you from Edwardia's home…" Colonel Grayford frowned. He seemed to search for the right words. "The only way I could remove your body from that location was to possess it."

Possess her. Fill her. Make her beg.

I gasped as my brain lit on fire. A tidal wave of passion crashed over me. I staggered in his arms.

"It is an unavoidable side effect of sharing the same…space. Our, how do you say, neuro-pathways are aligned."

"Excuse me?" I shoved at the solid muscle beneath the loose fabric of his shirt and vest, which caused his hands to tighten.

Touch me. Find me. Slide your soft fingers along my…

"Stop!" Another wave of ardor rolled over me, and it was a powerful, aggressive, masculine thing. I'd never felt desire that way before.

"I am trying. It's harder when you are near me." Grayford lowered his head until the loose tendrils of his thick brown hair brushed my cheek. "I know it is a shameful intrusion."

I felt a tremor run through him where my hands

rested on his chest. It seemed as though he were concentrating. The alien weight of manly desire eased away. I was left breathless. Blood sang through my veins in the wake of his passion. How could his attraction be so strong? We'd just met. Thoughts spun to life in my aching head.

"Have we just met?" The question whispered from my lips as I contemplated that first time I saw him in the graveyard. He'd seemed so familiar. And again, in Edwardia's dining room. Something about him felt like home. Like a large gracious home with a sprawling porch and a view of the river.

"In a way," he whispered close to my ear.

I pulled from his grasp and backed away from him. "Have you…" My voice shook. "Have you…" I couldn't even formulate the words. I wiped at my arms as something viscous and violating clung to me. A thought. A feeling. It was the same feeling I had every time a ghost entered my personal space without permission.

Grayford's guilty look said it all.

"Melisande."

"No."

"It is not what you think."

"Isn't it?" I cocked my head and the rainbows swirled. "You've been near me…watching me. Haven't you?"

Grayford's chest rose as if he were breathing real air. "I am drawn to you, yes. I protect you. And sometimes—" He hung his head again. "—I keep you company when you are lonely."

"Can you hear my thoughts?" I asked abruptly. I wrapped my arms around my chest until the ache in my ribs became a stabbing pain.

"Not until now. The Joining…".

"The Joining," I repeated. "Don't you think you should have told me about this little side-effect? I mean, shouldn't I have been given a chance to decide if I wanted that to happen?"

"Melisande." He said my name again, and it was as sweet and tender as mimosas on a breeze. "There was no time."

I shifted from foot to foot until my legs shook with exhaustion.

"Please." Grayford gestured to the bench once more. I lowered myself to the very end of the seat. He perched on the opposite end and folded his hands in his lap.

Exhaustion spread through my brain as well as my body. I felt defenseless again. I was also acutely aware of my need for a shower. In an ordinary circumstance, I would never let a man see me like this, but apparently he'd seen me in lots of ways.

After a long moment of studying the grass at my feet, I took the opportunity to look at Colonel Grayford in the bright light of day. And he was amazing. His pale blue eyes were circled with a thoughtful line of darker blue. They seemed to give his words conviction and his ideas clarity. In fact, every one of his handsome features seemed certain and complete. I wondered if my impression of him was part of that ghostly glamour.

His long, brown curl had fallen forward over his shoulder when he'd taken a seat. Even in my fuming state, I fought the urge to twine my fingers in its silky length. An image of my hand tugging his hair washed over me. I felt the pressure of his teeth on my neck, the thrust of his tongue in my mouth. Was I leaning toward him? He seemed so close. His eyes ran along the curve of my cheek and followed the trembling line of my lips. My lashes fluttered low.

"It seems you must learn to control your thoughts as well," he whispered. His voice was breathy, and he suddenly seemed unsteady.

"I…I'm sorry." I flushed.

"And I am sorry for the intimate nature of our first meeting." His mouth said the words, but his eyes did not agree. He didn't reach for me, but I could tell that his fingers ached with the need to. I could feel it as surely as I could feel my own desire to reach for him. I wanted to respond to that apology in so many ways, but for once I chose silence. And a smile. Apparently, I'd chosen right, because he smiled back.

"What now? Does Edwardia come for me at nightfall?" I changed the subject abruptly.

"Edwardia could come for you now. The sun's energy makes it harder for us to keep the pieces of our selves together. It is, at once, a nurturing thing and a withering thing, our beautiful star." The corner of his mouth turned up, and I felt another mote of desire drift down the connection between us. He reacted instantly, closing his eyes as if to strengthen his resolve. "But it does not stop us—at least, not those of us who fully possess those pieces."

"I have so many questions." I shook my head in frustration. "I don't know where to start."

"And I will answer them all, but first we must ensure your safety." Grayford's voice was strong and authoritative. I ignored him and launched into my questions.

"Last night, Mr. Pratt spoke my name. How does he know me? What did he mean when he'd said I'd been called? Called to what? And those shining people last night...I've seen them before, in my dreams."

"There is time to explain all of this, but first, I must ask you to follow these instructions. I will escort you to Trinity Church where you will meet with Reverend Braidfoot. I believe he is in possession of an article that might serve to keep you safe."

"Braidfoot? Reverend Braidfoot?" My thoughts returned to the engraved print in the back of Mrs. Spruill's album.

"Yes. Are you familiar with the Reverend?"

"I've been hired by the church to paint his portrait." I waved my hands at the synchronicity of it. I was so fully down the rabbit hole now that I didn't even know how to react.

"Well, now is your chance to commit his features to your memory." Grayford took my hand in his. The thrill of that touch passed through us, but with a little concentration, we managed not to overwhelm each other with our visceral reactions.

"The hands of an artist," he whispered and lifted my hand to his lips. He kissed the place between my knuckles. His mouth was cooler and somehow less substantial than the last time he'd kissed me. It left an ache inside me.

"You feel different." The words slipped from my mouth as I thought them.

Grayford's lips curved into a smile that had no mirth. He tipped toward me and my heart sped up.

"I can conjure strength from certain energies. Heat lightning. Storms." He raised his hand to the giant lens behind us, but his eyes stayed on mine. "It lends a…firmness to my constitution."

My body clenched, and I heard gears grinding to a halt. I looked over my shoulder to see the lens drift to a stop. The kaleidoscope of rainbows cast by the lens came to a rest, draping streaks of color across our skin. Electric green striped his brow, and his cheek burned with an aqua aura. His pupils swelled, devouring the pale blue inner ring of his irises, leaving only the dark and hungry midnight outlines. Somewhere deep at the bottom of those twin wells a fire glowed. My hands shook with the need to touch him. The sharp blade of his jaw, the solid sweep of his nose…they were mine, all mine.

Grayford leaned an inch closer to me then hesitated. I inhaled sharply, and then his mouth was on mine. He pulled me into the kiss. The ache in my ribs was a distant annoyance as he licked the round swell of my bottom lip into his mouth. With one arm locked around me, he filled his other fist with my hair. Grayford forced his tongue deep into my mouth.

For one crystalized moment we were one mind, one body aching to know itself in a vast press of emptiness, and then, woefully, we were back in the park in our bodies again. Our thoughts returned, and Colonel Grayford's sense of propriety rejoined him. His lips hovered a second longer above mine, and then he straightened. I had to think for a minute before I could remember how to breathe.

"Time is of the essence," he whispered quickly, and a pained look crossed his face. Before we could lose ourselves again, he tugged his olive-green vest with newfound resolution, and his fingers grasped

mine. He pulled me gently to my feet.
"We must depart."

Chapter Fifteen

A manifest plan

Trinity's churchyard was bathed in dappled sunlight. I followed the church administrator's instructions and waited just inside the tower door for my guide. When the old man appeared bathed in the glow of stained-glass light, I couldn't be sure that he wasn't another of Portsmouth's ghosts. I guess, in my case, he'd be the ghost of strayed Episcopalians past. I prepared to have my "on again, off again" commitment to the Church flash before my eyes. My faith was strong, but my attendance was not.

As it turned out, he wasn't at all interested in judging the level of my faith. He was more a historian than anything else. I felt a little underdressed, but nonetheless, I enjoyed a second wind of energy as we drifted from memorial plaques to stained-glass windows. The brightly colored Civil War window turned his long white mustachios to cotton candy tendrils that quivered and bobbed as he read its dedication.

After a tour of the altar and a few pulls on the church bell's rope, I thanked him kindly for his time. He promised to save me a seat on Sunday and then left me in the back pew to wrap up my experience with a prayer. He propped the tower door open to let in the breeze and disappeared into the sunlight.

It wasn't long until I felt the icy presence of a ghost.

When I saw Reverend Braidfoot, my first thought was that this was the wrong ghost. Either that or Braidfoot had chosen the wrong career. The remnant standing in the aisle next to me was a firebrand, a soldier, a willing combatant in a war of ideals. His eyes were twin barrels, and his mouth was a trigger. He was anything but a man of God.

"Your most obedient servant, Ms. Blythe." The spirit bowed. Again, my legs locked halfway between rising from my seat and bowing. I wasn't sure what the proper colonial response to that was, so I just sort of went with a nod and a hello. That seemed to work.

"Pray, has the colonel explained the purpose of our meeting?" I couldn't help but smile. His manner of speaking was almost lyrical, but his voice was a well-used gravel road of sounds.

"He said you might have something that could keep me safe." I met his intense gaze.

"Indeed, for it is my understanding that you've joined the Battle." My head shook back and forth, but he took a seat next to me and continued. "As you are still of this Earth, you must be vigilant. One like yourself might be able to close the Door, but you are vulnerable. There are agents that will endeavor to thwart you." I threw my hands up and shook them wildly.

"What door?" I finally managed.

Reverend Braidfoot pointed both barrels at me. "Why, the Door to Hell, miss."

I took a breath and then forgot to exhale. My ribs

protested the sudden pressure.

Reverend Braidfoot gave me a moment while I searched the church with my eyes in an attempt to find my bearings. "This fair land has been burdened too long with pain and suffering. There have been too many wars, too many battles. The heart of this place bends into a well of turmoil. We few sentinels minister to the city as best we can, but we are of the past. We can slow the trend, but we cannot reverse it."

"What about the shining people?" The question raced from my mouth.

"The Angelics are our only defense, but they are few and the Enemy's legion grows."

"How..." I paused because what I needed to ask him was so important and I had no idea how to ask it or if I really wanted the answer. "What does any of this have to do with me?" There, I said it and with only the slightest quaver in my voice. The Reverend looked at me, and I felt the weight of his assessment. Did he think I was undeserving of this strange call to battle? *Well...I was.* I was entirely the wrong chick for the job. Someone had made a big mistake.

Braidfoot studied me as my mind filled with the same questions it usually asked when someone scrutinized me closely. *What does he see? A scared, broken girl?* But this time there was no defensive heat to my thoughts. I was scared. I was a broken girl. I'd never been able to speak to a priest about my disorder before. I'd never been able to ask someone of the cloth if God had made me this way on purpose, or was I a mistake? Or, even worse, was I not "God's own" as my baptism had promised? Tears filled my eyes, turning the church into a stained-glass blur around me.

"Am I cursed?" I whispered finally as tears pushed past my eyelashes, spilling down my face and splashing on my hands where they lay folded in my lap. The swelling around my eye burned and throbbed, and barely contained sobs hammered at my cracked ribs. The rough-hewn man sat beside me and waited as years of fear and unvoiced sorrows rushed to the surface and then overflowed. I cried like I'd never cried before. My ragged sobs echoed through the sanctuary as I let it all pour forth from me.

He waited as I expelled a lifetime of loneliness and rejection, uncertainty and shame. He waited while I cried for the terror-filled nights and the days of hiding what I saw and heard. He waited while I remembered the way my father's eyes changed when I finally gathered the courage to tell him. I cried for the way he never looked at me the same way again. I cried for lost friends and eroding confidence.

Reverend Braidfoot was silent as I rode a tide of grief that I hadn't even realized had begun to crest with recent events. It had taken a long time, but I had finally adjusted to the fact that my brain worked differently than others. But now, ever since the night I'd woken up in the hall of my apartment with William Grayford holding me in his tingling embrace, I was changed...worse...caught up in some kind of natural evolution of evil. I was just wrong somehow.

"No," was the Reverend's answer. He had waited until I'd regained control over my hiccupping breath and my zombie-like jaw had reattached to my face. Crying and cataplexy were an ugly mix.

"No?" I repeated numbly, wiping my face with the backs of my hands.

"No," he assured me and handed me an embroidered bit of cloth. I took it and stared at him through tear-soaked eyelashes, waiting for him to say more.

"You are not cursed. You are called." His young, almost strident voice had softened, and his tone changed to that of a much older man. When I didn't use the handkerchief he gave me, he took it and gently dabbed my cheeks. It was a strange interaction that left me feeling like a child.

"We cannot decipher the Heavenly Father's intentions, nor can we judge them. We must be steadfast in our certainty that He has a manifest plan for each of us that only His eternal eye can see." His voice was a salve on wounds both old and new. "You are fashioned for a purpose, Ms. Blythe, and your positioning here at the last gate cannot be mischance."

I swayed in the aftermath of my emotional outburst. My body felt loose and somehow lighter. I scoured Braidfoot's face with my searching gaze. His work-chiseled cheeks were tanned by a sun that had set hundreds of years ago.

"Why are you here?" I examined his clothes, his hands, his wavy, chestnut hair.

"It is the Father's plan for me. I fight with the rest to close the wound of the world."

"This Door…last gate?" I whispered. The ghost nodded. "Where is this Door?"

"The Hell Mouth lies at a crux of deep sorrows near the center of the city."

"And why is it so hard to close this Door?"

"Because it is being held wide by one we cannot reach." My blood chilled at his words. How could there be something so fearsome in such a beautiful city? Auschwitz, maybe, or a terrorist stronghold deep in a desert somewhere, but here in sunny Portsmouth, Virginia? A town where people still drank lemonade on their porches and waged war only on the honeysuckle that tangled along their back fences.

And yet, I'd seen it myself in dreams, a darkness spreading across the land. I closed my eyes as my mind raced across the landscape of my home. The waterways zigged and zagged through my thoughts—neighborhoods, businesses, parks spread out across my mental map. I searched the city with my inner eye remembering the feel of the land. There were places of light and beauty, but there were dark places too. Injured places. Places that turned from me as I looked at them.

"Arcadia Park." The words slipped from my lips. Pieces of dreams pulled together, knitting a heart of darkness that pulsed over an inland parcel of land next to the city's water tower. It was the site of the old wartime shipyard workers' homes built in the early 1940s. I'd driven past the sprawling site on many occasions, wondering where the houses had gone. The driveways were there. The streets were there, but nothing stood on the land except forgotten daffodils and abandoned roses slowly choking away beneath unkempt brush and weed trees.

"What happened there?" I asked, searching the chambers of Reverend Braidfoot's intense eyes.

"The land became unlivable." He dipped his head. "Too many battles, even before the Colonies arose. The weight of subjugation and despair poisoned the land so that evil begat evil. Each generation added to the defilement until it rotted beneath the homes that had been built upon it. The very air is afflicted with sorrow and rage. Those of us that remain safeguard the rest of the city from it as best we can, but there are agents of evil that feed the rift."

"Edwardia."

"Madam Landry." His brows furrowed. "She is tied to this place as surely as I, but for very different reasons. If she takes control of the seventh and last Gate, she will become the Seventh Devil…the one that ushers in the end of mankind." My hands shook. Reverend Braidfoot laid a tingling hand over mine, and a sense of peace washed over me.

"The days ahead will be harrowing, and your part in all this will be revealed, but you must never forget that He is with you. His eye never strays from you. If you let Him, He will guide you through this trial."

Fresh tears sprang to my eyes as his hand left mine. I had been given the assurance that "God was with me" my whole life, and who better to believe than one from the other side. Yet I couldn't help but wonder, in a guilty way, where had God been when the nightmares burned through me as a child? Where had He been when the whispers of ghosts terrorized me as a teenager? Where had my Savior, Lord Christ, been when the Shadow found me?

"I have been entrusted with a relic of special import." Braidfoot's hand disappeared into a pocket and he withdrew a small object attached to a thin chain. "The Catholic Church retains a collection of relics—remains, if you will—of the Saints of our Lord. It is believed that the physical pieces of these individuals are somehow imbued with the Grace that God once bestowed upon them."

The Reverend held the tiny glass vial up to the light so that I could see the ornate metalwork that enclosed the vial. "We, however, are Episcopalians," he continued with a raised brow. "Our relationship with the saints is slightly different. This—" he began, peering into the dark glass as he jiggled the vial. Something tiny clinked against the glass. "—this is a finger bone." My stomach lurched. "But not of a saint." His eyes shifted to mine, making note of my horrified look. "This is the remainder of one much like a saint, one much closer to this new land, one born of its roots and soil." I squinted at the ghoulish necklace, trying to make out its shadowy contents.

"This is the bone of a man whose courage and love surpassed all others of his kind." Braidfoot lowered the talisman and said, "Let me tell you the story of a young native named Chanco."

The priest went on to tell me what the world had been like during the time of the first colonies. His eyes lit with a gunpowder glow as he explained the trials of the first settlements and the colonists' uneasy relations with the native people. He described life in one of the first English settlements to thrive on the East Coast. The place of which he spoke was Jamestown.

As he described the Powhatan Indians and the various ways their homelands were impacted by the English settlers, images from childhood textbooks came back to mind. Visions of bloodthirsty warriors and peaceable Pilgrims were soon replaced by more accurate images of two peoples trying desperately to find a way to live together and still preserve their cultures.

Braidfoot's voice lowered as he told the tale of one

young Powhatan boy who walked the edge of two worlds, following the mandates of his tribe's leader while exploring a friendship with the pale newcomers.

There came a time when the leader of Chanco's tribe, who had tolerated the colonists' incursion into their hunting grounds, passed from the world and was replaced by a man full of anger and resentment. Threats flew from his arrow-tip tongue, and the tribe prepared for war.

"This new leader made a plan to salt Jamestown's earth with the blood of the colonists, and Chanco, who had grown to care for the newcomers, had a decision to make. He could easily turn his back on his new friends that had shared their lives with him, or he could disobey his leader and his kin and side with the colonists."

Braidfoot cupped the small reliquary in his rough hands. "Chanco, who had been taught that the pale people were evil and a plague on the land, stole into the settlement and warned them of the impending Powhatan attack. Hundreds fell in the battle, but in the end Chanco's warning saved thousands of lives." Braidfoot's eyes fixed on a place further back in time than I could imagine. "Those of us who honor Chanco's memory believe that his single act of mercy endures forever. This remainder still holds a bit of God's Grace. It cannot be undone by evil's machinations."

With that, Reverend Braidfoot held the charm out to me.

I hesitated for a moment. I think anyone would have. Something this important came with a lot of responsibility. What if I dropped it or lost it? Again, I felt the overwhelming sense that someone had made a big mistake in choosing me.

The Reverend stared at me and then at my hand as I raised it to the necklace. I cupped my palm under the tiny metal cage, and Braidfoot lowered it into my grasp.

Silence filled the church as I gripped the cool glass and metal enclosure. The small thing had almost no weight. Braidfoot's eyes glowed a cannon fire yellow as he watched the relic cupped in my palm. I watched it too. Was something supposed to happen? If the finger bone moved even the slightest bit, I was sure I would throw it so far and so fast that it would break the sound barrier. Luckily, nothing moved.

The Reverend met my eyes with a road-weary kindness and asked me to bow my head. I closed my eyes and lowered my head as Braidfoot's voice filled the church.

"Eternal God, in whose perfect kingdom no sword is drawn but the sword of righteousness, no strength known but the strength of love, so mightily spread abroad your Spirit, that all peoples may be gathered under the banner of the Prince of Peace, as children of one Father, to whom be dominion and glory, now and forever. Amen."

I opened my eyes and whispered, "Thank you," to the emptiness where Reverend John Braidfoot had just been. I stood and headed for the tower door. I didn't bother trying to remember the fervor in his hazel eyes and the frantic energy of his chestnut hair. They were etched in my brain forever.

Chapter Sixteen

I need to check out now.

Josh must have fed Bougie already because the big, black cat barely touched his half of the tuna can. I sat at my kitchen table and read Josh's note while I scraped the other half of the can onto some crackers. Josh's handwriting was a series of sharp vertical lines separated by conservative curves and circles. The letters were like him—calm and contained until you got to the things that he cared about. Then his words were slashes meant to tear into the truth at any cost.

Mel,

Here's your medicine. The pharmacist said not to drive after taking it. He said a few other things too, but what's the point in repeating his instructions when we both know you won't follow them.

I waited for you. I don't know where you are. For all I know, you've been abducted again. I plugged your phone in. It needs another hour to charge.

This is crazy. All of it. You can't just disappear. These are dangerous people. We've got to get some distance from this. I have some money saved up. We could go on a vacation. Maybe just the two of us.

I'm going back to the hospital, then home to take a shower and eat. Please take the medicine and get some sleep. Call me if you need anything.

Josh

I fought to swallow the tuna around the lump in my throat. Bougie stared at me from the other side of the kitchen table. He blinked at me, then settled onto his favorite place mat. I read the note again. "…just the two of us." It had never been just the two of us. He had made sure of that. Was he telling me that he wanted that to change? And was that something I still wanted?

"Distance." What would happen if I got some distance? If Reverend Braidfoot was right, things had reached critical mass here. If Edwardia gained control of the Hell Mouth, she would become the Seventh Devil. The scales would tip, and our world would be lost to brutality and decay. If I left now, what would become of Colonel Grayford, Reverend Braidfoot, and all the souls that were, at this moment, putting themselves in harm's way to protect the rest of us?

I tried to stay focused on Josh, but another kiss swam into my mind, fresh and new and filled with a passion I thought I'd never know. I'd hoped Colonel Grayford would be waiting for me outside of the church, but when I'd emerged from Trinity's tower, he was gone.

"I'm no hero," I whispered to Bougie. His eyes had closed, and he'd begun to purr quietly. "But I'm not one to turn and run either." If Josh was willing to drop everything and leave, then that meant he was ready to abandon Ghost Towne Investigations and all the work he'd put into it. All our lives were turned upside down now. I needed to tell them everything. Right now.

****

I brought Seth a couple of barbeque sandwiches with coleslaw and hot sauce from his favorite restaurant plus an extra-large limeade. I ate his french fries. It was more than upsetting to see him lying in a hospital bed with metal protruding from his leg and a cast around his ankle.

I couldn't say that he was doing well, but he'd already made friends with several of the nurses. He was also on some top-notch pain meds, so it was safe to say things were on an upward trend.

Josh and Matt had gone home to shower and eat, and Gabe had ducked out for coffee. I sat next to Seth's bed while the nurse checked his blood pressure and his IV drip. I noticed that she touched him a lot. He didn't seem to mind.

"They treating you well?" I asked sarcastically, once the nurse had left.

Seth shrugged. "What can I say?" He grinned and crossed his hands behind his head. "I'm hoping for a sponge bath later." He winked.

On the outside, I shook my head in amused disapproval. On the inside, I cried with joy to hear him say something so Seth-like. I knew I'd never get the image of him motionless on the cargo bay floor out of my head. All I could do was build new memories with him and pile them over the thoughts of that horrible night until one day, hopefully, I'd lose sight of it. He must have seen what I was thinking because he reached for my hand.

"I'm okay," he reassured me, but his voice was soft. It was his "all jokes aside" voice.

I tried. I really tried not to cry, but it just came pouring out of me again. The cracks in my ribs stabbed me with each sob, but I couldn't hold it in any longer. I laid the bruised side of my head on his good leg and put his hand against my face.

"I'm sorry, Seth," I cried, and he smoothed my hair until I'd gotten it all out of my system. Streaked mascara was turning into my signature look. "I was supposed to go alone."

"I can't let you have all the fun," he joked gently, and I loved him for it.

"We're done with the fun for now, okay?" I gestured at the contraption that held his leg elevated.

"Agreed under one circumstance."

"And what circumstance is that?" I dabbed my face with a tissue from the box on his over-bed table.

"Don't blame this all on Lizbeth." Seth waved at his leg and his bandaged head. I went very still. "Mel, I know what it looked like. It looked bad, but Lizbeth said that Edwardia was going to kill us. She did what she thought would save me."

"She choked you unconscious!" I shouted.

"It worked. I'm still alive."

"She's affected your mind, Seth. She's made you believe that she's your heart's desire."

"It's not like that."

"Isn't it? You think about her all the time, don't you?" He didn't answer, which was answer enough. "You are trying to think of ways to see her…be with her. I know, Seth. It happened to me too, first with Edwardia, then with…"

"Colonel Grayford," he whispered. We looked at each other for a long moment. I felt sick. We sat in silence, listening to the beeping of Seth's heart monitor.

"Let's just take a step back for a second." Seth put his hands up to hold back time for a minute. "We've spent years searching for a trace, any trace, of life after death…and we've finally found it." Seth's eyes were filled with a knowledge that was too profound to process. "There are sentient beings that have found a way to exist between worlds. They are pieces of our history trapped in some kind of multiphasic amber. This is an amazing discovery."

"This is a dangerous discovery," I corrected.

"Mel, we have to document this. Mankind needs to know about them. The fact that there is awareness after death is life-altering…faith altering. I mean, what can these entities tell us about God and the universe?"

"I don't think most of these entities have even a passing acquaintance with the Heavenly Father, Seth. I hear you. I do. This information would be a real game-changer for people, but it would be a game-ender for us. If these ghosts wanted a public profile, they'd already have social media accounts. They are smart and capable and seem to have very loyal and very discreet members of the living to help them. Don't you see? We can't say anything, at least not yet."

"Shouldn't we put that to a vote?" he replied.

"We can vote, or you can trust me. There is something much bigger going on here than just a few hauntings." I struggled to find the words to describe all that I'd learned about the Battle that raged around us.

"There's so much I need to tell you. I just don't know where to start. I don't even understand it all myself." The medicine the doctor had given me for pain was wearing off and my head felt, well…cracked open.

"Just start anywhere, and we'll help you figure it out," Gabe said from the doorway behind me. He leaned on the door frame holding a latte. He seemed calm and concerned and as ready as he'd ever be to hear the truth.

I thought about how different our two perspectives were. I asked myself if I were in someone like Gabe's shoes, would I really want to know? I couldn't begin to calculate the consequences of such knowledge, but I could try and calculate the effect it would have on my friend. Gabe gave me the time I needed to work it out in my heart as well as in my head. I turned back to Seth. Gabe came in and shut the door.

****

"How much did Matt and Josh tell you?" I asked them finally.

"They said there were ghosts…lots of them on the ship," Gabe began. "They said some of them looked normal and some of them weren't put together right. Like only parts of them had manifested." Gabe seemed to have had some time to process the information.

"Josh said that you can control them. Is that true? He said that you were…changed," Seth asked calmly.

I started to answer him, but I didn't know exactly what to say. I needed to talk to someone about it all. I needed to get it out where someone else could try and make sense of it.

"Ever since I was a little girl, I'd always felt like there was another side to everything. I was sure it was there…like I was seeing it, but just not with my eyes."

I remembered the sensation. I remembered asking my parents and later my sister if they felt it too, but they'd never seemed to understand what I was talking about.

"As I grew up, I learned to accept that other people didn't feel it. They didn't hear the voices or catch the glimpses of things moving around us. It wasn't really until I was diagnosed with narcolepsy that I realized what being in the hypnogogic state meant."

I twirled the streak of white hair at my temple nervously. "Working with you guys has been the best experience of my life. Accepting the way my brain works and putting it to use has been the best medicine for dealing with my disorder.

"But everything I'd experienced in my life didn't really prepare me for Edwardia. I know I seemed okay after the cemetery encounter, but I wasn't. I felt vulnerable and scared of the unknown again, like I did as a child." I worked it out as I spoke and the guys listened.

"That's why I wanted to investigate the very next night. I realized that the one thing that always made me different and isolated from everybody else was also the one thing that made me special. I couldn't let her take that from me." I inhaled and blew my breath out slowly. "Boy, was that a mistake. I'm pretty sure I would have been killed at that party if Colonel Grayford hadn't helped me."

"Not *the* Colonel Grayford?" Gabe choked on his coffee.

I nodded. "Here's the thing—" I paused, while I waited for the "thing" to make sense, but it would never make sense, so I decided to just keep talking. "When Colonel Grayford took me from the party...he did something to me."

Seth pressed the button on the bed that brought him to a sitting position. "What do you mean by 'something'?" His heart monitor started to beep faster.

"I don't know how to explain it, but it was as if he moved us outside of space rather than through it." I felt like a little girl again, trying to explain seeing without seeing. "One minute I was at the party, trying to get away from Edwardia, and then the Shadow showed up. The next thing I knew, I was in my apartment."

"Did you fall asleep?" Gabe asked, holding his coffee in a frozen position halfway to his mouth.

"No...well, yes. I was just on the verge of sleep when the Shadow found me. It spoke to me, and then I woke up in my hallway."

"The Shadow spoke?" Seth repeated my words.

"Yes."

"What did it say?" Gabe asked.

"I don't know. It rarely speaks at all, but when it does, it's like the words just slide off my brain."

Seth's monitor kept a brisk beat as the guys shared a worried glance.

"It doesn't really matter now about the Shadow. I got away. It tore a path through Edwardia's party, though. The ghosts seemed as afraid of it as I am. Anyway, when I woke up, Colonel Grayford was there, and I felt...different."

"Can you describe what's different?" Seth asked.

I searched for the words. "It feels like the crackling of an open connection when you end a phone call on a land line but don't hang up. I think ghosts are at the other end and they're waiting for me to...speak." Saying it out loud sent a shiver down my spine.

"This is something Josh and Matt need to know about," Gabe said. Josh and Matt...I didn't know where to start with them.

"Was Josh right? Can you control ghosts?" Seth asked again. Everything I'd just said was leading me to this answer, but I was still working it out for myself.

"I think whatever is different now…it allows me to—" I tried a few words out in my head. "—command them." We all stared at each other.

"Josh…" Gabe rubbed his forehead and laughed. "Josh said something about chains."

"I don't know what that's about," I said in a rush. "To me it feels like I'm just exerting my will to make them stay with me. I can feel the stronger ones fighting me and some—" I looked at Seth and then dropped my eyes. "—I can't make a connection to at all."

"I remember…" Seth's voice sounded distant. "I remember ice. Lizbeth. There was a sting, and she dropped me." Seth looked up from the garbled memory.

I shook my head. "She was holding you by the throat. You weren't breathing. I tried to stop her…get her under my control, but I couldn't." His eyes held a hint of accusation. "Seth, she dropped you and pulled me in too." The numbers on his heart rate monitor were climbing.

"It sounds like a lot was happening in a short space of time," Gabe offered magnanimously. "Let's just take a breath and try to absorb all of this." Gabe sucked in the stale hospital air and blew it out. "So what do we know? We know that some kind of encounter with a spirit has changed Mel's…abilities. We know that there are ghosts here in Portsmouth that don't want us interfering with their business. We know they can hurt us. I say, we take a little time off. The internet is going nuts. Our latest video had almost forty thousand views this morning. It's been radio silence from us.

"I know the nature of our published footage seems unremarkable given what's happened since, but people still want to hear from us. We already have a dozen requests for podcast interviews." He looked from Seth to me. "We have options. With Mel's new tricks, we can ghost hunt anywhere. We can literally take this show on the road. Seth, you've always said that you want to work with the Psi Channel. Let's take a few videos. We'll be careful not to mention the names of real deceased people. We'll send them to a few networks."

I held my hand up. Gabe stopped talking.

"There's more," I said.

"More?" Gabe and Seth asked in unison.

"Yes." I took a big breath and pulled the necklace from my shirt. Their eyes followed my fingers to the capsule and its grisly contents. "When I got home from the hospital today, I met with someone, a priest." I shook my head. "Apparently, what was said about me at the Ghost Fleet is true. I've been called to…battle."

Gabe swallowed the gulp of coffee in his mouth loudly.

"Uh, what battle?" Seth asked calmly.

"The battle to stop the Seventh Door to Hell from opening here in Portsmouth."

Seth took one look at me and one look at Gabe then pressed the call button.

When the nurse's voice answered, Seth said, "I need to check out now."

Chapter Seventeen

Amusement park rides and a gauntlet of light

Josh and Matt met us at the hospital and helped Gabe get Seth into the van. The doctor refused to issue the release papers. Seth was nowhere near ready to leave the hospital. We all knew that, but Seth wouldn't listen to reason.

The nurse did her best to explain how to care for Seth's surgery sites. She ran out to the van just before we pulled away and handed us Seth's prescriptions.

"Elevate! And absolutely no weight on the leg!" she practically cried. Seth's face had taken on a gray tint again, and he'd broken into a cold sweat as we lowered him into the back seat of the van.

"This is a bad idea," Gabe kept saying over and over under his breath.

By the time we made it to Josh and Matt's house, Seth's shirt was drenched in sweat. We got him inside the house and on the couch, and then we all exhaled. I went to the kitchen and poured Seth a glass of water. When I walked back into the room, everybody looked at me.

"Mel, you need to bring Josh and Matt up to speed, and this time don't skip the details." Seth's voice was weak, but his face was all business. I handed him the glass and sat in the chair next to the couch. How was I supposed to explain what I didn't understand myself?

Josh pulled his chair next to mine and took my hand in his. I stared at his hand in shock, then gripped it tightly.

"Start talking, girl," he said, so I did.

****

"This makes no sense. There's nothing in Arcadia Park but empty lots and overgrown hedges." Matt wiped his fingers through his curls until his hair began to frizz. "I think someone from Housing and Development would have noticed a doorway to Hell on the city's grid."

"I don't know, Matt." I returned the sarcastic tone. "I won't know until I get a look at the site."

The room exploded with sound as everyone talked at once. Everyone was, pretty much, saying the same thing. "*YOU'RE NOT GOING THERE.*"

So, with that I started the show and tell portion of the class by lifting the necklace from around my neck and handing it to the guys. They each were hesitant to touch it at first, but after taking it in their hands, they rolled it around, examined the dark glass, testing its weight. Gabe even smelled it. Josh was the only one who refused to touch it.

"I can barely see anything. That could be a stick in there for all we know." Matt squinted at the reliquary. "How do you know it's not a stick? No, really?"

I rolled my eyes. Matt stood to pass the necklace back to me, and that's when we heard it.

Ordinarily, when you hear a knock at the door, you don't wait for another, you just head for the door to see who's there. But this knock was different. No one moved. No one had to because the next sound made it clear that the door would stay closed.

A long scratching sound started at the small, semi-circular window at the top of the door and dragged down its metal length almost to the weather strip at the bottom. The sharp, tinny noise froze us in place. We couldn't have moved if we'd wanted to.

My heart pounded against the crack in my ribs, and when the first blade-like finger sliced through the metal door, I sucked in a breath and slumped to the floor as cataplexy washed over me. I heard shuffling and male voices drenched in fear. A low, vibrating moan filled the room, and Gabe's boots came into view. Josh pulled at my limp arm and dragged me to him. Everyone crowded in front of the couch. From where I hung, I could only see their feet, but I could tell that they'd put themselves between Seth and whatever was coming through the door.

A sucking sound accompanied the moan as something large pulled itself through the particles of Josh and Matt's front door.

"Oh, God." Matt's voice was high and drained of reason as the entity strained against the threshold. Josh knelt and pulled me across his lap, turning me toward the front hall that opened into the living room. He gripped me so tightly that what little breath I could take in had nowhere to go and my ribs screamed in agony.

"What is that?" Gabe's voice teetered on the edge of insanity as he tried to make sense of the twisted limbs and knotted fabric that pulled free of the door.

"Lizbeth," Seth whispered as he peered around Gabe's legs. The rumpled mass of frost blue skirts and peeling skin reconstituted as we stared into the visage of a young, auburn-haired beauty from another time.

Her pale eyes searched the room until she caught a glimpse of Seth.

"No," Gabe mustered weakly as Lizbeth took a step toward Seth. The apparition turned astonished eyes to the big man. Her covetous look turned my blood to ice water.

"He is mine," she whispered in her child-like voice, and the whisper seemed more horrifying than if she'd shouted it. She hovered over the hooked rug that reached out from the living room floor to the front hall. Her eyes moved nervously from Seth to the door. "Do as she says," Lizbeth ordered hurriedly. I caught Seth nodding numbly in my peripheral vision, and then Gabe moved in front of him.

I struggled against my paralyzed muscles as the front door seemed to bend inward. Spidery fingers reached through the painted metal and fastened on the curved newel post at the bottom of the stairs. The wooden banister cracked under pressure as a tangled mass of black lace and green velvet forced its way through the door. A wet whisper threaded through the hall as Edwardia made her entrance. Josh shook as Edwardia's body pulled together, rebuilding into the very essence of feminine beauty.

Her teeth clicked into place, and her ruby lips curved into a heart-melting smile.

"What a lovely home you have." She inclined her head, but her ravenous eyes never left us. "You know, this was once the countryside." She giggled demurely. "It was long ago, and a creek ran just behind." She gestured languidly. "It was wide enough for a paddle boat, but now its waters have found new beds down which to roam." Her voice was a charming peal of bells that threatened to stir the song to life in my head. No sooner had I thought it than her voice found me in its intimate way.

"My Beautiful Dreamer." Her voice caressed. "Fallen into sweet slumber again." A new wave of fear crept over me, and my jaw separated. I tried to turn my head as she moved toward me. "Let me help you with that," she whispered close to my ear, and Josh's arms tightened around me. A moment later they loosened as a delicious warmth washed through my body. Josh exhaled, and I felt his muscles relax. I knew what was happening, but I couldn't do anything to stop it.

Frost blue skirts swayed impatiently at the far end of the room as Lizbeth appeared to shift her weight from foot to foot above the floor. The look on her face was chilling as she watched Edwardia drift from man to man.

Edwardia started with Seth. She hovered over him like a beautiful death shroud, pinning him to the couch. She whispered his most secret desires to him as he struggled. Lizbeth's hands clenched. Seth's mind was usually a complex system of moving parts. He could disassemble and reassemble intricate machines by memory. He could make projections and trace trajectories that left us all scratching our heads like monkeys. If something complicated needed thinking through, we all usually stepped aside and let Seth handle it. He put up a valiant fight, but in the end even Seth succumbed to the mindless rush of hormones that Edwardia flooded through him.

Gabe was next. He leaned against the wall on shaky legs as the painfully beautiful ghost drifted toward him. She toyed with him more than she had with

Seth. I smelled Gabe's fear. Edwardia sipped it like a fine wine. He broke out in a sweat as she drew a velvet-gloved finger across his lips.

"I didn't think they made men like you anymore." She chuckled. The sound slithered through our minds like a silk whip. She waited until his eyes began to glaze with shock, and then she triggered his limbic system. His breathing went from shallow to deep and hard.

"How lovely you are. I do hope you die young, so I can add you to my collection." Edwardia tittered and turned to Lizbeth. "Maybe I should kill him now and take him with us." A cruelly approving smile slid across Lizbeth's face. If she was upset about Seth, she hid it well.

Matt had found the strength to inch toward the front door, but Edwardia caught him in her sensual snare. I watched in horror as Matt's eyelids grew heavy with bestial thoughts. His handsome face curved into a mask of all the dark things he could become. She twisted his desire with her delicate fingers, sculpting a creature of violence and possession.

I tried to look away and finally felt my neck muscles respond, but the dark snake moved toward me again. She'd saved the best for last.

Edwardia watched me with her moonstone eyes as she twined her fingers through Josh's long, sandy-blond hair. She unwound the tiny braids that reached back from his temples to keep the rest of his hair in check. The unruly waves fell forward over his cheeks, giving him a feral look.

"There. Isn't that better, Melisande?" She winked at me. "Now he's irresistible." She stroked his cheek.

"His thoughts are already doused in desire. He only needs a tiny nudge." I twisted in Josh's lap. With her last word, Josh's body tightened. His jaw tipped, and his eyes burned.

"Why are you doing this?" I pleaded as I fought the cataplexy for control.

"My Beautiful Dreamer…you owe me a meal." Edwardia's voice had gone dark and predatory again. The purr had turned to a growl. "Don't worry. I'll make sure you enjoy it too." With that, a liquid heat ran down my skin. A warm tingling crept across my tender spots.

I turned to the men—my friends, the people that meant the most to me. Their eyes slid across my skin, beneath my clothes. I could almost taste the lust overwhelming their thoughts. Their hands trembled as though the need to touch me overpowered them.

My body responded to that need. I pressed against Josh. It was the only move I could make. At least, I knew that Josh's attraction to me was real.

I clutched his shirt as my muscles awakened. I straddled his lap. I clamped my legs around his hips. Our eyes met and then our mouths, and I was drinking him in. I knew that we were under Edwardia's spell, but his mouth tasted right. His hands felt right in my hair, trailing down my skin, delving beneath my clothes. A thin membrane of restraint tore inside Josh's mind, and he was on me. He gripped me and forced me backward to the floor. Clothes ripped as we tore at each other. I exposed the pale steel of his muscles. He was hard to the touch as though he were chiseled from milky marble.

He ripped my shirt in half, revealing the quivering spill of my breasts. I had a demi-cut bra on that barely contained them. I heard a low growl from somewhere behind me. I turned to see Matt moving toward me. He stepped on the talisman he had dropped on the rug and I heard it crack.

Edwardia giggled from the place where she hung suspended just below the ceiling. She was clearly enjoying the show.

Lizbeth inhaled sharply and an urgent, pain-filled sound turned my head back to the couch. Seth was attempting to sit up.

"No," I cried, but Josh flattened his body against mine and his hungry mouth closed over my lips. I would have kicked away sooner, but Josh pushed the stony length between his legs against me and I cried out with need. Audience or no audience, I'd waited too long for this. I needed Josh in me like I needed air in my lungs.

Another pained sound broke from Seth's lips, and I watched as he threw his injured leg over the side of the couch. I had to stop him. I couldn't fail him again. Though I was loath to do it, I channeled my energy and pushed Josh off me. I got my feet under me and launched toward the couch.

Seth and I crashed together, and my momentum pushed us down onto the couch. His silky hair spilled around us. He had been struggling to reach me, so I did the only thing I could. I came to him. His arms wrapped around me and I remembered how I'd felt when we'd first met. I had been as doused in Seth's glamour as any other red-blooded woman.

Carefully, I lifted my leg over his cast and placed my knees on either side of his hips. I stared into his mirthful, carefree eyes and was shocked to see his pupils blown out with mindless desire. His face was wracked with pain and passion, swirling into one sinister potion. His skin was covered in a fresh sheen of sweat. The need to lick that sweat from his skin was overwhelming. I tried to restrain myself, but he reached suddenly and pulled me into a kiss that I would never forget. Seth kissed with his whole body. He kissed with the confidence of a truly amazing lover. Seth was as advertised...delectable.

One second, I was lost in the amusement park ride that was Seth's embrace, and the next I was lifted into the air, suddenly looking down on the couch from what seemed like a far distance. Strong arms clasped me around the waist. Rough hands turned me in the air. My feet never touched the floor as Gabe pulled me from Seth. Worry and hunger warred across his dusky face as he looked from Seth to me.

If Gabe had ever had feelings for me, he'd kept them strictly under wraps. But now that he'd intervened for the sake of his friend, now that he held me in his arms...I felt Edwardia drift closer as I molded my body to the front of Gabe's. His boulder muscles clustered under his skin as he tried not to crush me. At that moment, I wanted the crush. I wanted everything his giant body could offer. He read it on my face, in my lowered lashes, in my parted lips. I squirmed against him, and a low rumble issued up from the barrel of his chest.

His breath was heavy as it heated my neck. He leaned his forehead against mine, and it felt almost like an apology. His left hand reached for my buttocks and I complied, lifting my leg. Gabe pulled me up onto his bulging groin and trapped me against the wall. I clamped my legs around his waist and cried out. I'd just found the biggest ride at the amusement park, and I wanted to ride it over and over. And I would have if something strong and solid hadn't slammed into Gabe from the side, breaking our lusty lock on each other.

Matt's face was a frenzy of emotion as he slammed into Gabe again. Gabe put a warning hand out to his feverish friend, but Matt was beyond reason. What had Edwardia done to him? His lush curls had gone wild, and his perfect face was pulled tightly into a grimace. His burning eyes darted from Gabe to me. He was clearly not feeling the same thing we were.

I stepped away from them both, but Matt's hand clamped onto my wrist like a vise and I cried out in pain. At that, Josh was up and moving. He nearly ran through me in his effort to get to Matt. The air simmered in the room and when Josh's hand locked on Matt's arm, it suddenly reached its boiling point.

Matt's other arm flew out, and his fist cracked hard against Josh's jaw. I stumbled away from the impact as the brothers locked together in a wrestling match of brutal force. Before I could get clear, their struggle knocked me to the floor. A sliver of something sharp tore at my arm. I looked down to see the crushed reliquary with its withered relic still caught inside the metal casing.

I pulled the glass from my arm and locked my hand around the necklace. The tiny bone spilled into my hand. Someone grabbed me from behind and tore at my shorts. I heard fabric rip as I was yanked backwards. My hip suddenly burned with a fiery trail of nail marks.

Gabe was shouting and someone crashed into the side table, sending the lamp to the floor. The light bulb exploded next to me, and the room was consumed in shadows.

I rolled over and my eyes went to the fiendish sight that hovered above the melee. Edwardia drank in the violence and lust in an attempt to quench her insatiable thirst. Only Seth had looked up to see the nightmare that hung above them. The others were unaware as they clashed and rolled beneath her spidery fingers.

Edwardia's mouth was wide as our life energy slipped through the ether toward her. Lizbeth lingered on the threshold of the room, seeking a way to Seth. Her ethereal silhouette cast an equally dark shadow on the room.

I raised my hands to my face in an attempt to block the horror, and I realized my hands were empty. I'd dropped the finger bone. I flipped over and scrambled onto my knees. I felt along the hooked rug, searching for anything hard and small. Someone rolled over my ankle twisting my foot sideways. The pain added to my panic. I slapped my hands against the floor and flung my arms out, making snow angels on the rug. Finally, my pinkie clicked against something small and stick-like.

I latched onto the finger bone and pulled myself into a tight ball as bodies rolled into me. I caught a glimpse of Josh's bloody face as I was knocked aside, and just like that the fear left me. Blessed anger washed my brain clean. It inflated my lungs and filled my limbs with strength. I looked at each of their faces and the straining lines of insanity that redrew them. Blood dripped from Matt's fingers and Gabe's mouth. Seth's jaw clenched in pain, and Josh's shirt had been torn away to reveal muscles straining past their limits.

I looked up at the woman-shaped stain stretching across the ceiling of Josh and Matt's charming arts and crafts bungalow and hatred burned through me with an incandescent light. My eyes burned with the phosphorus of it. I stood and Edwardia turned her ravenous gaze to me. Her gaping maw pulled into a hellish grin.

"Lizbeth." The one-word order scraped across the air. And without hesitation, in a twirl of shimmering skirts, the sublime spirit of Edwardia's constant companion tore through the air with blackened nails stretching for my throat.

In the blink of an eye, Lizbeth's face twisted into a mask of loathing. It happened so fast that I realized she must harbor that contempt at every moment of her existence. Her disdain for the living was not blindly summoned. Lizbeth had true scorn in her eyes. Whatever humanity Seth thought he'd seen in this vicious ghost was glamour only.

I thrust my arm before me and felt the tiny sliver of bone press into my palm. It warmed my hand and then my arm. It crept past the clenched muscles of my shoulder and chest, and I felt my rage draining away.

I panicked.

This was not what I'd expected. I'd expected fire and brimstone or a sparkling shield to just appear and stop the specter rushing toward me. I'd expected a lightning bolt or anything else, but the feeling of peace that spilled through me like warm honey. In the second it had taken Lizbeth to cross the room and throw herself at me, my mind had stilled, my heart had slowed, and a profound sense of perspective widened my being until I felt as though I filled the room. My awareness swelled, taking up every inch of space until I'd become one with everyone and everything in the living room except for Lizbeth and Edwardia.

I realized, in the slowness of time, that this is what had saved those colonists in a sweltering summer forest so long ago. This residue of Grace that still remained even after Chanco himself had moved on to the light of God, this echo of glory would save us all now.

So it was with a distant sense of shock and surprise that I watched as Lizbeth thrust herself at me, arms closing, fingers curving to do their worst, and then she passed through me. Or more to the point, I passed through her. My outstretched hand punched through feathery flesh and I both saw and heard fabric, skin, and bone tear around my arm.

The shredding pieces of Lizbeth shaped around me as she impaled herself on my outstretched arm. I gasped as my eyes met hers in one final glance. The withering heat of her stare banked as she looked from my wide eyes to her chest and the arm that protruded from it.

"No!" Seth shouted, and the sudden wave of horror that washed over him swam through my newly expanded mind. The agony of it twisted my gut, and I yanked my arm from the dust of Lizbeth's body. She whispered something high and soft in her innocent voice and her face began to cave in. Her lips peeled away from rotting teeth and her skin crumbled from her skull. A malevolent look crossed her dimming eyes and then, with a fluttering exhale, she slipped from the world.

I backed against the wall as Seth shouted, but the silent benediction that emanated from the relic in my hand had caught us all in its soothing snare. It quieted

Seth's raging heart and softened his wails. It eased the fever in Matt's eyes and relaxed Gabe's grip on Josh's throat. Josh surrendered to the blessing and collapsed to the floor.

Plaster streamed from the ceiling in powdery wisps as Edwardia knit herself together. Her black-booted feet folded toward the floor until she stood before us, no longer a mind-numbing nightmare, but a woman slight, graceful, and becoming. She stared at me for what seemed like an eternity. Then she stared at the talisman in my hand.

"My Dreamer is filled with surprises," she whispered in a tone quiet enough to hide her true feelings. She seemed to size something up for a moment, and then she took a step. Plaster cracked along the walls. She took another step, and the beam above the living room entryway splintered. She took another step and every wall-mounted picture in the room crashed to the floor.

If I hadn't been holding a tiny piece of God's Grace in my hand, I imagine I'd have been pressing a Mel-shaped dent into Josh and Matt's living room wall right about then. But that's not what I did. Instead, I pushed away from the wall and took a step toward Edwardia.

I lifted my hand and took another step, and my expanded awareness allowed me to feel every bit of fear the guys felt for me before the bone stole it from them.

Edwardia's moonstone eyes flashed with danger.

We met in the middle of the room, maybe as equals, maybe not. But there was one thing I was sure of...I was no longer a toy. I could see it on her coldly beautiful face.

I lifted the finger bone and held it between us. As I did, the supple velvet of Edwardia's dress withered away in a wide swath, exposing the even more supple skin of her right shoulder and teacup breast.

She smiled.

I moved my hand an inch closer to her, and that milky skin began to crack and peel. My nose filled with the stench of death. Before I could even register it, much less react, Edwardia's left hand whipped out and smacked me across the cheek. The pain of it shocked me as my head whirled sideways.

I turned back to her with disbelief and unveiled anger. I shoved the finger bone against her, and her flesh imploded. Edwardia grinned as her body shriveled. Tissue shrank and blood evaporated until she was little more than a skin-covered skeleton dressed in the frayed remains of her death shroud.

Anger slipped from me like water in the presence of Chanco's bone, but a large part of me still hoped it hurt. I'm no saint. I wanted this bitch to suffer.

I stood toe to toe with the leathery corpse. I steeled myself as her craggy lips split into a savage smile.

My cheek burned where she'd clawed my face, but I didn't reach for the injury. Instead I tipped my face away as the shade of Madam Edwardia Landry stepped into me. I felt bones pressing against the knuckles of my closed fist as she pushed against me. I pushed back until my arm was almost inside her chest cavity.

By that point, all the trappings of humanity had fallen away from Edwardia and she stood before us in her true form. Seemingly a collection of blacked bones, claws, and teeth, Edwardia had imploded, but not in a debilitating way. This entity before me was a neutron star of energy. Power cascaded off her in invisible waves, sickening the flesh and confusing the mind. I stepped away from this new horror as my stomach turned. Edwardia's feral eyes followed me.

"Am I to surmise that you do not care for this form?" she quipped, but her vocal cords had hardened, turning her lilting voice into something brittle and alien to the ear. "Well, you had better get used to it, Dreamer. When I open the Gate, my new form will be complete."

"The Seventh Devil," I whispered as I looked upon her sinewy body. She was lithe and horrid, deft and detestable. The thing that had once walked this world as Edwardia Landry was something beyond mankind's reasoning now. And it was too close for comfort.

I slid my foot backward in an attempt to put a little more space between us, but her hand shot out and caught me around the throat. My feet left the floor as she hefted me skyward. I heard the guys scrambling to get their feet under them, but I lifted my hand to hold them back. I clenched my neck muscles against the pressure of her finger bones, and my head began to swim.

"You will not interfere, or I will kill every person you hold dear and drag their souls through the Gate." Edwardia shook me like a rag doll for emphasis. I hooked my fingers between the bruising skin of my neck and her obsidian claws. I'd been without oxygen before and lived to tell about it.

I glared at her flashing, night predator eyes and coughed out, "I don't think so." She dropped me immediately and reached to the side. Seth's scream split the air as he was wrenched from the couch and dragged across the floor by an unseen force. Gabe reached for him, but the big man's reaction was too slow. Josh, on the other hand, was closer to me. Josh crouched and threw himself between Seth and Edwardia.

I made a decision and called Josh's name. Before he could object, I tossed the finger bone into the air. His eyes widened and his hand shot out. Josh caught the tiny bit of bone in mid-air and the whole room changed. My body tingled with a lightness of being I'd never felt before, and the weight of the world lifted.

"Josh," I breathed as I tried to make sense of what I saw. Seth had come to a stop in the tangled remains of the living room rug. Josh reached behind him with one hand on Seth and the other hand outstretched before him. He clutched the finger bone tightly inside the gauntlet of light that had formed around his fist and forearm. The whole room glowed with kaleidoscopic light. My newly regained breath caught in my throat as I looked at Josh. His bloody face was transformed in the light of the gauntlet. His whole being was transformed. His shimmering hair and golden beard suddenly looked knightly as they framed his strong face. I watched the fear melt from him as he stood and squared his shoulders. He was no longer a sketch of a man. He was complete.

A dark glee surged through me, filling up the spaces that Chanco's borrowed grace could not reach. I was expanding again, but in different directions. I felt my will roll out around me as oppressive as the July heat, but cold to the touch. Frost formed on my lips and crystalized along my eyelashes. It crackled in my hair and spread out from my palms. Slick links of ice clinked together as they manifested from my upturned hands.

I could feel them…every soul that had passed from the world and been laid to rest in a quarter mile radius. I could feel animals too—some newly passed, others as ancient as oil. Traces of their essence laced the leaves of the trees out front, the trees that Maynard and the bloody-vested man hid beneath.

"Tell him to drop the gun," I ordered Edwardia. The gruesome smile had fallen from the onyx planes of her face. She looked from Josh to me to the window where Maynard watched us through a pair of cross hairs.

"I do not answer to a lesser being." She looked me up and down. "You are beneath me. I will grind your bones to dust." The words were scary, but the tone was less so. In fact, I was almost sure I heard a trace of doubt in Edwardia's voice.

"The gun," I said again, and the whisper of ice storms sang through my words. Edwardia's body tensed, and I flung my arm backward toward the window. Glass shattered as heavy chains of ice shot out into the yard. I didn't reach for Maynard. The chains were not for him. I reached for the bloody-vested man and the snare of malicious thoughts that bound him to this plane of existence. I coiled my will around him until he understood. Without looking, I felt him rip the gun from Maynard's hands and toss it into the ravine. Edwardia's razor-sharp teeth parted in a snarl.

"You have taken much from me, human, but you will not take the throne." Edwardia leapt for the broken window. "You will meet eternal fire first," she promised, and every evil part of her elongated, threading through the broken pane and out into the gathering shadows.

****

Josh stared at the glowing bone in his hand. Blood seeped from the metal pins protruding from Seth's leg. I crunched the links of ice that sprang from my palm, releasing the soul at the other end. Maynard had run off, and Edwardia had disappeared into the ether. The bloody-vested man followed her.

"I'm sorry. I'm sorry. I'm sorry," Matt whispered over and over, staring at his bloody hands. He looked up and all our eyes followed his to Josh's hand. Matt and Josh's living room was on the north side of the house, one block in from the actual creek and screened by two magnolias and an overgrown crepe myrtle. It was the darker, cooler side of the house that needed little in the way of air-conditioning. Even in the late daylight, this room usually needed one or two lamps, but now it was filled with a glow so blinding that we all found ourselves squinting.

I raised my hand to shield my eyes, and Josh caught the movement. We both studied my ice-encrusted fingers as the light of his gauntlet danced along the frozen facets. Josh laughed and it was a quick, nervous sound. We stared at each other. He was beautiful in the light. And somehow…made for it.

He smiled one of those brief, unexpected, dazzling smiles and the ice melted from my hands and dripped to the floor. My hair and clothes felt damp, and somewhere deep inside I shivered. Josh extended his hand in a gesture to return the bone, but I stepped away from it. Josh froze.

"You keep it," I whispered. He shook his head, but I waved him off. "I think it's meant for you." I suddenly realized why Reverend Braidfoot had looked so closely when the relic touched my hand. He'd expected something like what had just happened to Josh.

"Mel, she will kill you. You need every bit of protection…"

"Josh, look at your hand. The relic didn't do that for me. It helped, but it didn't do that."

"Then…then, we will stay together, and it will protect all of us. I will protect us," he promised, and his words were filled with a kind of music.

"No." I shook my head. I took another step away from my friends. The room was in ruins. "I can't stay," I whispered almost to myself. I shook my head again. Seth needed to get back to the hospital. Matt and Gabe needed a doctor. I took another step back, this time toward the door. The guys stared at me questioningly in their various stages of shock.

"I have some place to be," I said and headed for the door.

"Melisande." Josh rushed to the only table left standing and let the bone roll from his fingers. The glowing gauntlet vanished, painting the room in shadows. "You can't. You won't be safe." He put his hands on my arms, but I shrugged out of his grip.

"No one is safe, Josh." I looked around at my friends. "You can protect them now." I lifted my hand and watched as frost drew jagged fractals across my skin again. "I'm okay. I'm more than okay," I said and meant it. I felt a strength inside me that I'd never known before. It was solid and complete and exhilarating. It had awakened from the broken parts of my mind, and it was reshaping me from the inside out.

Josh reached for me again. His mouth opened to say something more, but words wouldn't form. We stared at each other for a moment, he from the light of the hallway and me from the shadows by the door.

"It's okay," I whispered. I opened the door and smiled. I was okay with the shadows.

Chapter Eighteen

Three hundred years is a mighty big age gap.

I set the table for two, but he didn't show. I poured two glasses of wine, but he didn't appear. I put on my sexiest dress, which I realized as an afterthought might actually be a turn-off for a man from the Colonial Era. Women's clothes these days probably resembled a prostitute's attire more than I realized, but Grayford had watched the years pass. He was familiar with the changes in fashion.

I even put on a tiny dab of my lily of the valley perfume and waited in the candlelight, but Colonel Grayford didn't materialize. The open phone line in my head crackled with presence, but he held himself apart from me. I barely knew this man, and yet he felt like a puzzle piece carved just for my empty place.

I thought back to Edwardia's party and the way the world had rewritten itself when our eyes first met. I'd never felt that way before. I'd never even entertained the thought that there might be someone out there who could make me feel so disarmed. Or had I? My mind turned to a selection of impressions, a collection of hopes that I'd laced together in the shape of a mystery man. Grayford resembled that man almost exactly.

My thoughts curled into questions. I wanted to trust him, but I couldn't shake the feeling that he had motives I didn't understand. That brimstone glint that sometimes lit his eyes felt like a warning. Colonel William Grayford wasn't the man he had been in life. He was on the other side of the grave. That had to change one's perspective.

I wanted a clear explanation of what had passed between us during the Joining. I wanted to know what was between us now. I wanted…anything he would give me.

I trailed my fingers over the silky hem of my dress. Part of me felt ridiculous waiting for a man, any man, to manifest and take me into his arms. Did I expect him to knock on my door with flowers? Three hundred years is a mighty big age gap. What could we possibly have in common? Other than the burning need to touch each other, explore the aching places, inhabit each other's skin.

I needed to talk to him. I was changing so quickly inside. I needed him to be an anchor. I needed him to hold me still while I morphed into this new version of myself. Only Grayford could explain what was happening. I pictured him in my mind, tall and commanding, in hopes the thought might conjure him.

Almost immediately, the image changed. A picture of Josh flashed before my mind's eye. His golden visage sparkled with a power I couldn't feel. His dark-blond hair gleamed with an inner light where it brushed the tops of his shoulders. His gilded beard shimmered along the strong lines of his face. I'd never been more attracted to Josh than when I'd seen him standing there in his living room holding off the specter of darkness. I'd also never felt so separated from him. Was it the darkness inside me that pushed me out of his house, back to my sanctuary and begging for my lover's shadowy embrace? I loved Josh, but Grayford…fit.

What if the Colonel really could read my thoughts? Maybe the Joining had lifted the wall between us and every embarrassing craving that crept into my mind was broadcast to him for his amusement. Or maybe they were broadcast for his pleasure. Either way, it seemed like any red-blooded man living or deceased would have come running at the first glimpse of what I was thinking.

I waited until midnight and then blew out the candles. Maybe I had misread the connection between us. After all, what attribute could I possibly possess that would appeal to a three-hundred-year-old man.

I caught a glimpse of myself in the mirror on my mantel. My dark hair draped over my shoulders and hung in loose curls down the middle of my back. Dark lashes trailed over my amber eyes casting shadows down the bruised side of my face. That was me…pretty, but broken. And more than a little foolish.

I changed into my pajamas, slipped through the shadows of my bedroom, and climbed out onto the widow's walk. Bougie leaned against the wrought iron lace work, keeping silent guard over our home. He greeted me with a blink. We sat together and watched a distant storm roll in.

****

He was there. I could tell. His thoughts whispered down the phone line between us. They simmered— heavy, wordless, and thick with desire.

Lightning flashed outside my bedroom windows, illuminating every shadowy corner of my room, but the hall was dark. It didn't matter. I knew he was there. I felt him inside my head watching me…longing for me. Thunder rolled across the roof, pushing against my ward. My bed shook with the force of it. Even the sky wanted in. Maybe I'd make it suffer too.

He knew I was awake. I kept my eyes closed. I ran my fingers along the tendrils of my dreams until they spun apart and vanished in the strobing light of the oncoming storm. Then I ran my fingers along my skin. First, my mouth that I knew he longed to kiss…then the warm curve of my neck. I pushed the silky strap of my tank top over my shoulder, and it slid along the track his fingers wanted to take. I brushed the satin slick material with my fingertips until my nipples hardened to aching tips.

I felt his heart join his throbbing flesh as it beat out a rhythm of desire. He was moving toward me in the shadows, gaining strength from the storm. I slid the blanket off me, leaving the velvet curve of my hips exposed. He grazed my skin with the heat of his stare. I could almost see myself through his eyes—a supple form folding through his mind, setting every nerve he possessed on fire.

I lingered on the tight plains of my waist, drawing circles with my fingertips until places lower down began to tingle. I heard his breath, hard and low, in the hallway. Every dark, masculine drive he'd possessed in life flooded through him again.

Lightning bit the sky like a whip, and I slid the languid line of my legs open. He whispered to me in my mind, showing me, with fiery images, what he wanted me to do.

A smile spread across my lips. I teased at the lace edge of my panties until I knew it hurt him. It hurt me too, but it was a sweet ache. I waited until I could take it no longer, and then I slipped my fingers beneath the wet silk. My mouth opened in a breathy gasp, and my nipples sharpened again.

He groaned in the shadows just beyond my room, and his fist hit the door frame, rattling the mirror on my wall. I laughed as the thunder rolled. He felt the slippery ecstasy of my fingers as they danced along my burning flesh. Men are not to know the liquid pleasure of women. I wasn't sure he could handle it. I barely could. He was shaking with desire.

"Melisande!" he shouted, and his fists pounded against the invisible ward. I drew my hand away and raised to my elbows. Grayford's eyes were red flames. Lucky for him, I was in the mood to play with fire. I crossed the room and stopped just inside the ward.

"Take your shirt off," I whispered, and lightning seared the clouds above. He watched me through dark lashes as he slowly complied. It was my turn to ache as he took his time revealing every inch of hard muscle that he'd hidden under his modest, eighteenth-century gentleman's attire.

"The pants." I smiled and looked down. My breath caught. His hand rested on the straining fabric of his trousers.

"Ladies first." His voice was barely more than a growl. I wondered for a second if Grayford was still in there or if I had driven him mad with lust. He raised his arms and leaned against the barrier, spreading his muscular frame out in front of me. He was every woman's dream—narrow waist, carved abs, wide cobra-like lats, and shoulders that bulged beneath the weight of the world. It was my turn to be tortured.

I reached through the thin air that kept him at bay. I ran my hands down his chest to his waist. He shivered but didn't move. I looked at him as my hands slid lower. He closed his eyes but still didn't move. I took that as permission to explore the thick line of his desire. My hand found his hard swell, and a sound escaped my lips. It was all he could take. He wrapped his arms around me and pressed his mouth to mine.

I sobbed, but the sound was lost as he claimed my mouth again. I'd only been separated from him for a matter of hours, but it felt like I'd waited years for our bodies to be joined again. The joy we could not take on the night of Edwardia's soiree was now ours to drown in.

I clutched at the solid warmth of him. He was mine for as long as the storm lasted. I'd take everything I wanted and give him everything he needed.

His hand ran down my side as he reached for my leg. He fastened his fingers behind my knee and forced my leg up. He pressed me against the hard column of his desire. I cried out as he moved against me. He pushed his tongue between my teeth, and I writhed against him.

Then, in a roll of thunder, he pulled away from me far enough to grip my breasts. A low sound rumbled from him as he explored the warm, round weight of them.

My breath caught again. His fingers moved to the lace trim at the bottom of my tank top. Slowly, he lifted the fabric, inch by inch, keeping his eyes on mine. I raised my arms, and he dragged the cloth over my head, exposing my breasts. His eyes burned with carnal delight as he lowered them, drinking in every milky curve. I stood in front of him, naked except for my panties.

That's when I realized we were inside my bedroom. He looked around as though he'd been as unaware as me of our crossing the barrier. I was alone now, in my protected space with a hungry ghost. His eyes devoured me. He closed the space between us and kissed me. His lips were soft and urgent, and his hands held my face as though I were his most precious possession.

I wrapped my arms around him and kissed him back. I felt a sudden rush of emotion flooding down the line between us. I'd only known this man a few days. There was no way this could be love. Lust maybe, respect for sure, but there was something more, something beyond attraction. There was an endearment that we'd not yet had the time to develop normally. I felt it taking seed in that silent place that we shared. I knew things about him. Secret things. Things he'd never shared with another soul. I knew where his strength came from and his unconditional love. I traced them to shimmering moments from his childhood like the time he had chosen to take a beating rather than reveal which of his younger siblings had set the barn on fire.

I brushed a strand of chocolate hair from his cheek as I remembered the cold night he'd slept in the pasture wrapped around a rejected calf so that it wouldn't freeze. He'd been only a stringy adolescent then with a blanket and a prayer.

Grayford looked at me, and I wondered what he saw. I saw a man forged by love and pain, hard work and conviction. He was everything I wished I could be.

It couldn't be love, I thought as I looked into his clear blue eyes. Could it? I put that contemplation off for another time and lost myself inside the warmth of his tender embrace.

"Never fear me," he whispered as though he'd felt my concern only moments before. I nodded and kissed his chin and his cheek and his mouth. I reached behind his head and pulled the tie from his hair. Luscious brown strands swept over his shoulders in loose waves. I ran my hands through them. He smiled a wide, happy smile, and I felt a tidal wave of amazement and gratitude flooding down his end of the open line. I laughed. What did he find so amazing about me? Was he really that grateful for our time together?

He kissed me again, then moved his mouth to my neck. I shivered as his lips moved lower. He leaned a knee on the foot of my bed and lowered his mouth to my breasts. His tongue found first one then both pink tips. He filled his hands with the soft, pillowy mounds. A soft cry escaped my lips. I pressed my body against his.

His hands dropped to my panties. He pushed them down over the round curve of my bottom. His hungry fingers gripped my bare cheeks. I wanted him so much. If he could feel my thoughts in his mind the way I could feel his, then he knew that I was ripe for the taking. He plunged his hand between my legs, and a begging sound tore from my lips. The rush of desire almost overwhelmed us. He tugged at the ties on his trousers and pulled himself free. He found my hand and closed it around his erection. He cried out as I gripped him.

"Please," I begged, and avoiding my injured ribs, he gently pressed me backward onto the bed. Our movements were desperate. Our hands shook. He climbed between my legs, the place he should have been the entire time.

With his boots still on and his trousers barely down, he prepared to take me wildly. The room lit with a blinding white light and lightning scorched the earth somewhere below my bedroom windows. I spread for him, and he pushed his way inside me. He gave me only a moment to adjust, and then he plunged deep and hard.

My slippery flesh tightened around him as he found the end of me. With a quick breath he withdrew. I quivered against him, and he drove his marble column into me again. Now I understood the thick forcefulness of his tongue. It was a warning of what would come. He was letting me know how large he was.

I was stretched wide. I reached my arms above my head and braced myself against the headboard. Grayford drove into me again and again. His hair trailed through the strobing light. I felt his pleasure, his relief to finally be inside me. His muscles danced as he plunged and withdrew and plunged again. He drank in my ecstasy at being so completely filled.

He must have thought he could do better because no sooner had an image formed in my mind than he pulled his stony length from me and turned me carefully onto my stomach. Reading my fiery thoughts, he slid his fingers under me until they found my wet front. I cried out as he rubbed the swollen mound. I moved against his fingers as they danced across my secret spot. He took a shuddering breath as he drowned in my feminine pleasure. He knew what I wanted.

I screamed into the storm as rain beat against the

windows. He pushed his aching member into me and took me from behind as his hand worked between my legs. I'd never felt anything so wonderful. I gripped the bedsheets as he found the rhythm that caressed him just right.

I felt his pleasure mount with each thrust and tug. I rode the building wave of sweet agony as he matched his movements to mine. The Joining trapped us inside each other's pleasure while still feeling our own.

He cried out as his body rose toward release, and I was dragged along his straining masculine pulse. I'd never felt a man's pleasure before. It clenched and pressed and forced as it built inside my mind. It hammered and clawed and pounded like the beating of a drum. I could feel his possession each time he thrust inside my warmth. The quiver of my breasts made his mouth salivate. My soft, breathy moans lit his senses on fire.

His fingers massaged me just right, and suddenly I was back in my own body riding the lick of his fingertips, rubbing my liquid lust against his invading hand. He was with me, marveling at the sense of surrender as I welcomed his conquering flesh. He could feel my burning abandon as he filled me, pounded me, claimed me hard. It was more than I could take. He thrust inside me one last time, and my body spasmed around him. He exploded and I climaxed on the thunder. My body hugged his as we were claimed by the storm. We raged with the lightning in trembling release.

Grayford's knees buckled, and he caught himself, steering his weight away from my side. His trembling arms folded around me, and we rode the aftershocks of pleasure as we huddled together in the place where our minds and bodies touched. The line connecting us sang with the intimacy of our joining, and we both could feel the sanctity of it.

He caressed me with the sudden gentleness of his thoughts, and I embraced his being as if it were my own. We'd beaten time and distance and death itself to be together. Wind and rain rattled the windows in fitful gusts. Eventually, the storm would pass, but we would still be together. I was certain of it. I moved into the curve of his body and found where I fit.

****

"Grayford," I whispered as his lips chased the frost across my skin.

"William. You must call me William," he insisted as he licked a spiral of ice from my waist. The storm had indeed passed, but my body was already aching for him again. The memory of our superimposed pleasure pulled at me like an addicting drug. I could live inside that tsunami of sensation and not need anything else. No food, no drink, no rest. There was a warning in there somewhere, a silent alarm that cautioned me to take it slowly.

I ran my fingers through his hair. The thick brown strands crackled with static. He was fully charged. I wanted nothing more than to burn off some of that energy in bed, but I'd seen where the storm was headed. Every thundercloud in the sky was converging on the same place.

Arcadia Park.

I drew icy patterns across Grayford's skin and looked out the western-facing tower windows. The sky was a cauldron, bubbling to life.

"Can you feel it?" I whispered against his hair.

"Yes," he answered.

"What does it mean?"

"It means I have one last fight, and then we can be together." His tongue left my skin, and I instantly missed it.

"Don't you mean we…we have one last fight? I am called to the Battle too, right?" As soon as I said the words, I felt the change in Grayford.

He sat up and turned away from me. "Melisande…I've been thinking." He swiveled back and trapped me with the sharp, blue rings of his eyes. They were filled with plans, as usual. "Might I share my thoughts with you?"

I nodded, trying to see inside those plans. Grayford had locked down his side of our connection, and nothing was leaking out.

He got to his feet and walked to the windows. Every inch of his naked body glowed in the storm light, etching his silhouette into my brain as a tantalizing keepsake. He began to speak, but my eyes had overtaken my ears. All I could think on were the lines that cut along his abdomen and down to his heavy groin. He turned to me and the light danced down the outside of his chiseled arms. His hair folded along wide, strong shoulders.

"Melisande, please. You must hear me." His words were sharp, but his mouth was amused. He walked back and planted a knee on the bed, which didn't help things. So I offered him a corner of the sheet. He took it and tugged the material over his best parts. I was sad to see them go, but there was something wrong about that storm and the night in general. We needed to talk.

I used the technique I'd invented for refocusing after waking from the hypnogogic state. I picked one thing in my room, my dreamcatcher, and focused only on it, until the world rushed back in around it.

"…and though your newfound abilities are formidable, you, my dear, are still made of exquisitely vulnerable flesh." Grayford lifted my hand to his mouth and kissed it softly. I took my hand away and wondered at what I had just missed.

"What are you saying?" I asked, shaking my head.

"The Gate is a place of great evil. It corrodes living bone and shreds the—" Grayford searched for the words. "—synaptic pathways. Even if you can survive the Battle, the Gate itself will pull you apart." He knelt next to the bed and folded his hands before him as if in prayer.

"I can't allow that to happen." His eyes were wide and pleading, but his voice held a hint of command in it. And there was the difference between us. I knew Grayford spoke from a place of true concern and maybe even love, but the town's founder also spoke from a place of authority. I'd gotten enough of authority from my military parents.

"I hear you and I thank you, Gray…William, but this is the twenty-first century. As much as I appreciate your desire to keep me from danger, this isn't something you can allow or not allow." I stood and pulled a pair of black bike shorts from my dresser and slipped them on.

Thunder rolled across the roof tops and slammed into the western windows, shaking them in their frames. We both turned and looked out. The cauldron had begun to churn in a slow spiral, expanding the cloud wall outward with each revolution.

"I can't..." Grayford turned to me with tortured eyes, and I saw a man out of time, a man in love. His every instinct was to protect me, but this fight was bigger than him.

"You need my help." I let the words hang between us as I pulled on a bra and black T-shirt. The thunder rolled again, but this time light surged from somewhere behind the gray, spinning wall. We both knew what that meant. The Battle had begun. I laced up my paint-splattered Doc Martens and pulled my hair into a high ponytail. "Well, if I die, at least I've got someone waiting for me on the other side." I winked at him and headed for the front door. I had a few quick errands to run and then I would save the world.

Chapter Nineteen

The ghost in the closet told me everything.

The first stop was the library. It was closed tight for the night, and the downtown in general seemed drained of life. Lightning flashed from cloud to cloud overhead like spokes of a wheel. Every bolt streaked in the same direction.

I stood on the cracked pavement and stared down the stone lions that guarded the building's collected knowledge. Their marble eyes didn't see me. Instead, they peered out from their frozen perches at the roiling night sky. Emergency response sirens wailed in the distance as all attention focused on the weather phenomenon hovering over Arcadia Park.

I took one more glance around, then lifted my hands into the air. My will expanded out in tight translucent cords. Each chain felt cool against my palms and very solid, yet the frosty links whispered through the walls of the library without even tripping the alarm. They took my awareness with them, through the mortar and stone until I felt the inside of the library as surely as I felt the sidewalk pavement beneath my feet.

I ran my fingers through the collections at the front of the building first. I fanned through the fiction section and pushed my mind through the periodicals. I searched every stack on the main floor, then sank like a stone into the basement.

I'd just cleared the children's reading room on the library's lower level, when I brushed up against it. It slithered down the aisles of the book sale room, heading for the staff lounge. I dragged the icy tendrils of my will through the local history room in an attempt to cut it off, but grasping this slippery ghost was like trapping a tadpole at the edge of a puddle.

I closed in slowly as its movements became more erratic. It lunged forward and backward, spewing questions, weaving a caustic web of doubt around it. I brushed it with my chains, and it remembered me.

It turned its orbs of oblivion on me and began to whisper. I moved my mind away from the trap and tightened my will around it. Frozen chains wrapped around its swirling mass, fixing to the parts of it that still held the memory of form. I waited while it struggled. It put up a ferocious fight as it reached back through the evil path of its own evolution. It drew strength from all the minds it had stripped in the past. It pulsed with a devouring energy.

"Good," I whispered. "You're going to need it." And then I yanked.

****

My next stop was a tiny house at the back of the Swimming Point neighborhood. The small stretch of land extended out of the Olde Towne proper, connecting with Hospital Point along the banks of Grayford Bay. It had been a jog to get there, but I'd used the time to experiment with my chains. I'd started out with as many chains as I could wrap around the Murmur. Then, I tried merging the chains into wider, stronger cords. As I focused, my links became denser and the ice more compact.

I dragged the entity behind me as I ran along the waterfront. I turned onto the narrow walkway that led to the last house and crept along the shadows at the base of several ancient magnolias until the small cottage came into view.

I waded through the warped energy that wrapped around the house until I could feel my quarry—another entity, much stronger than the Murmur. I wavered at the edge of its awareness. It was already angry and ready to lash out. I'd tracked it too easily. Its unstable energy was like a beacon in the boiling night. I needed it even more than I needed the Murmur, but this entity was tricky. If I didn't get this capture right, I might lose both ghosts in the process.

I edged around to the front of the cottage. It was an old, squat building that was still oriented toward the water rather than the street. The home was much older than the city's streets. It was older than the giant magnolias that surrounded it. The historic plaque that stood in its tiny front yard read *Built in 1735*—back when people still rowed their boats right up to their homes.

Thunder rolled across the bay, and I put my back to it. I reached my arms wide as if to hug the structure, and I sent my chains slithering out in an arc to surround the house. My new, stronger links hissed and popped in the humid night air. They were a variation on the ones I'd manifested for the Murmur, not quite so solid that they wouldn't pass through walls, but hopefully infused with enough will to get the job done. This entity would not come easily. I needed every ounce of concentration

I could muster.

Slowly, I extended several more chains up and over the painted tin roof and wove them with the others until my will encompassed the entire home in a frozen net.

It knew I was there.

It had no intention of attempting an escape. It had claimed its territory, and I'd have to scrape the foundation clean to get it out. So that's what I did.

I took a quick look around, then closed my eyes. I breathed in the thick soup of low tide wafting off the water behind me and exhaled frost. I tightened my will into a force so sharp that it burned the air with icy splinters. My palms stung where the chains manifested. I breathed past the pain and began to reel in the net.

I pulled through the plaster and crashed through cupboards. The poltergeist crackled to life at the intrusion and whirled into a raging ball of kinetic energy. A shriek split the darkness, followed by another as the human inhabitants woke to madness. Lights flashed through the windows, and I heard objects thudding against walls. I tightened the net as furniture crashed and glass shattered.

The locus of destruction was tiny, small enough to fit through my net, so I split the chains and split them again. I combed the crawl space just above the ceiling of the home and dragged it from its hiding place. Ozone filled the air as the small star of annihilation demolished its sanctuary in a fit of rage.

Doubt loosened my grip on the chains as I thought of the people inside. They were more than afraid. They were in danger. Inside the home, shrieks turned to sobs, and the sobs turned to wails for help.

"What am I doing?" Just as the thought escaped my

lips, the poltergeist lashed out, severing one of my chains. I felt the ice shatter at a crack of uncertainty. Another fracture formed farther down the net, and the poltergeist found it. Another chain cracked, and another. I felt the poltergeist racing along the links, searching each one for weakness.

A side door crashed open, and a man emerged from the cottage carrying a small child in dinosaur pajamas. A woman followed behind them, holding pressure on a bloody gash running down the side of her face. I watched them dash across the narrow, dead-end street to the house of their nearest neighbors. The man risked a glance behind him at the strobing house. The tiny historic cottage was tearing itself apart.

One by one, the entity snapped every chain in my net, and I let it. It wasn't going anywhere. This nasty little convergence of evil was dug in like a tick. When I'd first encountered it at the Ghost Fleet, it had hidden its mass from me, but now as I peeled back the layers of malice surrounding it, I sensed its proportions more clearly. It wasn't little at all. Its time in the ship's gulag must have allowed the malignancy at its core to grow. That's why it had felt so different from any other poltergeist I had encountered. That's why it felt stronger.

Something huge pressed against the front door, and I heard wood splintering. I was in the line of fire, but if I moved out of the shadows of the magnolias, I'd be visible to the house next door. Already, lights were turning on in the home as the neighbors rushed the poor family inside. Soon the place would be crawling with emergency response crews.

I stepped farther into the shadows and took a deep

breath. I couldn't see the wall of the storm from my location, but I saw the flashing in the western sky. Time was running out, and I still had one more stop to make.

Anxiety pricked at me as I struggled with a decision. I could leave the raging poltergeist behind and go on without it, but my attempt to subdue it had just wrecked three lives. I couldn't let my efforts be in vain. I couldn't leave them or anyone else to face this horror alone. I had to fix this. After all, it was my fault it was loose in the first place.

"Okay." I exhaled slowly. "So you're a big guy, huh?" I closed my eyes and stretched my arms toward the straining door. This wasn't the Public Library. The next chains to manifest would be solid. I hated to add to the property damage of a historic site, but I wasn't leaving without my biggest weapon. Giant links of ice exploded from my hands. I braced against the cannon-like backlash, opening my eyes just in time to see the antique red door blow.

I found the biggest thing in the house and wrapped my chains around it. Fury reverberated along the facets of my ice and rang like a bell in my brain. I hooked my fingers and tightened my will around the bubbling mass. A twisted mimic of a human wail echoed out from the shaking house as I pulled with all my might.

The cottage's doorframe bulged then split as an invisible weight poured out across the small lawn. It flattened the wrought iron fence as I reeled it in. The hair on my arms stood up as the poltergeist's rancid thoughts poured over my skin. I turned my face away from it, and before I could react, it launched itself out over the water behind me. My body yanked backward, and suddenly it was all I could do to hang on to the fleeing energy and still keep a grip on the Murmur as well.

All fell silent on the shore behind me as I soared over the salty spray. Water splashed into my eyes as I did my best to hold myself above the water.

"Up," I screamed as the marina rushed into view ahead of me, and to my surprise the poltergeist pulled up. I dangled in the air above a tiny anchored sailboat as the entity slowed to a crawl. The Murmur drifted to a stop above my head, and its incessant whispering threaded through me. I whipped its chain out before me, and the ghost flung wide. The whispering died away. I pulled on the chain that held the poltergeist, and it moved…slowly, but it moved.

The night air above the river was exhilarating where it blew in around Hospital Point to circle the small bay. Below me and many yards ahead, the waves rolled toward the boardwalk, slapping and bumping the bulkheads in its endless grudge match. I'd never seen my town from this angle before. From this height, I saw all the way to the center of the city where angry clouds bent toward the ground like a giant lightning-laced hand. I hung in the gathering mist. It was way after midnight, and even the bar at the end of the marina's main dock had closed for the night. I was alone in the darkness with dangerous things. A wicked smile crept across my face. It was time to have some fun.

****

By the time I made it to the corner of Glasgow and Middle Streets, I felt like a completely different person. If I could have seen myself, I doubt I would have recognized me. Hopefully, Mrs. Spruill would. I hated to knock on her door at this hour, but her bedroom light was on and I had a feeling that Mrs. Spruill did most of her sleeping when the sun was up.

I glanced over at the dog park and the huge dent in the grass where I'd parked a particularly angry poltergeist. The Murmur drifted around it like a satellite caught in its gravity well of evil. I checked the chains that held them both to me as I waited on Mrs. Spruill's porch. The invisible links burned my palms.

If someone decided to walk their Pomeranian right now…I perished the thought.

I jumped as a jaundiced yellow porch light snapped on next to the door. The curtains moved as the little historian peeked out. I lifted my hand and waved my fingers at her. The smile on my face felt absurd, but I couldn't show up on her doorstep at this hour with two snarling entities and a grimace on my face.

After a very long moment of contemplation, Mrs. Spruill twisted the antique locks on her door, jiggled the knob, and then the door cracked open.

"Ms. Blythe?" She poked her pink head into the gap in the door and looked around me. It was just me on the porch. I waited until she was convinced of it, and then the door opened the rest of the way. "What are you doing here at this time of night?"

"I can't apologize enough for the late hour, but—" I wondered how to word it. "—you have something and I need to borrow it."

Mrs. Spruill raised her pencil thin eyebrows and blinked.

****

Because she was my new friend and because I had the distinct feeling that I could trust her, I decided to tell Mrs. Spruill the truth. Not the whole truth, but the parts that I thought she could digest. Something told me that this woman had seen and heard a lot already. Anyone that could share a home with what I suspected was lurking in her walls could handle a little Doomsday talk.

A few minutes later, we stood in her hallway, whispering as though we'd wake someone with our voices.

"How did you know the history of the home?" She blinked. Her tones were hushed out of habit. She'd clearly not been widowed long. In her heart, Mrs. Spruill was still a considerate wife, tiptoeing through the house to keep from waking a hard-working husband. "It's never been publicized that this was a stop on the Underground Railroad."

Our brief conversation clearly left the historian with more questions than answers as to why I was there and what I needed.

"As I said before, when I first visited your home, I felt their presence. I wasn't sure then about what I was sensing. But since then things have changed. I'm sure now."

Mrs. Spruill stared at me from her mild state of shock.

"I don't know if I can convince them to leave with me," I said. "But if I can, I'm sure your quality of life will improve. Their sorrow...their rage is not your burden."

As soon as the words left my mouth, tears streamed from Mrs. Spruill's starlight eyes. She looked from me to the closet door and back at me. She nodded and grabbed one end of the narrow table that had been placed in front of the hall's closet door. I grabbed the other, and together we nudged it out of the way.

A chill breeze breathed through the cracks around the old door, rattling it in its frame. I felt a tingling trace of cataplexy threaten the muscles in my knees, but the sensation dissipated as quickly as it had appeared. For a second, my thoughts were drawn inward, and I realized that I hadn't felt any cataplexy at all this evening. My last bout of it had been at Josh and Matt's house before I'd touched Chanco's bone and felt that strange expansion inside me.

I refocused on the closet door and realized that I didn't need the hypnogogic state to sense what was behind it. I glanced at Mrs. Spruill nervously. Could she feel it too, I wondered?

"This could become violent," I warned. "You might want to take a few steps back."

Mrs. Spruill's eyes went wide, but she didn't step back. Instead, she reached up and fastened her thin hand around the banister next to her head. The closet was under a wide, old staircase that reached up into the dimness above us.

"No, dear, I'll face this with you," she replied in a somewhat steady voice. I liked her. I liked her a lot.

Without giving myself any more time to think about it, I just reached out and opened the door. The sudden shock of winter wrapped around me, and I realized that I stood in snow. I'd never seen snow before, or at least the man I was with had never seen it. He shook with the chill of the wind, and I could feel that his clothes were not made for this type of weather. The blizzard had extended all the way to Virginia, but not to their point of origin in South Carolina.

I swayed under the weight of his worries. He didn't

worry for himself. He worried for his son and his wife. He had thought they would have made it across the Mason-Dixon line by now, but the storm had slowed their pace. The man gripped his son's fingers in his own frozen hands, willing whatever warmth he still had within him to transfer to his son's numb fingertips.

"I can't!" I shouted and broke the connection between my mind and the ghost's. As soon as I did, the closet door slammed shut and Mrs. Spruill shrieked. "Oh God, I can't." I breathed in the sudden warmth of the hallway. I leaned against the wall behind me and took a deep breath. I wasn't a parent, so until that moment I hadn't understood the agony of a parent's love. It was too much.

I squeezed my fists together testing the invisible chains that stretched through Mrs. Spruill's house and out into the empty park. The entities shifted restlessly in response to my distress. They fed on the agitation, but my grip on them was intact.

"What was that?" Her quiet voice sounded like thunder to my ears. A moment ago, I'd been tuned to a place so far back in time that it had strained every one of my senses to experience it. Now every sound, sight, and touch assaulted me.

"There was a house here. Not this one. A much older home," I recalled.

"Yes. There was a homestead here in the 1780s with a small farm," she confirmed. "This house is built on top of its foundation."

"It was winter. They were trying to reach Pennsylvania, but the storm..." I tried to put some emotional distance between me and the heart-rending scene, but pieces of it came back to me, playing forward. I remembered the signal light on the back porch of the home...two candles to mean the coast was clear. The closet door creaked open, and I remembered the man moving forward on feet he could no longer feel. His son in his arms. His wife falling behind.

"No," I pleaded with the ghost, but I was the one that had set this attempt at communication in motion. I had to see it through. Slowly, the closet door swung wide again. I stood in the hallway and hung my head as the ghost in the closet told me everything.

Chapter Twenty

Just one small woman with a hand-grenade and a neutron bomb

I stepped over the chain that marked the edge of the abandoned Arcadia Park. A sign swung wildly from its rusty links. It read No Hunting. It was a strange thing to read inside the city limits. It was like finding a No Sky-Diving sign in the subway. It begged the question, what lived in that urban jungle now? Clearly, there were things with enough body-mass to barbeque or they wouldn't have posted the sign. I hoped every living thing had made it out before the storm wall had gone up.

I fought the wind as I made my way down the abandoned street. Behind me, the world was caught up in a maelstrom of hail and hurling debris. It was almost impossible to make out any landmarks outside of the storm. It was as if the city had already been eaten by the darkness. The water tower was gone. The train tracks were gone. I was still close enough to the cyclone to hear the wail of ambulances and fire trucks outside, in the world that still made sense. If it weren't for those thin, random sounds, I might have lost my resolve. I'd hoped to land closer to the battle, but the wind shear had ripped us off course. Regardless, I'd made it inside the eye in one piece. Now, I just had to figure out how to stay that way.

I whipped the Murmur out in front of me and told it to be ready. It drifted along the battered pavement seeking minds to rend. I still wasn't sure exactly how that particular entity had come to be, but I'd learned a bit more about it on the flight in. We'd taken a southern route over the empty industrial parks to avoid being seen. As we'd glided over the deserted parking lots and lonely storage units, I felt the Murmur weakening. Yet, when we crossed over the tiny neighborhoods that clustered around the margins of the trucking companies and packing facilities, it suddenly strengthened.

Unlike normal ghosts, the Murmur needed thinking beings to sustain it. And not just any thoughts. Specifically, the Murmur could not survive without doubts. It thrived on hesitation and indecision. It dined on uncertainty and feasted on confusion. I still felt bits of its human origins slithering across it like an oily film, but without victims to poison with its vicious vacillation, it would eventually lose its cohesion. The Murmur had a healthy concern for self-preservation, and even though we'd left the living world behind, the fountain of negative thoughts geysering from a point somewhere ahead of us drove it onward with renewed zeal.

The poltergeist was a different story entirely. If the Murmur was a birthday balloon, the poltergeist was a Goodyear blimp. I had about as much control over it as a team of anchors has over a giant Macy's Day Parade balloon. Everything was fine as long as there were no stiff breezes—like, say, a tornado.

I yanked on its chain, testing the strength of our connection. The descent into the eye of the storm through a lightning-charged sky had shredded my grip on the unwieldy entity. Once we'd touched down, a quick patch to my chains had kept it from putting any space between me and it, but it still made me nervous. What made me even more nervous was the question in the back of my mind. *If it got loose, would it* put *distance between us or* close *the distance between us?* I could feel its loathing humming along the links that bound it to me. Could it feel my apprehension?

"Up," I commanded it, and the squirming cloud of destruction lifted me into the air. I glanced back at the storm wall just in time to see three dark shapes glide through the vortex. I hadn't been sure if they were still with us, but as we moved forward toward the melee, the ghosts behind me took up a flanking position. They were joining the fight of their own free will. I'd liberated them from the residual aspects of their prison-like haunting, but they didn't owe me anything. They were free to go to the Light that surely called them. As much as I needed their condensed psychic energy, I wasn't going to force anything on them. There would be no icy chains for this tiny collection of spirits.

We rose through the crackling night until all of Arcadia Park unfurled before us. From my vantage point, I saw everything. The broken road ahead led straight into the strobing lights of the battle. Another street circled wide to the left, almost reconnecting to the dead end of the first road farther on. There were no longer any street signs to point the way through this deserted wilderness, only empty cul-de-sacs and refuse-choked driveways.

We floated past the first intersection of round-abouts, and before we could make it to the second, the swarming landscape rippled out to meet us like a page of the Old Testament. My muscles tensed as I gripped the frozen chains streaming up from my palms. Before I'd seen the frantic ballet of violence, I'd been holding the loose pose of a hang-glider or parasailer, ready to make my dramatic entrance high above the fray. But now, as I twisted and dodged the catapulting movements of the larger combatants, I stomach-crunched into a tight ball of defense.

Blinding light seared my eyes as fists hammered and weapons clashed. Outside the confusion of my nightmares, I'd never been in a real battle before. Everything I knew about war was expertly executed in cinematic perfection with a rousing score playing in the background and seamlessly choreographed heroic engagements.

This was completely different.

I flinched at the trumpeting shouts and sickening impacts. All around the blasted center of the park were creatures sculpted into shapes only Hieronymus Bosch could understand.

I tried to find a safe place to land, but that place didn't exist. Shadows flitted through the air around me, sizing me up. They were small things, the type that usually kept to the periphery of my vision when a sleep attack loomed. But these shadows were bolder. They dipped in close as I searched the ground beneath me. My eyes locked on a tire-strewn clearing that shot off from the second intersection. Next to it, the faded footprint of a small home struggled against a tsunami of ivy.

"Down." I sent my will toward my captives, and the ground rushed up to meet my feet. My heels stung with the impact, but I absorbed it with my knees bent. My Doc Martens had been a good choice. The little shadows came with me. I tightened my grip on the Murmur and waited to see what the tiny pieces of darkness would do. First one, then another rushed me with tiny claws extended. Razor thin lines drew across my skin, leaving a slight sting no worse than a paper cut. I thought to set the Murmur on them, but their assault was so minor, I chose to ignore them instead.

I surveyed my surroundings and plotted a path toward the center of the battle. I'd seen it from the sky. I'd felt it too. The darkness around it thrummed like a bird's heart. Though my mind still couldn't make sense of it, I knew exactly where it was.

An enormous arm wrapped in a glowing archer's brace swept across the treetops above me, and I felt my feet fly out from under me. An endless moment later, the world shook with a shattering impact. I was tossed around, and I wasn't even in the fight yet.

I could fix that.

I pushed to my feet and started running. The entities at the end of my chains rushed forward, pulling me faster. Between one step and the next, I flew through the night, and just like in my dreams, nothing could catch me. It was intoxicating how quickly I owned the darkness. Shining people stole across the landscape in front of me. They moved with a cyanide certainty. The nightmares didn't have a chance. A feverish smile spread across my face as the enemy sized me up. By myself, I might not look formidable. One small woman running in the night—what's to fear? One small woman with a hand grenade and a neutron bomb attached to her by icy chains? Well, that was another matter.

I broke into the next intersection with so much force that I nearly cleared it before I slid to a stop in the crunching glass and loose gravel. I turned and oriented myself as quickly as I could. To my left, a defensive line bowed out around a massive, shivering darkness. To the right, a line of engagement zigged and zagged like a giant serpent across a ruined sprawl of dead grass and cracked pavement. Shining people hacked at a wave of raging bodies.

Though it made the hair on the back of my neck rise, I put the poltergeist behind me and slung the Murmur out in front. We moved forward into the space between the lines. The Murmur rushed forward, gripping everything in its path with paralyzing doubt. First one, then another, then another of the twisted creatures slowed to a stop. Some were trampled by the clawing frenzy of their own side, while others stood slack-mouthed as shining people hacked them to literal pieces. I watched as the remains of the dead creatures coiled together into a sickening vapor. Each cloud of dark energy was not wasted but reabsorbed by the pulsing darkness behind them.

These misshapen beasts were the same beings from my nightmares. The only difference was now I could look upon them fully. Fiendish faces that had clearly never been outfitted with the things that make us human stared at me with ravenous eyes. Muscles coiled along limbs that only knew reaction. Claws scraped along bones that hummed with a lust to devour. They looked vaguely humanoid. Lungs breathed, hearts pumped, but that was where the similarities between humanity and these brutish things ended.

Something clicked to my right, and I turned in time to see pointed teeth splintering as they crashed together beneath the crack of a shining mace. I flinched away as the creature's body collapsed at my feet. I looked from the imploding demonic body to the shining warrior next to me. His mace whipped across the night. He flashed a menacing grin at me and drew the shining weapon in an arc, taking out half a dozen beasts. The invincible glint in his eye infected me. I felt my own mouth curving as I entertained the idea that I might be able to inflict some damage as well. I lifted my arm into the air and whipped the poltergeist over my head. It crushed a wave of winged creatures descending on us from above.

"I can do this," I shouted to no one and dragged the poltergeist behind me again. A wedge formed in front of the defensive line, angling out. Its outer edge reached me in a concussive wave of struggling bodies. Before I knew what was happening, I was swept up in the press. Shining shields smashed at thickly horned skulls. Burning arrows sliced the night. I covered my ears against the howling as a swarm of bodies pulled me closer to the arc of defenders.

Panic gripped me, and my confidence drained as quickly as it had appeared. I dug my heels into the loose dirt and debris and slipped, jostling the soldiers behind me. Ghostly hands locked on me. One by one, their eyes focused on me with a white-hot fervor as their bodies took on a more solid state.

I recognized these men. They had fought under Mr. Pratt at the Ghost Fleet. I scoured the faces nearest me. Muskets fired in the center of the wedge, and I followed the sound with my eyes until I saw the Scotsman. Mr. Pratt hovered over the fray as a band of watery-eyed sailors beneath him hacked at a loose point in the defensive line. His steely voice shouted orders over the din of clashing sounds.

"Grayford," I shouted, searching the rushing crowd, but bodies were pressing ever closer.

"Touch me," someone pleaded, and I felt hands reaching for me. I tightened my grip on the chain holding the poltergeist, but the links vibrated with my uncertainty. The entity hovered above me.

Just then something huge descended on the wedge and ripped Mr. Pratt from his position above his men. Giant talons tore his body in two and the liberated parts spun away into the encircling trees. The crowd wailed with one horrified voice, and my knees bent as cataplexy washed over me. My stomach lurched.

"Take my hand." A soldier pushed into my vision and I felt his cool, partially materialized fingers squeeze against mine. He was trembling. I focused on him. He was young, too young for battle. I looked around at the soldiers crushing in close. They were all too young to be carrying rifles and muskets.

I shifted the chains in my palms and did my best to grip the young man's hand. He turned to grip the hand of the man behind him. I reached out with my other hand and brushed another soldier's shoulder. He, in turn, touched the man next to him. The Murmur drew in close behind me as more and more soldiers swarmed toward me. Their fears and doubts teased through the Murmur's frenetic mind. I reinforced my will along the links of its chain, but I knew I couldn't dampen its feverish nature for long.

One by one, the soldiers that I touched sped back to the center of the wedge, carrying a little piece of the mantle of life with them. Weapons clanged with a solid force. Corporeal arms wrapped around twisted throats. The surge in their manifestations spiraled out through the crowd. It was an extra bit of energy they hadn't had before. If I could help in no other way, then I would at least contribute to the vigor of the fighters.

"Up." I sent my will toward the poltergeist, and I felt a wave of dizziness wash over me. My feet left the ground, and the Murmur followed. Dark bodies dove at me instantly, but the Murmur intercepted them. The battlefield swam beneath me.

"Grayford," I called over the tumult. Another round of musket fire ripped through the night, and there at the front of the wedge stood Colonel William Grayford. His sword flashed like quicksilver in the gleaming light of the angelic warriors around him. He slashed at things too frightening to linger on. His boots kicked, and his shoulders shoved. He threw every bit of his crackling energy into the fight. And it was working. A hole formed in the defenders' ranks, and almost as soon as it appeared, the gap was suddenly filled with a choking onslaught as the offense rushed in.

I called to Grayford, but hundreds of battle cries filled the air, drowning me out. I lifted higher, watching in amazement as the defensive army split in two. I floated on a wave of cheers as the two remaining pieces of the line were slowly surrounded. It was a beautiful sight. It was the last thing I saw before the blinding darkness hit me.

Chapter Twenty-One

The balloon's revenge

"This way."

"Clear a path."

"Hold them back."

"Hurry."

Voices bumped against me like balloons, and I remembered a time when I was very young and my mother had bought me one of the good balloons. One that floated. She'd tied it to my wrist, and it had followed me all through the carnival. It bobbed and bounced and added a little lift to my step all day long. But, eventually, I was careless and let the ribbon slip from my wrist. The balloon floated away. My constant, obedient, loyal friend abandoned me at the first opportunity.

The sorrow of that moment morphed into something dark. It turned into something that crawled across my skin with sharp fingers of satisfaction. It took me long moments to fully realize whose satisfaction it was. It was the balloon's. The balloon had come back.

"Get her out of that thing!" someone shouted. I tried to take a breath, but there was none. I tried to move, but my body was locked into a tight ball. The crack in my head had reopened, and pain leaked out. I opened my eyes to see the ground hovering below me and men reaching above their heads. Swords shredded the air in front of me and guns fired, sending white hot meteorites zinging past my head. It wasn't until I felt the squeeze that I realized where I was. The poltergeist had me.

The air around me tightened, and my ribs popped along the fracture lines. I tried to cry out, but the air had been pushed from my lungs. The entity rotated, triggering the weakness in my inner ear. Vertigo swam through my brain, and my stomach flipped. The poltergeist had left no room in its greedy embrace for me to throw up.

I felt its anger and hatred burning along my skin like a gasoline fire. Invisible arms tightened, and the tendons in my neck strained. I caught a glimpse of Grayford. His face was ashen with horror as he cut a path toward me. My scalp tingled with his fear. I could only imagine what I looked like hanging in the air, contorted and pressed into a shrinking ball. The entity squirmed, and my backbone made a popping sound.

Grayford shouted orders over the clamor of too many voices. Life essence still sparked along his skin, but that same strength had opened him up to injuries. Angry red lines drew across his forearms and beneath his shredded shirt. His ponytail had come loose, sending manic tendrils of lush brown hair snaking out around his shoulders.

I studied his panicked face. His kiss was still fresh on my lips. I could still feel the warm press of his body against mine, and now we were here.

Blood trickled into his eye, and he wiped a bare wrist across his forehead. He took another look at me and launched himself into the air. I knew the expenditure of energy would cost him, but at the moment I was comforted by the sight of him lifting toward me.

His sword carved the night sky around me, but nothing seemed able to interrupt the entity's hold on me. Grayford shouted in desperation.

My heartbeat spread out along every inch of my body until I was one pressing beat of fear. The air glittered, then glimmered, then glowed with light. A shining giant broke from the battle and surged toward me. Its supernova hand swiped out to grab me, but the poltergeist sped away from it.

I lost sight of the battlefield and Grayford's contorted face as the entity stole through the trees, taking me with it. Wood splintered and branches snapped as I was pulled away from any source of assistance. Not that I thought anyone could help me. It was my mistake to pursue such a dangerous being and my further mistake to try and tame it.

We broke from the jungle of towering overgrowth and raced down the outer road of the park. The storm wall loomed ahead. Its angry winds had picked up cars and uprooted trees. Trying to pass through it now would only make a bad situation worse. The poltergeist couldn't be pulverized, but I could.

If only I could have reached the fetid mind at the center of this abhorrent creature—if it even had one at all. I knew very little about poltergeists. They usually dissipated after their host reached adulthood, but this entity wasn't formed from the psychic residue of an unhappy teenaged girl. It was born of something much worse.

One time, on a ghost hunt in the Northern Neck out

in cotton country, we'd come across a poltergeist in a turn of the century farmhouse. The guys had never collected readings like that before and wanted to stay the night to see what other data they could compile. I tried to tell them that the manifestation was unstable, but it took a smashed video recorder and a twisted tripod to convince them to leave.

That's when I'd made my "no poltergeists" rule. Had overconfidence gotten me into this mess? When had I abandoned my perfectly good sense of self-preservation? As if in response to my self-deprecation, the entity twisted, and I felt my organs wrench. It was toying with me. One good pull and I'd meet the same fate as poor Mr. Pratt.

Something moved inside my mind, waiting for my next thought. Or maybe it was the lack of oxygen desaturating my blood and suffocating my brain, but I thought I felt its...anticipation. The poltergeist was listening to me.

I stilled my wandering thoughts. Maybe if I starved it of emotion, it would release me? Silence drifted through my mind, and a moment later I felt another squeeze. My legs began to tingle, and I lost the feeling in my feet. One more squeeze, and I'd lose consciousness altogether. My heart struggled against the lack of oxygen. A regular person would have fainted by now, but my central sleep apnea had basically turned me into a deep-sea diver.

I had enough brainpower left to reason that if no thoughts and emotions pissed it off, then more thoughts and emotions might improve my night dramatically. If it wanted emotion, I'd give it emotion.

I set the table with a buffet of horrors that tore free

from my memory. It fondled the frozen fears of my childhood and licked the lingering nightmares of my adolescence. I watched with my inner eye as it picked through the delicacies that spread out from my recent memory. There were just too many treats from which to choose. I felt its grip loosen as it supped on the terror I'd first felt when my disease progressed into the hallucinatory stage.

There was the time when a ghost shouted in my ear in the middle of a restaurant and I nearly passed out.

Suddenly, I could breathe.

There was the time I saw a small, white dog racing across the front lawn of our house when we lived in India. I'd run with my arms waving toward the car speeding by. The driver had slammed on his brakes, causing his passenger to bang her head on the dashboard. I'd tried to explain about the dog that had run out in front of them, but no one had seen it. When blood trickled from the woman's nose, I thought my chest would burst with guilt.

Sensation rushed back into my legs and arms, and my feet caught fire with pins and needles.

And…of course…there was the first time I'd seen the Shadow.

The poltergeist swooned. To my mind, it felt almost inebriated after gorging on the parts of me that ached with unending fear. Those memories would never leave me, but now they at least served a purpose. They made me stronger. The tiny things that go bump in the night didn't scare me anymore. In fact, now, I scared them. I fell from the poltergeist's flaccid grip and hit the ground hard.

I lay sprawled on the cracked cement of a forgotten

road and stared up at the dark star above me. It was satiated. Had I only known what it craved we could have started out on a better foot.

I took a few hyperventilating breaths to resaturate my bloodstream then tore a strip from my T-shirt. With slow, cautious movements, I wrapped the cloth around my ribcage and tied a tight knot. I was sure the injured ribs were not aligned, but the pressure made them feel a little better.

I sat up and ran my fingers through my hair. Behind me, trees crashed beneath giant feet and beyond that was the clamber of a battle that sounded as though it had just taken a turn for the worse.

"I can fix that."

I stood and wrapped the hovering poltergeist in more chains than it could count.

"Up," I shouted, and the depthless sky bent down to greet me.

****

I rejoined the fight with only the poltergeist, but that was enough. The shining giants cleared a path for me as I scudded over the smaller skirmishes, descending toward the opening in Edwardia's defenses. I touched down in the crumbling cul-de-sac and let the poltergeist wipe it clean. Everyone stood clear.

I followed in the entity's aftermath as it carved a path straight to the Hell Mouth. It was a leisurely walk across the round-about and down the driveway to the thing that masqueraded as a house. It was small and unassuming, as I'm sure it had been in life. But pieces of it were just wrong. The steps were made of tree branches, and the porch was shaped of discarded tires. I came to a stop in front of the home and stared at the gaping maw where the front door should be. Bloody Vest was there guarding the threshold in a casual pose. He leaned against the refuse-wrapped doorframe and trimmed his nails with a short, gleaming knife.

The house shivered with a dark, skittering heartbeat. I peered through the glassless windows at the Frankenstein décor. Empty crates formed a couch, and the blue light of a tubeless television flickered on walls made of wooden pallets and flattened cardboard boxes.

I looked back at Bloody Vest. He had an inscrutable look on his face. He kept me in his peripheral vision, but otherwise seemed unconcerned with my presence. That made me nervous. But, then again, I'd seen how he'd interceded with Maynard at Edwardia's party. Bloody Vest had a mean poker face.

I wished I still had the Murmur. This was a perfect time for it to shine. The poltergeist was stronger, but it was a wrecking ball when I needed a precision strike.

"Well, waste not, want not," I quoted my mother again and suddenly noticed just how much my voice sounded like hers.

I yanked the poltergeist forward. I thought I saw a vicious grin slice across Bloody Vest's face and then he was a blur of motion. The knife he held flashed as it phased in and out of sight. I was impressed. I could see why Edwardia kept this spirit so close. He was quick, calculating, and not bad on the eyes.

I wove a web of chains from my free hand and whipped them through the air above me. Each time the poltergeist dodged, I struck. I didn't try to snare Bloody Vest because something told me I'd gotten lucky when I'd caught him off guard in Josh and Matt's yard.

"Sorry about the gun thing." I tried my hand at

taunting. "But Maynard was being a bad boy." I smiled, and Bloody Vest grinned back, seemingly unperturbed. Yeah, I wasn't good at taunting.

He lunged at the poltergeist, and his knife disappeared again. I wasn't sure what damage he thought he was inflicting, but if it wore him out, all the better. "Speaking of Maynard, where is he this fine evening?" I took an exaggerated look around, but in small part I was a little concerned. Arcadia Park was no place for the living tonight, even for a jerk like him. Also, Maynard was just the kind of guy to bring a gun to a ghost fight. The thought made the back of my neck itch.

"Maynard has other duties to attend to," Bloody Vest answered, and I thought I heard a slight accent, maybe central European. I couldn't be sure. I didn't allow my mind to wonder at the duties of which he spoke. If it had to do with Edwardia, I was better off not knowing.

"What is it that you two see in her?" I had to ask. "I'm pretty sure I've got Maynard figured out, but what's the allure for you?" Bloody Vest launched at the poltergeist and buried the knife and his arm into the shuddering distortion at the poltergeist's center. The entity closed around the ghost's arm and squeezed.

"We are of a similar bent," he offered in a gentlemanly, almost jocular tone. He struggled as the poltergeist enveloped his shoulder. "We travel well together." His arm twisted, and the poltergeist let go. I felt the poltergeist's shuddering growing more violent, and a putrid fear crept along the tether that bound the entity to me. I stepped back from the bloody-vested man and tried to assess the poltergeist's condition.

"It seems your pet is on its last legs," he taunted with a polished flair. He clearly had practice. I felt my chains slacken. The entity was shrinking. I tried to get a look at Bloody Vest's knife, but his hand moved too quickly. I reeled in the frozen links as the poltergeist continued to shrink.

"No, no, no," I muttered as my will tightened around the fading star.

Feed it! The thought burned through my mind. I scrambled for a painful memory, but the present moment was bad enough. The handsome ghost danced around the crippled entity and closed the distance between us. All I could think to do was put my arm up as the knife sliced too close to my face.

Fire stole across my skin as the burning metal tore my arm. I cried out and stumbled backward. Bloody Vest moved with me, fluidly maintaining the frame of our deadly dance. His knife slashed up, catching me across my elbow, and this time I saw blood finish the arc.

I backpedaled down the driveway, hoping that the good guys were just behind me. I risked a glance back, but all I could make out was a blur of bodies wrestling like one undulating creature. The tiny shadow creatures flittered over the melee like gadflies, biting at the beast. Where was Grayford?

I hated to leave myself open to another cut, but I had no training in hand to hand combat and my options were dwindling. I willed a glazier of ice into my free hand, and thin whips reached out for the wispy shadows buzzing above the battle. Chains encased the hovering horde, coiling them into tight little maces of mayhem. Bloody Vest's knife drew another searing line across me that tore through my T-shirt and across my sternum. I yanked away in an attempt to save my neck and face.

Anger found me like a lost child in a shopping mall, and I wondered where the hell it had been. I funneled the negative emotion down the connection between me and the poltergeist, and the shrinking stopped. Bloody Vest brought his blade down on the chains that connected me to the poltergeist. I blinked at the splintering ice, then lifted my arm into the air.

My obedient friend returned to me and wrapped his coiling rage around my wrist. I welcomed the repulsive embrace as it slipped along my forearm. I fed it morsels of dread and petit fours of foreboding. In return, it shaped itself into a shield.

Bloody Vest swung, and I blocked. He slashed, and I hammered. I held the frame of the deadly dance now, but Edwardia's formidable companion would not yield.

I swung the barbed cocoons of ice wildly, but each shadow-filled mace that connected left a disappointing amount of damage. My energy was draining quickly. I desperately searched the cul-de-sac for any sign of assistance. My heart sank until I caught sight of something wrapped in stillness off to my left. Three shards of burning night stood motionless on the crumbling curb.

"Why are you not fighting?" I called to the renegade slaves. Their eyes swept the park and the empty space between them and all the other darting figures. That's when I realized that no one would engage them. Every loathsome being that lumbered free of the Hell Mouth steered clear of the trio. I'd felt the weight of their presence as they slipped the bonds of their haunting. So many years of imprisonment, unable to breathe life back into their frozen bodies and unwilling to forgive the people that had promised them safe harbor. There were some wells of darkness into which nothing wanted to fall.

"Please." I met the torment in their eyes. They turned in unison and looked toward the second floor of the fabrication masquerading as a house. After what seemed like an eternity of contemplation, they turned and rained down on Bloody Vest like the Day of Judgement. Teeth tore and fingers ripped. The pent-up rage of every cheated moment, every stolen dignity poured out of the man, woman, and child in a cannon of destruction. In the end, they were a psychic weapon that no one could withstand. I knew it was wrong of me to try and tap that well of ruination and use it to help our cause. But I didn't regret helping them slip the last of their earthly bonds. I turned away from the obliteration. Some things are better left unseen. When I turned back, Bloody Vest was gone. The slaves stood in a line, staring at me.

"Thank you," I offered weakly, but they didn't respond. They just pointed toward the second floor of the structure.

"Go."

Their eyes burned.

"Quickly."

Chapter Twenty-Two

It's all written in molecular ink.

My body shook with blood loss as I climbed the Styrofoam stairs. Coolers, cups, and picnic plates crunched together beneath my feet. Stinging cuts and oozing slashes crisscrossed my body, but none of my arteries had opened in the fight. I could make more blood. It was the other losses that frightened me. I'd done bad things. Really bad things. And now I feared I'd lost my place in the world outside, where dawn was breaking over the river. I'd lost the lie that life was good and balanced and in our favor. I looked around and saw that it wasn't. And, worst of all, I'd lost my chance to claim a place in His house...the one with many mansions.

Jesus said that he was going there to prepare a place for us...but not me. Not anymore. I'd embraced the darkness inside me. I was pretty sure that voided my baptism.

I took a sobbing step and then another as the weight of that realization settled on me. I also realized, that I was the only one to approach the Hell Gate. Did they all know? Did every soul swept up in this fight know that this was an impossible task? Did everyone know I was about to die?

Did Grayford?

No. I couldn't believe that. Grayford had loved me long before we'd even met. He'd kept me company through the lonely moments. He'd stood with me when I faced my own demons. Some part of me had known he was there, my mystery man.

I could only hope that Grayford would make it out of this in one piece. The city needed him. There would be another woman, somewhere in time, that would love him. My heart clenched in my chest as I thought of all the moments we would never share. For one brief instant, I'd thought that I'd found the one. If ever there were a man constructed of the things most admirable, most endearing, and most suited for me, it was William Grayford.

For a split second, I thought about turning around. I could search the battlefield until I found him. We could slip into the Joining and leave this ugly world. I wasn't qualified for this job. I knew nothing about the Hell Gate. What was I doing here?

Before I could even begin to contemplate those questions, my foot reached the final step. The tiny hall at the top of the stairs had only two doors. One was a howling place of endless terror that stretched on into eternity. Evil things twisted through its threshold, crawling free to join the battle.

The other door was closed and quiet. It wasn't a hard decision picking which way to go. I picked the quiet door because it was the one Edwardia was guarding with her life.

Edwardia didn't wait for me to come to her. As soon as my foot touched the funhouse floor of the hallway, she launched. I crouched along the sloping surface of an old playground slide as the blackened skeleton tore across tricycles and broken bits of baby dolls. Her bony feet ripped through the discarded remains of someone's childhood as she sought my throat with her outstretched talons.

I raised my arm, and the poltergeist spread out like a shield in front of me again. Edwardia leapt, and the thunder of our impact shook the house around us. I went down in a tangle of jump ropes, and Edwardia pinned me to the mildewed refuse. Sweat and mold stung the cuts along my arms as I struggled through the loose debris.

Edwardia's eyes radiated with the same pulsing kaleidoscopic shadows as the Hell Gate behind me. We slid to a stop only feet from the distortion. Her moonstone gaze was shadowed with more than the reflection of the Gate's multi-hued blackness. Her eyes were becoming the blackness.

"It's too late, Dreamer. The Gate is mine." Her raspy words were accented by the clicking of her skeletal teeth. The sound was like a grating wind chime meant to chase rabbits from a vegetable garden. A dawning realization swept through my mind. I hadn't contemplated until that moment what Edwardia must have given up in order to become the Seventh Devil. She'd likely started life the same way I had. She'd had a childhood, I thought as I dug my fingers into the scattering of toy trains beneath me. I was willing to bet she'd had a family and friends and things she'd desired before this. Where had all those comforts gone?

"What happened to you?" The question slipped from my lips, and there was no chance of reeling it back in. Edwardia's bony face split in an ear-shattering scream, and my stomach lurched as the Gate behind me swelled.

"Look!" She laughed a sandpaper sound. "The Door listens to me. Only me. Not you. Not him. Me!" I tried to make sense of what she said. Her talons dug through the poltergeist's defenses until the tips of her claws pressed against my skin. "You will never be the Seventh Devil!" Her face contorted. Her eyes blazed. I gaped at the phantasm hanging above me. Papier-maché eyelids held her eyeballs in their sockets. Lipstick lips tattooed the bone surrounding her teeth. Her organs had finally abandoned her, leaving just a leathery skin to upholster her bones.

So this was the reason for all the attacks? Edwardia thought I wanted her job. My mind reeled as I pushed against her weight. How dark is my soul to her eyes that she would make such an assumption? Was that the real reason why Chanco's bone wouldn't work for me the way it worked for Josh?

Holy shit.

Did Grayford know? Is that why he didn't want me here at the battle?

Burning talon tips punctured the skin just below my collarbone, and my fractured ribs stabbed me with little bolts of lightning.

"Come on," I screamed at the poltergeist, but it was wounded. If I kept pushing, it might fall apart. It cried out to me from the emptiness at its core. Even in its wretched state, it didn't want to die. I had nothing left to give it. I couldn't do this. I was already too late. Where was my Lord and Savior? Where were the Angelics? Tears slid from my eyes.

"Help!" I screamed with all my might. I didn't want to let go of my will. It was all I had left. I'd be defenseless without it. But here at the edge of the world there were no other weapons. With a parting thanks to Creation for allowing me to hold on to such strength, even for a fleeting moment, I relaxed and then…I let go.

My will exploded out from me in all directions. The wave moved like a sonic thing, flattening everything around me. The second floor of the house peeled away. Edwardia's talons scraped down my rib cage as she hung on to the only anchor in this storm…me.

I gasped, and the Gate behind me pulsed again, but this time it responded to me. I turned horrified eyes to see that the aperture was still there. The doorway was gone, but the rip in time and space still bled into our world. I kicked at Edwardia, and her claws came free. She scrambled through the detritus, trying to regain her footing.

I knelt on the quivering mass of broken things and stared at the Hell Mouth. Information far beyond my pay grade swirled along its surface. Explanations of the universe so unimaginably simple yet too blindingly large for my human mind to comprehend danced before me. The immateriality of mass, the solidity of thought, and the certainty…oh, the blood-chilling certainty that all things have already been assigned a purpose…It all came crashing down on me at once.

For a split second, I claimed the moment because it was mine. I shared equal ownership of it with the Lord, and my authorship was written in molecular ink across every aspect of it. And then it was gone, and I knew my mind would never be able to encompass knowledge that vast ever again.

But it had infected me. I turned knowing eyes to Edwardia. She'd sipped from this fountain too many times. She was drunk on the possibilities of power that immense. The Gate was an invitation to godhood.

"No!" Edwardia shouted, and I turned in time to see her launch at me again. I looked at my arm and the place where the remnants of the collapsed poltergeist still clung to me. I whispered a secret to it, and it began to grow. The hungry locus of negative emotion swelled into a shield again, but not a shield of protection. This time it shaped into a ramming shield. I pushed to my feet and lunged forward.

Edwardia's bones unhinged, and her tendons stretched. She darted through the air like a poisonous barb of hatred, and I caught the assault dead center on the conical front of my shield. Bones cracked and the ground beneath me shook, but not from the impact. The ground shook with applause.

I spared a glance at the gathering of bodies pressing around the Gate. Combatants still roiled along the edges of the crowd, unwilling or unable to give up the fight, but the vast majority of the battleground had gone still. I searched the din around me for a single voice. With the walls of the second floor gone, every pair of eyes in the park was on me. All, but two precious circles of blue. Where had Grayford gone?

Creaking joints popped back into place as Edwardia gathered herself for another assault. I scrambled backward across the insubstantial floor as I attempted to get my feet under me. Gasps trembled through the predawn air as a sallow light peeked through the scribbling lines of the storm wall. It was the rising sun.

Outside the horrors of this nightmare realm, the pearly glow grew in the eastern sky. It was such a welcome sight. There was only one thing stopping me from drinking in that blessed glory.

The quiet door.

Everything on the second floor had blown away in my outburst except that door. And—as I slowly realized—Edwardia still guarded it.

"Dreamer," Edwardia whispered and a hint of her former voice sang through the dimness. It was so unexpected that I froze in mid-motion. "My Beautiful Dreamer," she tried again, and this time the minuet of her words spun to life in my mind. I felt a twitching in my muscles as a sense of relaxation washed over me. But Edwardia's gruesome new visage no longer matched the lie in her voice.

"You have seen the coming Age. It haunts you." She took a predatory step in my direction. "You know the world's fate, perhaps even better than I. So why fight it?" The patches of skin still clinging to her skeletal face smoothed. "We can open the Door together." Her lips shaped into the memory of a heart. "We can rule together," she purred, and I heard the swish of velvet.

I was so tired. Of all the dreams that I'd had of the world's end, this one was the worst. My CPAP was probably leaking. This is what happened when my mask knocked loose. My nightmares would intensify. I blinked at the woman that hovered before me. I'd dreamt of her before.

"Melisande," someone called. I'd heard my name called my whole life, even when I was alone. "Melisande, wake up!" A beautiful voice with a colonial accent called to me.

"Wake up," a tiger purred.

"Wake up, child. Pay attention!" my second-grade teacher barked.

"Melisande, please. I can't live without you," the first voice whispered, and I remembered circles of blue. I blinked as the phone line crackled to life. I shuddered at the intimacy of it. Grayford's essence swam through me, and with it came his strength in the face of insurmountable odds. His sense of justice aligned my thoughts, and his fortitude wrapped my insides with an indestructible mettle.

I risked a quick glance to my left. He hovered above the crowd. His muscles danced with tension. His body clenched, ready to strike. There were no words for what I felt when our eyes met. I knew that he'd given himself to the cause, but I could see in his face that he had not given me. It was all there circled in blue—he would sacrifice the world if it meant saving me. And in that moment I finally knew what it felt like to be loved.

Here, at the end, I finally knew.

"You have anchored me in this world now, Melisande," Grayford said, and I heard his words echo in my head even as his voice rang out across the throng of onlookers. "You cannot leave me here to walk this world alone."

I watched as his feet reached toward the ground, and as he sank earthward his body changed. I'd seen his corporeal form before. I'd touched it. Tasted it. Cherished my fleeting moments with it, but as his feet settled on the quaking ground, I saw that he was remade.

The man I loved was whole without the need for

electricity or even the benefit of my touch. Grayford was fully of the world again. It was God's grace. The Father Almighty was here, among us, strengthening us and paving the way for miracles. It was all I needed to know.

I tore my eyes from my beloved. I would not ask for his help. There was nothing further he could do. This was my fight. If Grayford was human again, I would not risk his well-being for any amount of assistance. I would end this.

Dawn's thin light silhouetted the skeletal woman that crouched before me, ready to spring. Edwardia's last hit had pushed me dangerously close to the Gate. Close enough to feel it pulling at my cells and unraveling my thoughts. But when she came at me again, this time I was ready. I whispered to the poltergeist. Edwardia launched. The shield elongated, and I caught her on the lance-like tip of an angry entity. I dug the other end of the lance into the refuse at my feet and dragged her through the sunrise.

I looked into Edwardia's eyes and saw her life the same way I'd seen Petal's and the ghosts' in the closet. Her memories opened for me in a flash of brilliance.

Life as an earl's daughter had been restricting in the 1800s, but the move to America had brought some freedoms. She was not allowed to entertain the young men of the city as they were far below her in status. There was no one of her station within two day's ride, so Edwardia spent many lonely days studying and watching the boat traffic from the upper windows of her father's waterfront estate.

After the dreaded yellow fever took her father, a young businessman by the name of Landry made his intentions toward Edwardia known. I almost laughed at the impression of the mud-covered man grinning from Edwardia's memory. It hadn't been love at first sight for either of them, but over the courtship period they'd managed a friendship. His carefree, undisciplined life had thrilled her to the core. And her staid manner and cultured grace was an endless marvel to him.

Mr. Landry was forward thinking, and during the first years of their marriage, he'd taught Edwardia the business of selling swamp water from the Great Dismal to the ships leaving port. I tasted the earthy presence of tannins in the water they barreled and sold. The tart bitterness and musty odor meant the water was good and would not turn rancid while the ships were out to sea.

Edwardia's life had been good enough until her husband's death. Those years seemed to pale in my mind as she looked forward to the years she struggled to make a name for herself as a female business woman. Such a thing was virtually unheard of in her time. Nevertheless, Edwardia was good at every aspect of what she did. Her business acuity was even better than her husband's.

Edwardia wasn't afraid to push up her delicate sleeves and tend to manual labor either. In fact, the time she spent in the Great Dismal Swamp were the happiest moments of her life. Her country home amid the cypress roots and dangling moss was her refuge from the life of a proper lady. She spent her days on the barge overseeing the water collectors and assuring the barrels were properly sealed.

My body flushed as I remembered the way Edwardia had spent her nights—in the arms of a chocolate-skinned lover with shining eyes and a gentle mouth. I understood her attraction to Gabe better once I'd seen the powerful man in her bed. My hands smoothed across his muscular body. Each bulge and cocoa curve were carved by years of heavy lifting and harsh swamp life.

He was a Maroon, part of a community of freed and escaped slaves who inhabited the marshland wilderness that stretched across Virginia's southern border into North Carolina. She'd loved him fiercely. But the world outside the swamp was intolerant.

I tried to turn away as she showed me the ruins of her happiness hanging from a cypress limb outside her house, but she forced the pain into my soul. She forced her sense of helplessness on me. She smothered me in her hatred and loss of respect for human society.

I watched her heart wither. Her desire to boil the corruption of mankind from the bones of the world drove her mad. It followed her to her early grave and back.

Do you see?

Edwardia's spear-point eyes stabbed at me from the tip of my lance.

"This is a fallen world," she keened. "Let them fall."

Her memories slipped from my mind like eels. I shuddered at their passing.

Dawn's light sparked across the pulsating rip in the world. It blushed Edwardia's boney features for one brief moment. She passed over my head like a trapeze artist who'd just lost her grip. Her clanking limbs flailed through the air. Her clicking talons scraped against the poltergeist's gleaming surface.

A high shriek echoed through the park as first one then another piece of her slipped across the swirling surface of unknowable things. My legs went limp as I watched Edwardia's lower half swirl like paint in a can of turpentine. Maybe the door was only one way and trying to enter it from our plane in one piece was impossible.

Edwardia screamed as more of her sank through the gravity well into another dimension. The horror of her bending body was too much to bear. I yanked on the poltergeist, and it broke free of her grasping hands. I lost sight of her in a scrambling mass of stuffed animals and game board pieces.

Cheers rose from the park, and I looked out at a sea of leaping bodies. Grayford was there, bathed in a halo of morning light. Edwardia was gone. There would be no Seventh Devil. Yet the great, sucking maw of darkness in which she had just fallen was still open.

I looked to Grayford and then the slaves. None of them were cheering. In fact, their eyes were locked on me with an intensity that promised no rest. Grayford lowered his gaze to the ground, and the crackling connection between us drained to silence. I watched as he placed his palms together and rested his chin on his steepled fingers. It was a nervous, fretting sort of body language as if his thoughts were weaving into prayers again. I couldn't know because he'd closed himself to me.

Ripe, red panic swelled to life inside me. Was he hiding something from me? How could this be the moment to keep secrets?

When he lifted his gaze again, his eyes were filled with a love I was not yet sure I'd earned from him. I could still feel how the Joining had accelerated things between us. I knew more about who he was on the inside than I should, and I wondered in that moment how much he knew of me. My skin went cold as I followed his eyes. He looked toward the east and the rising sun peeking through the tornadic wall beyond the tree line. The quiet door had opened, and to my unraveling horror the Shadow stood just inside it.

Frost filled the air around me as the pieces of my will, that I'd only just reclaimed, shattered instantly. The poltergeist drifted above me like that long-ago balloon. I watched it lift into the sky, abandoning me for a far-off land. I wished it well.

My knees buckled first, then my jaw unhinged. I fought my neck muscles to keep my head up, but it was a losing battle. I could defeat the Seventh Devil of Hell, but when it came to cataplexy, it kicked my ass every time.

Questions erupted from my mind like swifts from a chimney. Had I fallen asleep again? How was the Shadow here? What was Grayford hiding from me? And the question at the front of my brain…why wasn't the Shadow attacking? Tears rimmed my eyes as I thought of Josh and the plan we used to get me out of this sort of situation. What I wouldn't do for a cold, hard slap to the face right about now.

"What do you want?" I whispered. It was the only defiance I had left in me. I'd never spoken to it before. The idea of addressing such a monster seemed like a sure-fire way to bring it down on me faster. It had spoken to me, on occasion, but always in a language I couldn't understand.

Imagine my surprise when it said, *"COME HERE."*

The words rattled my brain so hard, it felt as though my skull would spring a second leak.

"I can't." I spat the words at it from where I crouched in the confusion of tiny green army men and dismembered baby dolls. My rebellion was short-lived because no sooner had I said it than the Shadow moved. Cataplexy swept through me, and I collapsed against the trembling floor. Ice formed across my skin as something even colder gripped the back of my shirt. I felt my body lift, and then the Shadow began to drag me.

My knees bumped along the slide, and my foot tangled in the jump ropes. The Shadow pulled me over the tricycles and tossed my limp body into the tiny room beyond the quiet door.

As soon as I crossed the threshold of the bedroom, the rest of the world slipped away. I used the sudden silence to gather myself. The Shadow was gone. The door was closed. I lay in a cold pool of moonlight even though the moon had set hours ago. I waited as my body slowly returned to me. My arms and hands came back first in a chemical fire of pins and needles, then my legs, then my face. A hundred little injuries suddenly cried for attention, but at that moment nothing hurt enough to keep me from sitting up.

I looked around at the sparsely decorated room. One window, one bed, one dresser, and a tiny mirror hanging on the wall that said, "Is this the face of a good boy?" scrawled along the frame. Something about that mirror sent chills down my spine.

I got to my feet and looked out the window. A quiet cul-de-sac reflected the moon's light outside, but nothing moved in it. Nothing moved in the room. I looked in every corner. I checked the neatly folded covers on the bed. There was nothing there. I tried the door, but the knob wouldn't turn. What was I supposed to do? What did the Shadow want from me?

No sooner had I thought it than the bedroom door creaked open. Something tall slithered into the room. I watched in nauseating wonder as the thing's face changed. Sometimes it was a man with whisky on his breath. Sometimes it was a woman with dead eyes and a hungry mouth. And sometimes…it was the Shadow.

I backed into a corner as a small boy appeared beneath the covers. He held the thin fabric over him as if it were armor. I looked away as the thing stripped him of his armor and then of everything else.

I dove at the bed. Shadow or no Shadow, I wasn't going to stand there and watch a child be abused. But when I clawed at the figure, my hands went right through it. I wedged myself between the Shadow and the boy, but the thing passed right through me. I kicked and punched until my ribcage throbbed, but nothing helped.

"What do you want me to do?" I sobbed in the direction of the door. I held my hands over my ears to block the child's cries and shouted at the top of my voice. "Show me!"

The door opened again and this time there was no mistake. The Shadow bent to fit its full size into the room. It moved across the room until it loomed over the child. The first version of itself was gone, replaced by this second version that I knew all too well and, apparently, so did the child. Fear drenched my brain, but I kept my legs under me. My hands tingled as the Shadow looked from the little boy to me.

"*GO.*" It pointed at the boy but spoke to me. "*GET HIM.*"

I sucked in a breath, tore my eyes away from the worst fear of my life, and looked at the boy. A second ago, the child had been awake and cringing at the Shadow from beneath his blanket, but now he was lying down with his eyes closed. He was asleep. I reached out to gather him in my arms, but my hands passed right through him. I tried again, and again my hands met thin air. I turned back to the Shadow and waited.

"*GO!*" Its voice boomed in my head, and I sank to the floor. Cataplexy dropped me like a rag doll, and my head landed on the child's pillow. My eyes closed. All I could do for the boy was be there with him. We lay in the silence, unmoving, as the Shadow loomed over us. It was almost as if…the boy…had…narcolepsy too.

Oh God.

My lungs fought for air as I realized what was happening in that tiny room. Or more accurately, what had happened in that room. The boy. The abuse. The Shadow. The child was narcoleptic. He must have died in his sleep and he was…still dreaming.

Adrenaline rushed through me as I realized what I needed to do. I thought of Petal, the little ghost in the graveyard. I remembered how her little hand felt in mine. If I could just figure out how to reach the little boy, maybe I could help him. My hand moved along the bedspread, just an inch, but it was something. I thought of all the times that I'd used adrenaline to force myself awake. I let the urgency of the moment flood through me. My hand moved. My eyes fluttered. The Shadow flickered, and I was back. I grabbed at the child's ethereal hand and willed my life into him. His fingers tingled with presence, and that was all I needed.

I called to the ghost, and the ghost came to me. The room spun around me as a shrill voice asked, "Is this the face of a good boy?" It was a memory of the boy's mother, but I could hear Edwardia's voice behind the words. Edwardia had found herself a narcoleptic to use. She'd been feeding the little ghost's pain to open a rift between worlds.

I understood. All at once, I understood how it could happen. Narcoleptics were like living ghosts. When in the hypnogogic state, we literally straddled both worlds, living and dead. If we were to die while in the hypnogogic state...The thought drained the blood from my body. I wished like Hell that I could reach inside the Gate and drag Edwardia out just so I could push her back in and watch her scream.

I turned my mind from the child's memories. If only I could make him turn away too.

"Wake up." My voice echoed in the space between us. "It's okay. You're safe now," I soothed, but the child didn't move. "It's okay." My voice caught in my throat. "The bad people are gone." Still the child slept.

I tried shaking him, but it didn't help. Maybe he's paralyzed by fear, I thought. "The Shadow is gone. It's never coming back!" I stared at the boy's angelic face. I had to help him. I couldn't leave him there helpless, like me.

I looked down at my hands and remembered that I wasn't helpless anymore. Frost laced my palms in sparkling fractals, and I remembered.

I looked at the child again, then I raised my hands above him. As gently as I could, I cast tiny chains about him. I wrapped the links around and around him. They crisscrossed under his blanket, enfolding him in ice. I sent a prayer to God and then flooded the chains with my will. Something moved against the links like a fluttering bird.

"Wake up," I called in the same way that the voices from my life had called to me only moments ago. The tiny soul stirred.

"Wake up," I whispered again, and the boy moved.

"Wake up," I commanded, and his little eyes opened.

Something cracked the fading night in half, and I fell.

Chapter Twenty-Three

That's a stupid tie.

A sweaty hand locked on mine, and after a few pulls and a lot of kicking on my part I finally fought free of the massive pile of rubble. I half expected to see a fireman or a police officer, but I guess a member of the City Planning Committee was just as good.

The park around us was utterly empty. Every disembodied soul had spent all that it had in the battle. The sun swept across the devastation, chasing shadows back to their rightful place. This was the time for spirits to sleep. I wondered if that still included Grayford.

"Ms. Blythe." Ben Martin gasped for air, then brushed his hands on his sale-rack slacks.

"Mr. Martin." I looked up at him from the scattered remains of the Hell Gate. Now that the storm wall was down and the gate was closed, I could see that a new day had dawned, bright and clear.

"That's a stupid tie," I said, chuckling soundlessly.

"I know." He chuckled too. "Do you want a ride home?"

"Yeah."

It took a while to hike through the destruction the tornado had left behind, but we finally made it to his car. I buckled the seat belt and pushed the chest band away from my ribs. The engine started, and I leaned my head against the window. I fell asleep almost immediately, and no nightmares came. I had no dreams at all. Just blessed nothingness.

Chapter Twenty-Four

What else have I missed?

Bougie stared at me from his placemat on the other side of my small kitchen table.

"What? I gave you your share. It's right there!" I pointed to the tuna on the paper plate next to his water bowl. As usual, he ignored me.

I'd made it about halfway through my crackers and tuna when the soldier showed up. I sighed as heavily as my ribs would allow. I guessed I'd rather have him interrupt my meal than my shower. So really, it was an improvement.

He drifted into arm's reach, so I put my hand out and touched him. A look of shock washed over his young face as the mantle of life settled over him.

"Have a seat, friend. What's on your mind?" I gestured to the other chair at my table and put another cracker in my mouth. The soldier didn't move. I looked back at him. He was solid, and the brief blush of life colored his cheeks. I could even smell gunpowder on his clothes. I was sure he'd heard me, but he just stood there like a statue.

Now that I could see what he really looked like, I knocked another year off his age. As I stared at his frozen face, I realized he couldn't be older than seventeen. He probably left a girl behind that he'd hoped to marry after the war. This was going to be a long, painful conversation, but if there was one thing I remembered from that moment in front of the Hell Gate when I'd gotten a peek at the universe, it was that talking to ghosts was part of my *raison d'être*. If I wanted to earn my keep on this planet, I needed to start helping as many lost souls as I could.

"Mitzi," he breathed, and his voice was high with a tight, strangling emotion. I followed his eyes to the side of the table where Bouguereau sat.

"What?" I asked flatly.

"You found her," he crooned, and tears fell from his eyes. I looked from the soldier to my cat.

"No, no." I wiped the crumbs from my hands and shook them in front of me. Just then Bougie stood, and with a lingering look back at me, he turned and leapt into the ghost's arms. My breath caught in my throat. Tears washed the boy's cheeks clean as he whispered into Bougie's thick black fur. He apologized over and over for leaving her. Bougie purred and nuzzled the soldier's chin.

"This is who you've been looking for?" I asked weakly.

"Yes."

He smiled, and my heart spasmed.

"She's a girl?" I tilted my head in confusion, and the soldier nodded. I guess I'd never looked under her skirt, so I just assumed because of her size she was a boy. I'd also assumed she was alive.

My mind raced back through my time with the big cat. He was always hungry, yet when I fed him it seemed like he never ate. I thought the neighbors were feeding him, but I guess not. They probably didn't even know he was there.

I thought back to the times I'd seen him slinking out of their apartments. They hadn't really made any comments about him...ever. And the hole in the screen that Bougie always came in through...sometimes he managed it even when the window was closed. I thought I'd just forgotten he was inside already.

But the ward around my bedroom? Maybe it didn't work on animals. Or maybe, like Grayford, it didn't work on ghosts I'd invited in.

The tuna and crackers in my stomach shaped into a stone.

What else have I missed? I wondered.

"Thank you," the sweet boy said, and I smiled.

"You're welcome," I answered and took one last, loving look at Bougie. "She's a good cat," I said, voice cracking. They disappeared into the mansion that Jesus had gone before to prepare for them. And I cried.

Chapter Twenty-Five

It wasn't my first choice for a name.

Midtown was back to normal, at least business-wise. Bulldozers still scraped at piles of debris, and giant machines still mulched the remains of Arcadia Park's jungle of downed weed trees. I took a left at the battered water tower and drove down until I saw the business I was looking for.

Grayford's presence whispered somewhere nearby. A shiver. A lick on my lips soft and slow. Anticipation tickled down my spine as a beautiful man in eighteenth-century attire materialized next to me. I giggled to myself. Just the thought of sharing a few moments alone with him diverted my blood flow to all the right places.

As a corporeal ghost, Grayford had been delectable, but now in his new flesh and blood manifestation, he was downright irresistible. Each time he materialized, his skin was warm, his hair smelled of open fields, and his heart…its thunderous beat filled me with hope for the future.

There was no understanding the nature of his current form, so we didn't try. We were too busy enjoying the blessing that it was.

Time hadn't passed for Grayford in centuries. He'd watched the ages flow, but he'd not felt the moments slip through his fingers into oblivion. He was remembering with each passing day what it was like to watch his shadow grow longer at the end of the day. He was learning to move with the world again. I'd searched his thoughts for any regrets, but I'd never found any.

I reached for his hand and curled my fingers around his. He looked so uncomfortable trapped inside the roller-coaster ride that was my jeep. I was only going about thirty-five miles an hour and he was still able to dematerialize should the occasion call for it, but nevertheless, his strong hand gripped the dashboard with fervor.

I pulled my car into the small lot and parked in the farthest spot. Grayford gave a sigh of relief. He took a moment and then turned to me.

"Are you sure, my love?" He focused his blue inside blue eyes on me intently.

I was someone's love. Not just someone's. I was his. I tried to hide the smile that spread across my mouth, but my face resisted. My lips were traitors. In the space of an exhale, he closed the distance between us and pressed his warm mouth to mine, saving me the embarrassment of grinning like a fool.

Grayford didn't need an energy boost anymore to kiss me the way he wanted to. He could still drain my car battery, tilt my chair back, and remind me what a super-charged flesh and blood man felt like, but he didn't need to anymore. It was a change that made him exceedingly happy.

I'd thought that a large part of my attraction to Grayford was attributed to his ghostly glamour, but now I knew it was good, old-fashioned chemistry.

"Yes," I whispered against his lips. I'd thought

about it a lot and I really wanted this. "But maybe you should hang back...just for now." I hated to leave him out of something so life-changing, but he nodded in acceptance. A trace of a grin pulled at his mouth.

"I understand." He withdrew his hand, and I instantly missed it. "My countenance can be...off-putting to some, I suspect."

I shrugged gently. Grayford might not be a true ghost anymore, but he wasn't quite human either. He could still cause a galvanic skin response in those with heightened senses.

"I will take my leave, then. May I call on you this evening?"

I nodded, maybe a little too vigorously. I watched as the crisp blue rings of his eyes faded from sight.

****

"Ms. Blythe?" the woman behind the counter asked.

"That's me."

"Thanks for calling ahead." She smiled. "Cool hair." She gestured to my temples.

"Thanks," I replied and let my fingers drift to the newest streak. At least now my right temple matched my left. I liked symmetry. The twin streaks of white hair were like a badge of honor that I wore proudly. I think anyone who'd survived two brushes with the Shadow would do the same.

The nice woman waved me back, and I followed her through a large door.

"Wow," was all I could say as she closed the door behind us. I took a minute and then another. I must have taken a couple more, because the assistant turned and gave me a questioning look.

"It's a little overwhelming sometimes," she offered sympathetically.

"I didn't know it would be this hard." I was a little embarrassed, but she just smiled.

I stood in front of the wall of cages and peered at the cats. Each one was cuter than the next. Some were sleeping. Some were wrestling with their cage mates. Others rubbed against the little door to their cage and purred.

"How does anyone choose?"

"There is another way." The assistant checked both doors to the room and made sure they were tightly closed. Then she instructed me to sit on the floor. "You can let them choose you."

She waited until I was seated with my legs crossed in front of me, and then she did something I'm pretty sure they are not supposed to do at the animal shelter. She started opening cages.

One by one, fluffy cats dropped from their perches and slinked around the room. Some came over, sniffed me, and then moved on to the toys in the basket by the corner. Others shied away or chose another cage to hide in. But one small, gray cat with a missing eye knew exactly what she wanted.

She jumped down from her cage, sprinted across the room, and leapt into my lap. I made sure this time that I had my pronouns right, then I made as much room for her as I could. She circled my lap a few times, then dough-punched my painting shorts until they were the level of softness she preferred. At last, she settled down and purred while I ran my fingers along her silky fur.

"I think Shadow likes you," the assistant chimed,

and I nodded dreamily.

"Shadow, huh?" It wasn't my first choice for a name, but it certainly was fitting. "Well, Shadow, I have just one question for you." She fixed me with her single, emerald eye. "How do you feel about ghosts?"

A word about the author...

Hunter J. Skye is a high-functioning square peg, which turns out to be a prerequisite for writing quirky, crossover urban fantasy and paranormal romance.

Her debut novel, *A Glimmer of Ghosts*, has won four Romance Writers of America awards.

When not typing away on her next novel, Hunter can be found cracking nerdy jokes or waxing existential over a bowl of spaghetti.

She firmly believes this world is ready for a disabled heroine.

http://www.hunterskye.com

Thank you for purchasing
this publication of The Wild Rose Press, Inc.

For questions or more information
contact us at
info@thewildrosepress.com.

The Wild Rose Press, Inc.
www.thewildrosepress.com

Thank you for purchasing
this publication of The Wild Rose Press, Inc.

For questions or more information
contact us at
info@thewildrosepress.com.

The Wild Rose Press, Inc.
www.thewildrosepress.com

9 781509 230044